Patrick Abbott. A tall, lanky private detective from San Francisco, now an intelligence officer with the U.S. Marines, home to New Mexico from war with two Japanese bullet wounds to his chest and three citations for bravery.

Jean Abbott. His pretty, inquisitive, and intensely loving wife, she owns The Turquoise Shop.

Julia Price. She's the attractive young manager of the Indian jewelry shop.

Hugh Kennicot. A former pilot, he raises cattle and sheep in Sky Valley.

Scott Davies. County Health Officer. He's spent much of his life recovering from TB.

Sheriff Jim Trask. A friendly bulldog type of man.

Max Ottoway. The State's Attorney, he's thinks the sheriff's office is outmoded.

Bee Chandler. The short and curly-haired co-owner of the amethyst spectacles.

Karen Chander. She's the spitting image of her mother, Bee.

Edwina Ames. She's more glamorous than her sister, Karen.

Maurice Ames. Edwina's rich husband, he fancies himself to be a Spanish don. He fancies himself to be something of a foodie.

Ray Thayer. When his battered body was found at the bottom of a canyon, some said murder, some said suicide. All anyone really knew was that those amethyst spectacles were found at the scene in his car.

Dorrie Thayer. The dead man's wife, called Little Dorrie by one and all, and something of a problem child. There are those that say Ray reconsidered his marriage to her and jumped into the canyon.

Geronima. Maurice's Indian cook.

Pancho. Jean's dog, diminutive but fierce.

Books by Frances Crane

Featuring the Abbotts

The Turquoise Shop (1941)
The Golden Box (1942)
The Yellow Violet (1942)
The Pink Umbrella (1943)
The Applegreen Cat (1943)
The Amethyst Spectacles (1944)
The Indigo Necklace (1945)
The Cinnamon Murder (1946)
The Shocking Pink Hate (1946)
Murder on the Purple Water (1947)
Black Cypress (1948)
The Flying Red Horse (1950)
The Daffodil Blonde (1950)
Murder in Blue Street (1951)
The Polkadot Murder (1951)
Murder in Bright Red (1953)
13 White Tulips (1953)
The Coral Princess Murders (1954)
Death in Lilac Time (1955)
Horror on the Ruby X (1956)
The Ultraviolet Widow (1956)
The Buttercup Case (1958)
The Man in Gray (1958)
Death-Wish Green (1960)
The Amber Eyes (1962)
Body Beneath a Mandarin Tree (1965)

*Reprinted by the Rue Morgue Press

Non-Series Mysteries

The Reluctant Sleuth (1961)
Three Days in Hong Kong (1965)
A Very Quiet Murder (1966)
Worse Than a Crime (1968)

Non-Mystery

The Tennessee Poppy, or, Which Way Is Westminster Abbey? (1932)

The Amethyst Spectacles
by Frances Crane

The Rue Morgue Press
Lyons, Colorado

About Frances Crane

AFTER SHE WAS EXPELLED from Nazi Germany prior to the start of World War II, Frances Kirkwood Crane, recently divorced and with a daughter heading for college, needed to find a new way to make a living. The old market for her writing—primarily poking gentle fun at Brits from the point of view of an American living abroad—was suddenly out of fashion. Americans no longer wanted to laugh at the foibles of the English now that brave little Britain was engaged in a desperate struggle for its very survival against the forces of Hitler.

Up to that point, life had been relatively easy for Frances. Her husband, Ned Crane, was a well-paid advertising executive with the J. Walter Thompson agency, whose dubious claim to immortality was the Old Gold cigarette slogan, "Not a cough in a carload." Frances herself was a regular contributor to a new sophisticated humor magazine called *The New Yorker*. Many of her short sketches for that magazine were collected in book form in 1932 as *The Tennessee Poppy or Which Way Is Westminster Abbey?*

Back in the states, newly divorced and in need of money—living in the United States was more expensive than living in Europe—she had turned to the mystery field at the suggestion of one of her old editors who told her it was a "hot market." Not long after arriving in Taos, New Mexico, Crane, now around 50, heard about an incident involving a jewelry store in that artists' colony, which inspired her first Pat and Jean Abbott mystery, *The Turquoise Shop*, published by Lippincott in 1941. Although she changed the name of town to Santa Maria and even commented that it had not yet been spoiled in the fashion of Taos and Santa Fe, there is absolutely no question that it was based on Taos. In fact, Mona Brandon and her hacienda in *The Turquoise Shop* are loosely based on Mabel Dodge Luhan and her famous adobe home (now a bed and breakfast inn).

Jean Holly (she sounds terribly experienced and world weary, yet she's only 26) meets up with a handsome San Francisco private detective in that first novel. *The Turquoise Shop* was followed by 25 more books featuring Pat and Jean Abbott, who marry toward the end of the third book, all with a color in the title. Many of them take the Abbotts to locales across the United States and around the world, although they were to return to Santa Maria several times in the course of the series. While some contemporary critics weren't always kind to her books, readers loved them, and still do. The series was so popular that it spun off a radio program, *Abbott Mysteries*, which ran on the Mutual Network in the summers of 1945, 1946 and 1947.

Nor was Crane ignorant of the trends in contemporary detective fiction. She was extremely well-read in the field. Along with fellow women mystery writers Lenore Glen Offord and Dorothy B. Hughes, she was one of the most influential mystery reviewers in the country, dwarfed in influence only by Anthony Boucher (for whom Bouchercon, the World Mystery Convention, is named). She relished her place in the literary world and numbered among her friends such literary lights as James Jones and Sinclair Lewis as well as her editor at Random House, the very urbane Bennett Cerf. Yet she realized she was not in that same league with these literary heavyweights, remarking once to Cerf that she was but a "minor light."

But all good things seemingly must come to an end. The Abbotts cracked their last case in 1965 with *Body Beneath the Mandarin Tree*. In the 1960s, Crane also wrote five stand-alone mysteries which were published in England but failed to find an American publisher. The last of these, *Worse Than a Crime*, appeared in 1968 when she was 78 years old, and though she would live another 13 years and enjoy relatively good health, her career as a mystery writer was over, and she settled into a well-earned retirement. Yet she had a better run than many women writers of her era, and, unlike most writers, male or female, she earned a good living at it. While many other female mystery writers who began in the 1930s and 1940s saw their careers end with the death of the rental librar-ies and the advent of the male-oriented paperback original in the early 1950s, Crane not only survived, publishing well into the 1960s, but endured, as any out-of-print book dealer who has ever offered one of her titles in a catalog and been overwhelmed with orders can testify. Her fans don't just enjoy her books, they revel in them, then and now.

She spent much of the last forty years of her life in her adopted New Mexico, mostly in Taos (though the "hippie invasion" in the 1960s drove her eventually to move to Santa Fe). She returned frequently to Lawrenceville to visit family. Three months before her 91st birthday, failing health forced her to enter a nurs-ing home in Albuquerque, where she died on November 6, 1981. She made one final posthumous visit to Lawrenceville, a trip that many old-timers in that town still recall with amusement. The postmaster sent word to her nephew Bob, a local doctor, that a package had arrived for him from New Mexico. "Only," he explained, "you'll have to pick it up yourself. I'm not touching it."

The package was marked "human remains." Bob and other fellow family members scattered the ashes it contained on the family farm. Frances Kirkwood Crane not only came home, she did so in her usual unconventional style.

Note: For additional information on Crane and her connections to Taos read Tom & Enid Schantz' introduction to the Rumorge Press edition of *The Turquois Shop*.

Chapter One

It was a fresh clear afternoon in the early spring. I sat in the corner seat back of the adobe fireplace in the Turquoise Shop and looked down the length of the room through the big show window into the plaza. The sunshine twinkled on the new green leaves of the cottonwoods and made the new grass golden-green. It made special magic with the pink or blue shawls worn by the Indian women going about their marketing, and it dealt gaily with those harsher colors, the scarlets and cerises, the heavy greens and lush yellows, which the Mexican men and women favored. The Anglos, men and women, stuck to blues and browns, going bright only with a scarf, or at most a loud shirt.

I kept seeing people I knew. I saw Karen Chandler, in khaki jodhpurs and an old tweed jacket, with no hat on her short gay blue-black hair, laughing near the birdbath in the middle of the plaza with a ruddy, square-shouldered young cow-man. I saw Sheriff Jim Trask. He stood for a while under the edge of the arcades on the north side of the square listening to what seemed to be a harangue from a plump-looking youngish man in a navy suit and felt hat.

"Who's that with Mr. Trask?" I asked Julia Price.

Julia looked up from the high stool behind the jewelry counter, where she was polishing silver jewelry.

"That's Max Ottoway," she said. "The state's attorney."

"He seems trying to talk the sheriff into something."

Julia Price sniffed. "He's been nagging at him ever since he got elected, Jeanie. The truth is, he wants to get rid of Mr. Trask."

"He must be crazy!"

"You said it. But Max Ottoway wants to be up-to-date fast. He says the office of sheriff went out with the Ark. He wants to call on the state troopers for everything, in spite of the fact that there's not enough state police to go round, specially now with a lot of them gone to the war. Ottoway doesn't seem to know that Santa Maria County is the best watched over in the state, even though it's one of the biggest. Why, this country is bigger than all of Connecticut, and Mr. Trask and five or six deputies, and two of those among the lame and halt, have to preserve law and order. And they do it darn well, by gosh! Ottoway's jealous, that's all!"

Julia snorted indignantly, her chin quivered, her Indian bracelets and bangles jingled. She always wore eight or ten silver and turquoise bracelets on each arm, earrings, several necklaces, and a silver concha belt. She was one of the nicest people in the world, and to me one of the most attractive. Her brown eyes were too big, her nose was too small, her mouth too wide, and her chin was too tiny for her smooth broad forehead but it all worked up into something very pleasing to my eye. Her hair was at present auburn. Her long-legged shape was encased in a red-and-blue checked shirt, and navy trousers tucked into fancy cowboy boots.

"The thing they really clashed on was Ray Thayer's death," Julia said. I looked at her suddenly. I hadn't heard that Ray was dead. "Ottoway said it was suicide after he couldn't prove it murder."

"Julia!" I felt shocked. "I didn't know Ray was dead."

"I wrote you myself, Jeanie. It was when you were in England. Poor Ray was—well, he fell—into the Rio Grande Canyon, there at The Rock." In my mind I saw The Rock jutting like a headland above the feverishly colored canyon. I saw Ray Thayer falling, his arms waving foolishly, and his legs taking those futile steps in the air. "His body was utterly crushed," Julia said. "I don't want to talk about it," she said then.

Neither did I, so I looked out on the plaza again, and my eyes fastened on Karen Chandler.

"Karen looks exactly like her mother, Julia."

"She's taller than Bee, and broader in the shoulders the way gals are these days. Otherwise, exactly."

"Those sort of gaunt women certainly do have style. I saw a lot of that kind in England. If those English girls only had clothes they would be the best-looking on earth. Who's the boy?"

Julia said, in a slightly different tone, "His name's Hugh Kennicott."

"Very elegant name, Julia."

"Very elegant guy. Or at least I thought so, at first. You know that log hunting lodge up in Sky Valley we used to be so nuts about? Well, it belongs to Hugh's father. The kid cracked up in an airplane shortly after the war started and they shipped him out here to get well. Right away he started raising cattle and sheep up in Sky Valley and did so well that by the time he wanted to get back into service the government told him to go on ranching instead."

I saw Sky Valley, an emerald-green bowl three thousand feet above Santa Maria. It was ringed until mid-summer with snow-capped peaks. I saw it teeming with white-faced cows and snow-white sheep, which was purely in my fancy, because when I had really seen that valley there hadn't been anything noticeable in the greenness save the hunting lodge and a small clear lake.

Julia said, "That ought to make a match. Unfortunately, Edwina saw Hugh first."

Edwina was Karen's older sister.

"Edwina? Isn't she still married to Maurice Ames?"

"And how," said Julia.

I drew a long breath.

"Things happen in this place, Julia."

"But definitely," Julia said.

Sheriff Trask strode across the plaza in the direction of the shop. He looked just the same, something over six feet of solid muscle and sinew dressed in a gray flannel shirt, corduroy pants in high laced boots, a stained windbreaker, a blue cotton bandanna, and a time-worn Stetson hat whose brim curled away from his lean sun-burned wind-seamed gray-eyed face. There might be a few more crow's feet raying out from his keen eyes, and maybe a little more gray in his hair, but the sheriff looked no older than when I had last seen him, two years ago.

He came into the shop. He ducked to avoid bumping his head on the top of the door frame. He took off his hat. He held it in one hand as he gravely advanced across the shop. We had both got to our feet. We shook hands. We both felt a little awed by the sheriff.

"Mighty glad to see you, Miss Holly," he said. "Excuse me, I mean Mrs. Abbott, ma'am." He asked after our health. We asked after his. We mentioned the weather. We all remained standing, because the sheriff wouldn't sit down. He held his hat in both hands and his bronzed capable fingers worked at its curling brim. "I saw you come in here, Mrs. Abbott. I been wanting to ask after Pat, ma'am."

"Well, he's doing fine," I said. "Too fine, in my opinion. This climate is much too healthy. He's already rarin' to go. Before we know it, he's going to be able to go back into active service, and I'd rather he wouldn't, you know, but it's what he wants, Mr. Trask."

Julia said, "I suppose you've heard that Pat's a hero, Mr. Trask? Pat came back with four Jap bullets in his chest and three citations on it."

"Oh, Julia!" I said. "It was only two bullets, Mr. Trask, but three citations."

"Anyhow, he was a hero," Julia said. "He saved another man's life."

"It was just what any Marine would do for any other Marine, Mr. Trask," I said. But proudly.

"They don't come any better than our Marines," said the sheriff.

"They were on reconnaissance, not in combat," I said. "Their plane was shot down. It's a miracle they got out alive. He was in the jungle for days—they were, I mean—and Pat got pneumonia along with the bullets. But he's going to be fine."

"He should have stayed in Europe," Julia said.

"Pat's a Californian," I said. He had been born in Wyoming but he now called San Francisco home. "He didn't rest till he got sent to the Pacific, and he hated it over there like sin, but still he won't be happy till he's back. Why don't you drop round and see him, Mr. Trask?"

"That's just what I stopped in to ask you if I could do, ma'am."

"He'd love to see you. Come any time, Mr. Trask. We haven't any phone, you know, so, whenever you feel like it, drop in."

After the sheriff went out I asked Julia about Ray Thayer.

Julia said, from the high stool, where she had again taken up her polishing, "Well, the truth is, Karen Chandler was sort of mixed up in that business, Jeanie. It was too bad."

"Karen?"

Julia frowned. "I might as well tell you, darling. You'll hear it anyway, and maybe not from somebody as friendly towards Karen as I am. I know she's a tomboy and always banging away with a gun, but I love Karen. You said a while ago that Karen looked like her mother. She certainly does. She is even a little nearsighted, the way Bee is. She has to wear glasses to see clearly at a distance—when she drives, goes hunting, or to the pictures, or to be sure who somebody is at the other side of a large room. You remember Bee's purple-blue glasses?"

I nodded. It was the frames that were purple-blue, with the color and semi-translucency of uncut amethyst, and they were charming. They had been specially designed for Bee Chandler's beautiful violet-blue eyes by somebody in Paris. The frames conformed to the lines of Bee's eyes and straight black eyebrows. The color flattered her eyes.

"Bee gave those specs to Karen, Jeanie. Well, they found them in Ray Thayer's car."

"In his car?"

"After he was killed. His car was parked there beside The Rock, in that flat place where we always park. It was parked with the headlights facing up that trail which leads to The Rock from the Sante Fe road. Well, since everybody thought that Karen was going to marry Ray Thayer . . ."

"Karen?"

"Ray was crazy about Karen in his quiet sort of way. Well, Karen wanted to finish college. She was down at the state university in Albuquerque, you know. She finished in less than three years. Karen is smart, Jeanie. Well, anyway, when he came back from Hollywood with a bride . . ."

"Ray?" I saw Ray in my imagination, sleepy-looking and moony-eyed. He walked with a slight limp. Ray wrote western stories and made lots of money because they were very exciting, which was funny, because Ray Thayer was really rather dull. *"Bride?"* I said. I felt rather dizzy.

Jeanie, wait until you see Dorrie! Then you will be knocked for a loop."

"Dorrie?"

"Dorrie's the bride Ray brought from Hollywood. She's the current problem child, Jeanie. First it's one thing then another from Little Dorrie, as she's generally called. She has a constant feud with Maurice Ames. The truth is, nobody has been very nice to Dorrie except Scott Davies, but of course Scott is nice to everybody and besides he and Ray were pals and neighbors and he says himself it's easier to treat people civilly than not, so why bother to fight. Maurice plagues the little woman, baits her."

"Julia," I said, "I wish you wouldn't mention this to Pat, if you don't mind. It's no time for him to get excited about the local murders."

"Murder?" Julia said, with her eyes going very round and her lower lip hanging. "Oh, nobody thinks now that Ray was murdered. When it happened and Max Ottoway grilled Karen so mercilessly at the inquest, on account of her specs being in the car, it made a sort of tempest in the local teapot, but now that everybody knows Dorrie better they think Ray took a good look at her too late and then went out and jumped off The Rock." Julia polished vigorously. "But of course, and why not," she said lucidly.

Some customers entered the shop, and, after a while, when it was obvious they were going to hang around interminably, I said good-bye to Julia and went home. I had walked the quarter mile from our house to the plaza. Walking back along the dry yellow rutted road, with the lush blue-green alfalfa field on my left and on my right the yellow mesa—where our low white house perched with its box-seat view of the village and the Santa Maria Mountains—I couldn't get the Thayer business out of my mind. I kept thinking about Ray Thayer, Scott Davies and Maurice Ames. Their ranches adjoined each other along the Silver River road. Also I thought of Bee Chandler, Karen and Edwina's mother. Mrs. Chandler was an attractive woman, with that thinness like Karen's which was so amazingly chic. She was always rather standoffish. She was a widow. During her married life she had lived abroad. The girls had been educated in Europe. Seven years ago, when Edwina was seventeen and Karen twelve, they had come for a summer in Santa Maria. In 1939 Mrs. Chandler had bought a small rancho two miles northeast of town.

The older of the two girls, Edwina, looked like a Spanish fairy princess. The summer she was twenty she had married Maurice Ames. Maurice was twenty-four years older than Edwina, and she herself was now about twenty-four.

As I turned up the steep lane Patrick appeared at the front door, waved, and walked along the flags to meet me at the gate in the white adobe wall which enclosed the white adobe house, the garden, and the long cottonwood which stood near the stoop. I thought suddenly of the first time I'd seen him, a lean lanky darkly tanned Westerner with blue-green eyes, white teeth, straight black brows, and those precise attractive lines the weather etches in Western faces. He looked just the same, except that his dark hair was now in a crew cut. He wore jeans and a navy wool shirt. His tight pants were belted low, cowboy style, on his lean hips. He'd got tanned so black in the Pacific that weeks in a San Francisco hospital had merely bleached him back to his normal brown. I kept thinking of him as I walked up the hill and I regret to say that I felt a sudden panic because he looked so disgustingly healthy. That meant he'd be going back to the war.

Two or three days went by. Each day was a little more beautiful. The sun would sail up gaily over the mountains. In the afternoons big white clouds would roll out of the west and sometimes there would be a short rain. The leaves of the cottonwood tree which shaded the flagstones that made a sort of terrace near the stoop were full-sized already, and each leaf was as perfect as though newly designed for this special season when we happened to be in the house. The alfalfa in the meadows which bordered the mountain rivers and irrigation ditches turned greener, if possible, and all over the valley the wild plums bloomed. Their thickets made little occasional drifts of white and their pungent scent filled the air. Some mornings there would be fresh snow on the peaks and in the valley their bases would look powdered with the whiteness of plum and apple trees. It was hard to remember, in the spring, that most of this valley was desert most of the year.

Mornings I stayed in bed till Mrs. Dominguez arrived, some time around eight or nine o'clock, then I would get up and take a bath and dress and bring Patrick his breakfast in bed. I loved that. He hated it. He grumbled but gave in, because Dr. Johnson said that if he stayed in bed till eleven every morning he could stay up the remainder of the day. If the weather was warm enough we lunched out-doors under the cottonwood tree. If it wasn't we had it in the little dining room, where a pinon fire blazed in a little Indian fireplace set in the wall three feet above the floor. Big, brown, handsome Mrs. Dominguez cleaned the house morn-ings and got lunch and went home after she had finished the dishes, so that in the afternoons we were alone together—that is, except for Pancho the dog and Toby the cat. We would have tea out of doors if the weather was fine and supper in the living room by the fireplace.

I considered this life ideal. I wished it could go on forever, but Patrick was already restless, wanting to do this or that which the doctor said was too much exertion for him at this time. He started smoking too much. He sent to the plaza for a lariat and practiced rope tricks. He had been raised in the saddle and he was smart with the rope, but I felt worried because I was sure that even this was too strenuous.

I even encouraged him to paint, and if you had ever seen any of the painting which was his private passion you would understand the extent of my anxiety over his restlessness when I bought oils and brushes and canvas and urged him to do a still life.

Painting was strictly no sale. "A still life!" he snorted. "Any news on the plaza this morning? Doesn't anything ever happen around here? Do you ever run into Jim Trask?"

"The sheriff is coming to see you, darling," I had reported, after seeing him in

Julia's shop. When he did not come I had asked about him and found out he was off in another corner of the county on the trail of some rustlers. That made Patrick even more restless. Rustlers are specially verminous now because they sell their stolen meat on the black market. They put Patrick in a state. What he needed to make him feel fit was a good successful chase after such rustlers, he thought.

I quoted Dr. Johnson. He snorted and said plenty about the doctor, which, boiled down, was approximately no guts.

People dropped in. Bee and Karen Chandler, whom Patrick liked. He didn't think Bee too standoffish, but I could see that her enigmatic character fascinated him. He thought Karen was marvelous-looking, and I couldn't decide if she was or was not. Maurice Ames did not come, but Edwina drifted in, and we talked about how different she was from her mother and her younger sister. Julia Price and Scott Davies stopped in one afternoon after work. Scott was about thirty, blond and slender, with candid blue eyes and pale shining hair. I was afraid he would talk about Ray Thayer and say perhaps that his death was a mystery, or something, and get Patrick excited, and I could laugh, too, when I thought about that, because how often I had egged Patrick on into working on a case and now I was just as anxious to prevent any such happening. Scott was running the public-health office now and, to avoid the possible mention of Ray Thayer, I kept asking him questions about that.

"It's temporary," he said. "In normal times there's a doctor in charge, but I guess I can hold it till after the war."

"What happened to your special research work?"

"That was WPA. It's washed up."

Scott had delved endlessly into early New Mexican history and had written up his findings for permanent filing in Washington. He was tragic, in a way, Julia said, as we sat under the cottonwood after Scott was gone. She told Patrick how Scott had got t.b. when a student at some college in the East, and had been sent for a cure to Albuquerque, and after he was through with the hospital stage he had got the WPA job which had brought him to Santa Maria. He had managed through the Federal Housing plan to buy himself a little rancho and built a small and very clever house. Patrick asked if there was no objection to his running the public-health office, with t.b., and Julia threw up her hands and her bracelets jingled.

"But he's cured, Pat! So long as he stays in this climate. Don't you think he looks healthy?"

"He looks fine," Patrick said.

"Oh, he is fine," Julia said. "Doc Johnson fusses over him, the way he fusses over everybody, but Scott hasn't been seriously ill now for years."

I sat feeling grateful to Julia and to Scott because they had not mentioned Ray Thayer.

I couldn't understand, quite, why I was so jumpy about that case, if it was a case.

Why should it have been murder? Nobody any longer thought about it anyway, Julia had said. Maybe he had jumped off The Rock. Maybe he got dizzy, and fell off. And why not? It was a wonder it didn't happen often. People were always picknicking at The Rock, and standing on its edge, peering over. Only why did Ottoway jump on to Karen, and then lay off entirely?

"Has Scott got over Edwina?" I asked Julia.

She shook her head.

"He never had a chance with Edwina," Julia said.

"Why not?" Patrick asked. "He's certainly attractive."

"No money," Julia said. "Edwina wanted money. It's just as well. She would have made him miserable and as it is they're all good friends. Scott and Maurice and Edwina and Bee and Karen. They're always together the way they always were."

Only Ray Thayer isn't with them, I thought.

It was teatime again, and the third day after Julia Price had told me about Ray Thayer, when the sheriff came to call. We were sitting outdoors and saw his old Buick come lumbering along the rough road at the foot of the mesa.

It wheeled grandly into our lane and zoomed up the hill.

Within ten minutes Mr. Trask was telling Pat all about the mysterious demise of Ray Thayer, and both were drinking neat Scotch whisky.

"I cain't get it out of my head that feller wasn't murdered, Pat," said the sheriff. "Say, Thayer used to be in the Marines. That's how he got that stiff knee, which was why he was classified 4-F, I reckon."

That does it, I thought. A Marine never lets another Marine down, remember.

2

We sat on the terrace. The men faced each other across the white-painted iron table which held the tray of drinks. My chair was between theirs but further from the table, which seemed to put me somewhat apart. Toby the cat lay on a branch of the tree and watched the stranger with yellow eyes which he had made narrow and suspicious. Pancho sat on guard beside me. When the sheriff first mentioned Ray Thayer I tried to stall him off by clearing my throat that Pancho mistook for displeasure, so he pushed out his oversized dachshund chest and emitted an ominous growl.

The sheriff gave him a benign glance.

"Funny little dog," he said.

Pancho bristled. He doesn't consider himself amusing. He is seven inches tall and twenty-some long from the tip of his nose to the end of his rat-tail. He considers these dimensions ideal.

Ridicule makes Pancho furious. It does anybody.

I warned the sheriff that the dog understood every word that was said, and then tried to distract him from Ray Thayer by asking about the recent rustlers. But he had come to talk about Ray Thayer.

"We found Thayer dead in the canyon, Pat. You know a place they call The Rock? That's where it happened. They held an inquest. There was an open verdict. Some people thought maybe it was suicide. Could've been, but I cain't get it out of my head it was murder." The sheriff took out the makings of his cigarettes. He slipped a tissue from the folder and filled and rolled it with one hand. "We got a young prosecutor here now—Max Ottoway. At first Ottoway called it murder and he got after a young lady here, named Karen Chandler, high, wide and handsome because her spectacles were found in Thayer's car. When he discovered he'd started something he couldn't exactly finish, he decided maybe it was an accident or suicide and since he seemed to be running the inquest that settled it." The sheriff's grin was wry. "After all, what evidence had we got that it was murder, except that there wasn't enough blood."

"Not enough blood?" I said.

Mr. Trask said, "When a person dies, ma'am, the blood stops circulating right away. I cain't say exactly how quick, but in no time at all after death if you break or cut the skin there's no bleeding to speak of. That's a big fall, six or seven hundred feet, anyways, and the body lit on sharp rocks. Every bone was broken and there was plenty of gashes which cut deep into the flesh. There was one big gash in the upper left forearm cutting into an artery which alone would account for a right smart lot of blood. But there wasn't any blood worth mentioning on his clothes or on the rocks or in the little spot of sand around the rocks that cut him up so. The body lay a few feet away from the river, but it hadn't been in the water, so the blood didn't wash away. It happened to be a cloudy day, so the sun hadn't dried up the blood, and even if it had the stains would have been all around. Nope. Thayer was dead before he fell off The Rock."

"Oh, I hope so," I said, thinking of the horror of being conscious of falling to death. "But, Mr. Trask, why should that mean he was murdered?"

"It don't, ma'am. I just happen to hold that opinion. If I could have proved it at the time I wouldn't be bothering Pat with talking about it now, Mrs. Abbott, ma'am."

"Any place where the body could have been held up during the fall? On a ledge, or a bush?" Patrick asked.

"Yes," the sheriff said. "It wouldn't have been likely, but it could happen."

"Anybody want to get rid of him, Jim?"

"That's the point," the sheriff said.

There was a tiny silence. Nobody spoke. The sheriff lit his cigarette.

"Thayer had just got married. I reckon I don't exactly get that little widda-woman, Pat. She didn't seem to grieve much, or take much interest of any kind in Thayer's death except in what property he left. When it turned out he had made a will leaving everything he owned to Miss Karen Chandler, she started hollering like hell—excuse me, ma'am—and then what does Miss Karen do but without so much as a word waive everything to the widda."

"Oh, what a shame!" I said. Karen could have used that money.

The sheriff nodded. "Well, a widda has first claim, ma'am."

"Why would he leave his money to Miss Chandler?" Patrick asked.

"They was engaged." There was a pause. "That was funny, too."

I remembered Karen's vivid happy face there on the plaza a couple of days ago laughingly upturned to Hugh Kennicott. She certainly didn't seem devastated by what had happened to Ray Thayer.

"Miss Karen is kind of a poker-face," the sheriff said slowly. "I reckon she knows more than she's told anyone about Thayer. I don't mean about the way he died. Maybe she knew more about that than she told and maybe she didn't, but Miss Karen or nobody else ever explained how her purple glasses came to be in that car."

"Purple glasses?" Patrick asked.

"It's the frames, darling," I explained.

The sheriff nodded. "Thayer drove a big light-blue Cadillac convertible, which is how we happened to locate the body as soon as we did. The car was parked there at The Rock. That's desert around there and pretty empty country. Maurice Ames, who's a neighbor of Thayer's, saw the car through his telescope early the next morning after Thayer—well, met his death—and for some reason Ames felt suspicious, so he phoned Scott Davies at the public-health office here in Santa Maria, and Scott called up Mrs. Thayer and learned that Thayer hadn't come home that night. Scott called me then and I picked up the coroner, just in case, and we went out to The Rock. The coroner—it's Pete Martinez—found the purple glasses lying in the seat of the car while I was peering over the rim looking for Thayer. Pete's a kind of gossip, and news gets around mighty fast anyhow in Santa Maria, so in two shakes the widda's yelling holy hell—beg pardon, ma'am—against Karen Chandler on account of the glasses. And then the will is read and it's Karen who is in the money, so right away the widda's shouting murder, in spite of Karen's waiving any claim to the property. I had a private talk with Karen about the glasses, and she declared it was the first time she'd seen them in months. She said she supposed they'd got lost. I asked her when she'd had them last and she said she couldn't remember. She said she didn't have to wear glasses all the time and that she had several pairs because she had a bad habit of leaving them around. I asked had she seen Thayer since he got back married and she said no. She didn't seem much broken up." The sheriff took time out, and then said, quietly, "She ain't a girl that shows her feelings much. I wouldn't be surprised, though, if she ain't a young lady who, if she was a mind to, would charge hell with a bucket of water."

Patrick grinned. "She sounds very okay, Jim."

The sheriff nodded.

I said, "Karen wouldn't lie, Mr. Trask."

"No, ma'am," said Mr. Trask.

I wasn't quite sure, though, that he wasn't agreeing with me out of his natural politeness to a lady. Probably Karen would lie. Anybody with spunk will lie if there seems a good reason.

"It's sometimes kind of hard to get justice done in Santa Maria," the sheriff went on. "You know how it is here, ma'am. When we've got an honest prosecutor and enough good men to enforce the law we get along right well. I don't say Ottoway's crooked, mind, I just say he's got the wrong point of view. He's too ambitious. For one thing he does more private business than he's got time for, and one of his clients is Mrs. Dorrie Thayer."

There was another of those silences which lie like cushions in the talk of Western men.

"Before or after Thayer's death?" Patrick asked then.

"After. They'd only been back three days when Thayer was killed. Mrs. Thayer seems to need a good deal of advice, and from other people as well as from Ottoway. I doubt if she takes it, though. She's a born troublemaker, Pat. For instance, she came to my office a few days ago and wanted me to arrest Karen Chandler. I asked for what. She said somebody had broken into her house and stole something. What, I asked. Well, she didn't know what, and she hadn't seen Karen hanging around her place, or anything, so I sicked her onto Ottoway, but she informed me that he's out of town. I knew that, of course. He's taking a vacation." The sheriff snorted. "Resting up from hard work."

Patrick grinned. "Have a post-mortem?" he asked.

"Nope."

Patrick said, after a moment, "You're suspicious of the widow, aren't you, Jim?"

The sheriff blew a couple of smoke rings and watched them float up into the cottonwood tree.

"I cain't prove she murdered Ray Thayer."

"How come Thayer married her? If he was already engaged?"

"Yeah," the sheriff said. "How come?"

"Didn't anybody tell anything?"

The sheriff made a small movement with his big shoulders, and said, "Well, the widda said they got married in Las Vegas, Nevada, the night before they got back here. We checked that. She told the truth. If Thayer did any talking nobody passed it along. He might have talked to Karen Chandler or Maurice Ames or

Scott Davies, and he might have talked with Mrs. Chandler, Karen's mother, but if so none of them admitted anything to me. Another thing, Mrs. Chandler said she would have been just as likely to leave the glasses in the car as her daughter, since they really belonged to her. She's a poker-face, too."

The silence continued a little longer than usual. At its end, Mr. Trask stood up.

"I didn't get anywhere with any of them last fall and I don't know any more now than I knew then about who or what killed Thayer, but it's satisfying to be able to say outright to somebody with something above the collar that he was murdered. Don't let it worry you, Pat."

Patrick had risen. His grave glance met Trask's.

"Sorry I wasn't around, Jim. But I couldn't've done any more than you yourself."

"I reckon you could've, Pat."

We said good-byes at the gate and the sheriff got in his old Buick and rolled down the hill. The state troopers used late-model cars, with the latest devices. But new cars are built close to the ground and in all Santa Maria County, which, remember, is the size of Connecticut, there are only thirty miles of hard-surface highway, and even that is relatively new. The sheriff's old Buick could navigate over rocks, gulches, irrigation ditches and thorny deserts. It was built high off the ground and equipped with tough rayon tires. His job really called for a jeep.

While the sheriff sat on our terrace a rainstorm had blown across the southern end of the valley. It had struck many miles away but it had left the air buoyant and spicy with the smell of the sage. Now the sky was purest azure. There were no clouds remaining, even on the mountains, which were now taking on the amethystine hues they assumed in the late afternoon. We sat out until after sunset, when the Santa Marias turned a deep plushy red, a daily phenomenon in fine weather.

The next afternoon Patrick announced that he was going for a drive. No, I said. We went, but I drove. We drove south on the Santa Fe road. I noticed that Patrick's gaze followed the Rio Grande Canyon which paralleled the road a few miles to our right. It snaked hugely across the great desert plateau, and it was repellent, because when you got close and looked into it you saw violent and upsetting colors, oranges and purplish reds and even a glistening and vicious black.

When we got to the spot where the dirt road led from the highway to The Rock, Patrick said we would go to The Rock.

"No," I said.

"Do as you're told, for a change," Patrick said.

"Darling?"

"I'm a little fed up with this coddling business," Patrick said. I had stopped the car, but I hadn't turned off towards The Rock. "I would have put my foot down long ago if you hadn't been enjoying yourself so much."

"Darling!"

"I'm sorry, dear. But I'm all right."

"Pat, the doctor said . . ."

"Now, listen to me! There's not going to be any more Dr. Johnson in my life, and no more breakfasts in bed, and just now we're driving out to The Rock."

I put the car in low and drove into the narrow and horrible side road. "Okay, sweetie," I said. "If something inside you comes unhitched, you asked for it. And if we ruin the tires . . ."

"We won't, with proper driving. I can take over, any time."

It was an insult. So I drove. I guess I know how to drive. It was slow and torturing, both to the car and ourselves, but I managed it. We parked in the place many cars had made into the accepted parking place and I hung after Patrick as he prowled around on the wide flat reddish surface of The Rock. When he lay down on his stomach and peered over the rim into the canyon I sat on his feet.

"A body falling off the rim might get stopped at a number of places," he presently said. "It wouldn't be likely, but it could happen. There's at least two ledges which might catch a man, and one or two tough-looking little trees. It's amazing what can grow out of what looks like hard rock."

I said, "Why did you ask Trask if there was an autopsy?"

"Thayer might have died from a heart attack."

"And then rolled off?"

"Um-m."

"Nope," I said. "He couldn't've. Unless he died very close to the edge and it crumbled or something. Because he would have to roll uphill, *darling*."

"That's one good reason you needn't sit on my feet, *dear*."

I continued to hold down his feet, meanwhile looking about The Rock. It wasn't as level as it looked. It rose evenly from the place where we had parked the car to its rim. Some people would drive their cars right up onto The Rock and turn around on it, and some would walk right to the edge and stand gazing down into the canyon. Well, edges can sheer off. You can get dizzy.

When Patrick got up he walked about The Rock, observing every little thing, and then he examined the countryside.

"How far to the Ames' house, Jean?"

"They say three miles across country."

"It looks further."

"That's because the air is so clear. Are you wondering about Maurice's discovering Ray's car? Here, after he was dead?"

"It's an item. Ames is married to Karen's very beautiful sister."

All men admired Edwina.

"Maurice wouldn't have any motive for murdering Ray Thayer," I said. "If that's what's on your mind."

"I remember Ames distinctly," Patrick said. "If I'm any good at guessing, his motive for doing anything wouldn't be very obvious. He isn't exactly an open book."

"Maurice is a very open book," I argued. "If a thing is to his advantage, he does it, or acquires it, whichever is indicated. If not, he lets it alone. For example, there's Edwina. Maurice built the house on his ranch in Spanish colonial style and furnished it with antiques he brought from Spain himself and when it was all finished and quite perfect along came Edwina. She looked Spanish, even though an American, so Maurice up and married her. She made the house perfect. Maurice doesn't have any feelings. Only taste."

"I take it Edwina is not a young lady who would charge hell with a bucket of water?"

"No," I said. "She isn't. But she manages to do all right for herself. Look, I don't want to talk about people I don't like. It makes me feel unpleasant inside, darling."

Patrick asked, "Is Karen the kind that would deliberately let somebody go unpunished for murdering the man she had expected to marry?"

I had had that on my mind. "Well, I'll tell you, darling. That's been sort of bothering me. I saw Karen on the plaza the other day with a boy named Kennicott. He's a rancher up in Sky Valley. They're in love, I think. Or anyway she is, and she doesn't try to hide it. She wasn't being poker-faced with Hugh Kennicott. I mean, if she fell in love with somebody else right away after Ray died, she wouldn't be apt to say much about Ray, or want anything stirred up, would she?"

"I'm asking you. I don't happen to know Karen Chandler well."

"I don't know her too well myself. She looks like her mother, but I don't know Mrs. Chandler very well, either. I wonder when Karen met Hugh Kennicott?"

"Maybe it doesn't matter," Patrick said. "Beautiful view west from here."

It was magnificent, with one escarpment after another floating up, many miles apart but, from this high red precipice, looking telescoped into dreamy blue terraces stretching to the mountains on the far horizon.

"I never want to set my eyes on this place again," I said.

When we returned to the car Patrick got in at the wheel.

Back in town he announced we would have dinner at El Castillo.

Julia Price would probably be in the restaurant, or come in while we were there, and I would ask her when Karen Chandler met Hugh Kennicott.

She was already there. She was sitting at our favorite table gloomily drinking a martini. "What's the matter?" I asked, several minutes later, after we had sat, and she had inquired after Pat's condition, and Joe Padilla had fetched us our drinks, with a second martini for Julia.

"Just one of those things," Julia mourned.

"Nasty customer?" I guessed.

"Right the first time, Jeanie. Dorrie Thayer came in and accused me of cheating her on a ring she bought the other day, and I haven't been the same since. I offered her money back for the ring, and thereupon she decided maybe it was worth the price after all, and went out, keeping the ring, but leaving me feeling terrible. Which reminds me, Maurice Ames said the other day that the only thing you could do with a triple-plated little bitch like Dorrie—oh, excuse me, Pat."

"Go right ahead, Julia. Don't mind me."

"Well, anyway, Maurice was mad as hell."

"What did she do to Maurice, Julia?"

"They had a fight. She accused him of entering her house and stealing something."

"What?"

"She didn't seem to know what. I wish she'd move back to Hollywood. I think that if it weren't for her Ray Thayer would be alive today."

"How do you mean that?" Patrick asked.

"It's just an idea," Julia said. "I wish I hadn't said it, Pat. I wish I were a noble character, or at least could see Dorrie's side just a little. I wish I hadn't said that, too," Julia said. "I wish I would stop talking."

"How about a dividend?" Patrick asked.

"I think that's a lovely idea, simply lovely," Julia said.

Patrick motioned Joe Padilla for the drinks.

"Julia," I asked presently, "do you happen to know just when Karen Chandler met Hugh Kennicott?"

"Certainly, dear," Julia said. "They met in the shop. It was last fall, while Ray was out in Hollywood. Karen was up from school for the weekend and Hugh stopped in to buy something to send East and Karen came in. I remember thinking right then they would make a good match. They looked so well together, simply lovely. And Hugh's got a lot of money—even more than Maurice Ames, I shouldn't wonder—and that would be lovely for Karen, simply lovely. If it only weren't for Edwina! There I go again," Julia said.

3

The restaurant and bar of El Castillo—we always called it the Castillo—had not changed in appearance while I had been away. But the patrons were different. For one thing there were fewer pseudo and more real cowboys, now that there was a good price for cows and Santa Maria County had gone in for ranching in a big way. Only a few people that we knew came in during dinner. But the place itself looked the same. The restaurant and bar were two long low-ceilinged rooms connected near the front by a wide archway. This presumedly gave a sort of privacy to the bar. Cowhands are very modest and they don't like to drink in a bar in the presence of what they consider ladies, and since the bar did a lively business in the late afternoon, females were expected to take their cocktails in the restaurant. Both rooms had cream-colored adobe walls and golden-varnished *vigas*—beams—which supported the adobe ceilings. Paintings by the local artists adorned the walls. The price of each painting was delicately penciled on a sticker somewhere on its frame and, in case you overlooked that, a sign in the archway said that the prices could be had at the cash desk.

We had a good dinner. I kept watching Patrick for signs of wear and tear from an afternoon which had left me dog-tired, but he didn't seem weary at all.

We were having our coffee when Maurice Ames came into the bar. Our table looked directly through the archway and we saw him some time before he discovered us. The first thing that always popped into my head when I set eyes on Maurice Ames was a crack Julia Price made once. She had remarked that he even had his jeans tailored for him by his tailor in New York. Maybe he did at that. For one thing he couldn't be a stock size. His shoulders were too wide and his torso too long and his legs too short for his height. He couldn't have been more than one or two inches above five feet tall, maybe not that, but he had the shoulders, long arms, and large head that belonged on a man over six feet. He had coffee-colored eyes, swarthy skin, thick wavy iron-gray hair, a big fleshy nose, and a narrow but thick-lipped mouth which smiled into a tight V. Yet he was somehow attractive.

"That's his vitality," I was observing to Patrick, when Maurice spied us through the archway and came over.

"I say!" he said. We said hello and shook hands. Patrick stood up. Maurice declined to sit down. "It's jolly you're back in circulation," he said, looking at Pat. Maurice had been born and raised in New York but he preferred to talk like the British. "We've got to throw you a party, Lieutenant. We don't see a hero every day. Ha, ha." He had a queer shadowy laugh, as if he always had a slight cold in the head. "How about tomorrow night? Dinner." That was impossible, but Patrick promptly said fine. "We dine at seven. Black tie," Maurice said then. Black tie! Just as though there wasn't a war on. Maybe he forgot for the moment that Patrick, dressed in corduroys and a windbreaker, was still in the Marines. "A black tie would look very funny with your blues or your greens, my darling," I thought.

Standing beside the table they made an odd pair. Maurice was so short and wide and so bristling with vitality. Patrick was so tall and lean and so diffident. Maurice was dressed like a cowman, as befitted a rancher in our valley. Under his arm was tucked a very clean, very wide-brimmed, cream-colored hat. "I'll do you a New Mexican dinner!" he was saying, with vigor, his coffee-colored eyes rolling from Patrick to me, and back to Patrick. "I've got some new recipes, jolly good ones, you know, if I do say it myself."

"He's got a jolly good cook," I said to Patrick, when Maurice had bustled away. "The food will be swell. Do you like him, Pat?"

"I don't know that I don't. How did he make his money?"

"In advertising, to start with. I guess he's got his finger in a lot of pies. He doesn't make any mistakes. May I remind you that you don't care much for Mexican food?"

"He said New Mexican," Patrick said.

"I stand corrected, darling. Maurice is nuts on his New Mexican recipes, by the way. He's traveled all over the state collecting them." I stopped and thought. "We've got a lot of peculiar people in Santa Maria."

I was the one, for a change, who got tucked into bed that night.

I went straight to sleep.

I was awakened by Pancho. He was standing on his hind legs and rooting aggressively at the mattress. I reached down and touched his head. It felt soft and satiny but he pulled it away and made small whimpering noises, barely audible, and very urgent.

Oh, Lord, I thought, why does anybody keep a dog!

I got up and tiptoed to the living-room door, thinking he wanted to go out.

Pancho stationed himself by the window open on the lane. He grunted ominously.

Patrick was lying perfectly quiet. I didn't want Pancho's whim to wake him. Tiptoeing back, I picked the dog up and chucked him in the bathroom and shut the door.

"That'll learn him!" Patrick said, as I slipped back in bed.

"Darling! I thought you were asleep."

Patrick put out an arm and pulled me against his shoulder.

"Dirty trick you pulled on that dog, Jeanie. It's discouraging. Generations of breeding have gone into making him a good servant to his mistress and then she double-crosses him—won't let him do his stuff."

"Stop drooling and say what you mean, Pat."

"We had a lurker."

I shivered and moved closer, and felt safer.

"Maybe it was just some Mexican celebrating something," I said.

"Huh-uh. I was awake. Pancho knew that and came to me before he woke you. The so-and-so lurked all over the place. Probably intends to steal your emeralds."

"Good," I said. We couldn't afford the emeralds, which Patrick had blown himself beyond his means to give me for a wedding present. "I mean, they're insured. We could pay up the insurance and the storage bills and buy some bonds . . ."

"Don't dream, Jeanie." Patrick lit a cigarette with his free arm. "I've been dying for a smoke, but I wanted to see what the guy was up to. I got interested in the dog, too. He's a good little beast, Jeanie. First he came to me, knowing I was awake. . . ."

"How would he know that?"

"People smell different awake than asleep. At least, to a dog. As you know, dachshunds have very fine noses." Patrick kissed my nose and said, "Of course, you have too. Pity you didn't wake sooner. Between you and Pancho we might have had some real detective work. Maybe a man intending to break in and steal a ham sandwich smells different from a man who means to steal emeralds, or with intent to murder."

I yawned.

"What lovely ideas you have in the night, darling."

"Well, he's gone away."

"There wasn't anybody, really?"

"There was."

Pancho scratched on the bathroom door. Patrick got up and let him out.

The dog did two or three delighted swishes around the room and then leaped into his basket, where he snuggled in with delighted nuzzling noises and cheerful sighs.

"The lurker doesn't seem to weigh on his mind, darling. I don't believe there was any. I think you made it up."

"The lurker departed while you were putting Pancho in the clink. That's civilization for you! Society breeds a fine dog and trains him to bark at the right time and when the time comes society forbids the dog to bark."

I yawned again. "If you don't mind, society will go back to sleep, darling."

The next evening, when we were driving along the Santa Fe road on our way to the party, Patrick asked how long Ames had lived in our valley. I said maybe ten years. "What brought him here?" Patrick asked.

"He came first on a trip. He liked the country and moved out. Maurice is feudal, Pat. I imagine the special attraction of Santa Maria was because he could live out here sort of like a Spanish grandee. Darling, be sure to notice the tiles in the risers of the main staircase. They are copies of the ones in El Greco's house in Toledo—Toledo, *Spain*. . . ."

"Thanks," Patrick said.

"Now, don't be stuffy—there are lots of Toledos. You've been in Toledo, Spain. You probably remember El Greco's house. The whole main staircase in the Ames house is supposed to be an exact reproduction of El Greco's. It would be fun if you remembered, and would know if Maurice is telling the truth."

"If he's faking, want me to tell him so?"

"Darling! Now, listen. Maurice Ames is full of little tricks. It would be a lot of fun if you discovered that his staircase is a bluff, I mean, not a copy of El Greco's at all. We'd keep it to ourselves, of course. I wouldn't run around telling people that Maurice lied about his staircase."

Patrick's glance was impudent.

"I did go to Toledo," he said. "But I'm afraid I'll have to disappoint you, because I didn't see El Greco's house. I didn't even know there was one."

"What a pity! Well, anyhow, Maurice gives beautiful dinners. It's fun to dress up."

Patrick groaned. He was wearing his forest-green uniform and his service and medal ribbons with their stars looked very gorgeous. I felt so proud. But he complained that the uniform felt stuffy and uncomfortable. His muscles, he said, were slack, and he had put on weight. I laughed at that. He was lean as a grasshopper. I was wearing a green lace dinner dress, an old one but new to Santa Maria, and it was precisely the green for my emeralds, my emerald engagement ring and my bracelet and the synthetic emerald loops I wore in my ears which everybody said looked like real emeralds. I loved to dress up. I liked Maurice's making his parties occasions.

The mountains were putting on their famous red plush act as we angled off into the Silver River road. This road was made of crushed white rock as far as the Ames' place. We began to climb a little as soon as we left the highway. Ahead on the right were the houses of the three friends. The first was quite near the road. That was Scott Davies'. It was a pure-white adobe in the modern manner. There were no windows on the flat white façade toward the road. Spruces and tamarisks planted in close thickets shut away all of the house except that blank wall from passersby, who got no inkling of the colorful, ingenious, lively house and terrace and garden beyond. Scott had perched his house on the edge of the cliff along the Silver River flood plain. Stairs went steeply from his flagstone terrace down to his gardens and orchard below. There was a path, too, which led along under the cliff, made by Mexicans and burros who had tilled the Silver River plain for generations.

The Thayer place was a half mile along from Scott Davies'. It had never been interesting. Now it looked rundown and dirty. Adobe needs constant care to look fresh.

The bright-blue Cadillac stood in the drive, seeming to have stopped at the wrong place.

The road veered left away from the flood plain, circled widely, and climbed more steeply. Now we had the Ames ranch on both sides. We had traveled through typical upland desert country all the way from Santa Maria, that is, yellowish earth sprinkled with grayish cactus and sage, freshened by spring but not verdant. Now we had grass. It was a short close-growing grass and looked at this season from a distance fine and vivid as a putting green. Dark plump evergreen juniper trees grew casually all over the landscape, and the Ames' cattle browsed on the grass. The ranch was fenced. We rattled over cattle-guards.

There was lane a quarter-mile long leading from the road to Maurice's house, which also stood on the bluff above the Silver River, but well away, so that a proper lawn surrounded the big two-storey white house. The house was built solidly of stucco simulating adobe, but solider and sounder if less artistic than adobe. It had large double verandas.

A pretty dark-skinned maid in a Spanish peasant costume let us in and took our wraps. We could hear Maurice talking back to the people in the drawing room as he bustled out to welcome us. His eyes were shining in their queer brown opaque fashion. He loved giving parties, and he projected his excitement. You enjoyed coming here even when you thought you might not.

He shook hands vigorously.

Patrick saw the staircase and delayed our entrance into the drawing room by going over to gaze at it. "You like it, eh?" Maurice asked. His mouth shaped its tight V. He rubbed his dry short-fingered hands.

"I like it very much," Patrick said. "I seem to have seen it before some place."

Maurice beamed like a light. "It's a copy of . . ."

Patrick lifted a hand. "I've got it. I saw it in—in El Greco's house, in Toledo."

"I say, old boy!" Maurice said. He was hushed. He gazed on Patrick with profound admiration. "That's amazing, you know. Really. You're the first! A lot of blokes that call themselves experts have missed that. I say-y! Really!"

When I got Patrick's eye I gave him a knifelike stare of utter disapproval. He looked innocent. But had he guessed what his astonishing memory of a staircase he had never seen was about to get him into, he wouldn't have been enjoying teasing me so much.

4

Maurice was dressed like a Spanish don, in black broadcloth, with an embroidered jacket and a white satin shirt.

The outfit suited him, enhanced his bizarre appearance, and it made him belong with the house.

As he linked his arms with ours and guided us into the drawing room I was conscious of his dry short-fingered clasp on my bare wrist, and I wondered why it is that so many people who aren't physically attractive like to touch you. I had such mixed feelings about Maurice Ames. He had always made a fuss over me, called me his yellow-eyed gal, and such, and I had always disliked it, but I had come to take it lightly because it was well-meant. He simply wasn't sensitive to people. He assumed, I think, that because he was pleased with himself for acquiring power and money and the beautiful things he craved and could now possess, that others were pleased for him, too. He was a generous, enthusiastic host. He lavished everything on Edwina and would have done the same, I had always thought, for Bee and Karen, if they had let him. You couldn't give things to Bee and Karen.

All the same, in spite of my rationalizing, when he squeezed my arm now, and told Patrick his yellow-eyed gal was lovelier than ever, I felt that deep tingling resentment. It's because you don't like being touched by all and sundry, I reminded myself. It's a matter of taste. It's nothing.

Edwina, her mother, Bee Chandler, her sister Karen, Scott Davies, and Hugh Kennicott sat around the huge hooded fireplace at one end of the great room. Here was dark Spanish-style oak in the massive furniture and the wood paneling and beams, and garnet red in the deep-piled carpet, the draperies, and the seats and backs of sofas and chairs.

Edwina wore a garnet-red dinner dress which showed off her full bosom and tiny waist. Her big black eyes went limpid as she rose to welcome us, and she smiled her sweet drowsy smile. She laid her lips lightly on my cheek. She offered Patrick one of her plump satiny white hands as if she expected it to be kissed. It is one of God's greatest gifts to a woman, I thought, to let her have a white skin and straight shining black hair and a face and head shaped so the hair looks wonderful parted in the middle and worn in a bun on her neck. But her musky perfume was her own choosing, and I didn't like it. I wondered what Pancho would make of a lurker dabbed with Edwina's perfume. Society certainly does make things tough for a dog.

Mrs. Chandler, not Karen, was using the amethyst spectacles.

Bee held them before her eyes to look at us as we entered with Maurice, and she laid them down on the coffee table near the sofa where she was sitting. She took them with her to the dining room. Later I couldn't remember having seen them after that.

Bee Chandler wore with complete indifference and much style an anything-but-new violet-blue dinner dress. It matched her fine eyes, which those specs had been designed to show off. You saw Edwina's beauty in a flash. You'd be jealous to deny it. But Bee's face haunted you, and Karen's would too, when it was older and more interesting, because you kept looking again to discover the secret of its charm. It was a triangular face, deeply tanned, with flat hollow cheeks, and a wide lively red mouth. Like Karen's, Bee's black hair curled naturally and she wore it in a feathercut. Karen was a size larger than Bee. She was more impulsive and more talkative. Bee had some white in her hair, and she smoked a lot and with a special elegance and Karen didn't smoke at all, but the resemblance was always remarkable. It is trite to say they looked like sisters, but they did.

There was trouble in the atmosphere and I sensed it the minute we were settled in the circle by the fireplace. The reason was soon obvious. Or was it? Could such a superficial annoyance be enough? I mean, could the fact that Karen and

Hugh weren't dressed up be enough to explain Maurice's waspishness? Scott
Davies had come in his dinner jacket, which was going rather rusty, but Karen
wore a rose-pink sweater and a gray tweed suit, and Hugh Kennicott's tall handsome figure was dressed in a dark-green flannel shirt, gabardine cheyenne pants
and cowboy boots.

As Maurice fetched from a sidetable the silver tray of cocktails he said, breezily, but with acid, "I've just been telling these kids not to come here again dressed
as if they expected to feed in a hamburger joint."

Hugh Kennicott's dark eyes glinted. "I apologize, Maurice," he said, in that
deep-toned, slow voice. *"Again."*

Maurice was handing the cocktails. He did not answer Hugh, or look at him.

"Shades of Emily Post!" Karen snapped at Maurice. "What were we to do?
We couldn't get away from Santa Fe in time to go home and change. You would
have hated us more, Maurice, if we had been late."

"You know my rules, darling," Maurice said, airily. He handed her a cocktail.

Taking it, Karen looked as if she might throw it back in his face.

"Well, don't be such a shirt! This is the Wild West, Maurice," she said.

"This house isn't," Maurice said, and though he spoke it gaily, there was
anger here, something smoldering underneath, which must be more serious, even
to Maurice Ames, than two kids turning up in daytime clothes.

Besides, Maurice had been out here ten years. He ought to have got used to
Santa Maria's unconventionality by this time. People dressed pretty much as
they chose. People had turned up at his affairs not formally garbed often enough,
and anyhow you didn't pile extra miles on your tires in wartime just to put on a
boiled shirt.

Maurice put the tray where he had got it and, standing in the circle, lifted his
glass.

"To the globe-trotting Abbotts!" he said. "And if Jeanie will forgive me, specially to Pat! We don't have a hero to dinner every day, really."

He smiled his tight V-shaped smile at me and at Patrick and sipped at the
cocktail.

I felt that deep embarrassment Maurice was always stirring up inside me and
I stole a look at Patrick, sitting next to Edwina, and seeing him accept the self-
conscious ovation without a shadow of irritation I knew it gave him, I envied
him.

Maurice dragged up an ottoman and sat at my feet.

"How do you like this drink, darling?" he asked.

I looked at it and tasted it. It looked like an old-fashioned. It tasted of Cuban
rum. It was delicious, and I said so. Patrick hated this kind of concoction, but I
loved it.

"It's my own invention," Maurice said. "I call it the Scorpion."

"It's got something in it which makes it a strictly New Mexican drink," Scott

Davies said, and he smiled as he said, "The formula's a secret."

"It packs a wicked wallop," Karen said. "Or should I say sting, Maurice?"

Maurice ignored her. Karen glanced at Bee, who did not look at her. Hugh Kennicott stared glumly at his glass. He looked about to burst with fury, I thought.

I glanced at Patrick, wondering what he was making behind his diffidence of the touchy undercurrents in this room.

He sat gazing down at Edwina. She was asking a question. She listened to his answer with her sweet sleepy smile.

"The cocktail belongs to the book," Maurice said.

Bee Chandler said, "Are you really still serious about that cookbook, Maurice?"

"Never more so, Bee-a-treech-ay, darling. Remember that Ray Thayer and I were planning a cookbook, Jeanie?"

I nodded, it being a thing you were never permitted to forget, because Maurice was eternally talking about it, but the truth was it hadn't come into my mind since I had left Santa Maria. Ray was to write it, I remembered, and Maurice had the recipes and would plan the advertising and selling.

"You always said it would make a mint," I said.

"But rather," Maurice said.

"I never could see that," Scott Davies said. "There's millions of cookbooks."

"My dear boy, there's millions of everything on this earth. You merely make something better, or, to be exact, you make the public think it's better, and they rush to buy it. The ideas for our book were—are, I should say—entirely original."

"Naturally, if it's a man's cookbook," I said.

"My sweet!" Maurice cried. "My innocent little angel, there are countless cookbooks by men. All the great creative cooks have been men. This one will merely be the cookbook to out-cookbook all other cookbooks."

There were smiles and a little laughter, and Scott Davies said, "What a pity Ray couldn't have done the thing before he died, Maurice. He was so sold on it. He thought it would be fun. He disliked so much of the writing he had to do. He always talked about your confounded book as if it would be a picnic. I must confess, not being a gourmet, or even a fair cook, that I never could understand what you two got so excited about."

"Because it was a jolly good idea, Scott! Well, cheer up. Writers are a dime a dozen. Another will turn up."

There was a queer crisp silence. Everybody, I thought, was shocked. Maurice didn't mean it, I felt, the way it sounded.

Edwina said, in a voice like black velvet, "But of course you must have been so brave, Pat. Don't pretend you weren't! We know better."

"Another writer may turn up," Scott said gently, "but he won't be Ray." It was a reproof.

"Well, he asked for it!" Maurice said. "Whatever made him get hooked up with that little bitch? He ought to have had some consideration for his neighbors, if not for himself." Maurice bounced up and bustled over to fetch the cocktail shaker, and coming back he said, "I don't know why I let her put me in such a dither, really. If Karen can stand for her, I daresay I can."

The red sailed up under Karen's tan. She said nothing. She shook her head when Maurice offered to refill her glass.

Hugh Kennicott lit a cigarette and turned down another cocktail. Maurice should thank his stars for his gray hairs, I shouldn't wonder.

"Look at Pat's ribbons!" Edwina cried, softly. "Look at his stars!"

There was a little rush of craning at the ribbons, and asking questions. The unpleasant moment was past. But there was too much eagerness for the change of subject, and Hugh Kennicott looked angrier than ever. He must have a whale of a temper, I thought. He hates Maurice, anyone can see that, I decided. Maybe there is something in this business with Edwina. Maybe it's an affair. Edwina had that look of clinging, that ageless quality, which made every man want to to take care of her.

She doesn't give a hoot about Patrick's ribbons, I thought, or the war, or anything else save Edwina. She's one hundred per cent undiluted Eve.

"Drink it down, dearest!" Maurice said to me. For the girl in the gay calico costume had come in to announce dinner.

The dining room was another large room, with pale walls and more of the massive dark oak furniture. There was candlelight. The table was set with snowy linen, and silver and crystal, and cream-colored English china. Other candles in tall candelabra on the sideboard lighted up Michael O'Hara's portrait of Edwina. In it she wore a white dress and the rubies Maurice had given her when they married. They were larger and more numerous than my emeralds. Everything had its price, I supposed, glancing down the long table across the flat centerpiece of freesias and tiny yellow tulips, and observing with one of my twinges that Patrick was still absorbed in Edwina. They all were. Hugh was watching her now, with a small soft gleam in his dark eyes, and Scott, as always, let his devotion glow all over his blond face.

But Maurice centered his upon the soup.

It was delicious. It had cream in it, and spices, and butter, and chicken and numerous mysterious herbs. The entree was a chicken dish with wild rice and toasted almonds. What dry white wine tantalized its sauce? And why was the parsley-and-butter sauce on the subsequent filet mignon different and better than any other we had ever tasted, and why did a simple avocado served in the bed of crisp cold lettuce taste so wonderfully at Maurice's table? It would all be told, Maurice always said, in the book.

This was one of his very special New Mexican dinners. The New Mexican recipes were his particular secrets. He had collected them with great patience, and he had perfected some, and some he had even invented.

"My cook's an Indian," he always said happily. "You'll never get my secrets out of Geronima. Indians never tell. You'll have to wait for the book."

The dinner was the reason for the party. It lasted long, and afterward there was no time for bridge, even if anyone besides Edwina had wanted it. Hugh Kennicott was the first to go. He said good-bye to Maurice in a brusque way that suggested he never intended to darken his door again. Scott went next. Then Maurice took Patrick for a tour of the house, and almost at once I went upstairs with Bee and Karen, leaving Edwina by the fire.

Lazy sensuous creature, I thought. She hated making any move she needn't. Of course she would sit by the fire. Why trouble to go upstairs with three women, two of them her own mother and sister? Why bother? What's the point? Such sweet ideas were tripping through my mind as I climbed the famous staircase with Bee and Karen Chandler. I stopped suddenly, attracted by the blue in one of the tiles above a step just below the landing, a blue as heavenly as that in a *Della Robbia* plaque, and then behind me I heard a rustle, and my nose picked up Edwina's perfume. She was coming up after all, I thought. I had been unkind to her, in my mind. I turned back smiling, but only to see her moving swiftly along the lower hall, a rapt expression on her oval face.

Bee and Karen had gone on ahead. I moved a step to the left and leaned over the railing.

Hugh Kennicott came silently out of a door near the rear of the hall. I knew that door. It opened into a short flight of steps which met the steps from the kitchen on a small landing, from which another flight led up to the cook's quarters.

Edwina gave Hugh both hands and swayed toward him. He put his arms around her.

I was furious. I ducked back and hurried on upstairs.

"What's the matter?" Bee Chandler asked, when I entered the guest room where the girl had left our things.

I said, "Matter?"

"You look so white."

"Oh. Maybe I need some make-up." I dived at a dressing table.

"Maurice's dinners are very swell," Karen said, "but you really ought to bring along your bicarbonate."

"Maurice enjoys himself so," Bee said.

"Maurice belongs in the Stone Age," Karen said.

"Karen, darling, stop it. The way you tease Maurice . . ."

"I'm not teasing," Karen said, tilting up her mother's chin and giving her a little kiss. "It's okay by me if Maurice and Edwina choose to live back in the Holy Spanish Empire or whatever they called it, but this is the last of these ordeals by food I'm going to endure. It's—why, it's awful, in times like these!

It's obscene. Besides—I—well, don't ask me why, but I can't come here any more."

Bee put an arm around her. They stood side by side, Karen two or three inches the taller, but so much alike.

"Have you got the specs?" Bee asked.

Karen felt in her pocket. "I've got one pair, darling," she said.

"When will you come to see us, Jeanie?" Bee asked.

"I can't promise, Bee. Pat shouldn't go out really."

"I suppose he's getting restless?"

"Very."

"Well, did you have a good time?" I asked Patrick, on the way home.

He was driving. I had my head on his shoulder.

"Very interesting, dear."

"The dinner was fascinating. Wasn't it?"

"Very," Patrick said. I knew he had disliked everything from the Scorpion on until he got the plain strawberries and cream.

So I laughed and said, "You're lying."

"I am not. The dinner did *fascinate* me. I didn't say I liked it."

"And Edwina?"

"Very lovely gal."

"God dammit!" I said. I couldn't help it. "Those droopy drowsy females ring the bell every time. What's she up to with Hugh Kennicott, Pat? I saw them meet in the hall. And I don't see why the hell Maurice Ames puts up with her."

"Maybe she drinks his Scorpions," Patrick said.

"Don't be funny, darling."

"I didn't know that I was."

I said, "It was seeing her meeting Hugh that made me mad. Karen is such a peach."

Patrick said, "Ten to your five that Karen gets him, Jeanie."

"You don't know anything about women, Pat. Karen won't have him if Edwina's been first. Did you like the house?"

"It's a bird," Patrick said. "Specially the kitchen, only I didn't get too good a look at the kitchen, because when we got there Ames buzzed around to all the doors and windows to make sure nobody was listening and then he offered me a job. He wants me to shadow his wife."

"Darling! What kind of detective does he think you are? I hope you socked him one?"

"Why? You aren't offered such nice work every day, chum." I allowed it to pass. "I didn't say yes or no, however, because just then we heard a noise which I thought was on the back stairs. I yanked the door open. Hugh Kennicott was standing on the landing, which is six or seven steps up from the kitchen. I shut the door. Ames couldn't see into the stairs from where he stood and he assumed that nobody was there. But after that he was worried that somebody might be listening and he asked if he could come and talk it over at our house. Day after tomorrow, he said. Evidently there's no grand rush."

"Pat, you've got no business . . ."

"Shush! He has such faith in me. What a memory I've got! Look how I spotted the El Greco staircase."

"Pat, that was awful. I honestly didn't know you had such a low streak."

"It comes out, Jeanie."

I said, "Hugh Kennicott's got something on his mind."

"I shouldn't wonder."

"He was mad all evening. Look, Edwina's working on him high, wide and handsome. It's too bad."

Patrick said, after a few minutes, "I rather like Ames. He got such a kick from his party."

"He's got a superiority complex, Pat."

"Inferiority," Patrick said. "I suppose he'd get it as a child. He's almost what's called a pituitary dwarf. Something goes wrong with the glands. The glands make up for it sometimes by giving such people super-normal energy. But the inferiority sticks. Other children laugh at such kids and they often turn their extra energy toward making themselves successes in this or that."

"People still laugh at his looks," I said, and I felt sorry for him, and ashamed of myself, because I too was critical of Maurice's appearance.

"He's an unhappy creature, Jeanie."

"Unhappy?"

"He is one of the unhappiest people I ever saw in my life," Patrick said.

"Do you think it's Edwina, darling?"

"I don't know. I think it's more than that. But, I—don't—know."

We had a lovely time next morning. We got up late and Mrs. Dominguez served us breakfast under the tree. Patrick had a line of lusty jokes, very hammy, much on the that-wasn't-a-lady-that-was-my-wife order, which Mrs. Dominguez adored. He would tell her a few and send her into fits of giggles and afterward for hours she would hold her sides every time he so much as looked her way. He dished them out that morning till she could hardly get on with her work. We didn't go to the plaza, not even to the post office. There was a thunderstorm along in the afternoon. The air smelled sweet then, and spicy, and we made a fire in the living room and had tea and pulled out some of our favorite books. The unpleasant side of last night's party hadn't been so much as mentioned all day long, and when Mr. Trask rolled up our hill along about six o'clock I was feeling so carefree that I didn't have even an intimation of looming evil.

The sheriff didn't get out.

"Maurice Ames is taken sick all of a sudden, Pat. Doc Johnson's out there now. He phoned a little while ago and said Ames wanted me to fetch you out there. Ames got on the line and yelled that he wanted a post-mortem. The doc tried to shut him up. Ames hung on, I reckon he was on another extension, and said to tell you there was a hundred thousand in it for you if you apprehended who'd poisoned him." The sheriff's eyes were suspicious. "Sounds pretty loco to me, Pat. Suit yourself about going out there."

5

Hugh Kennicott stood up from the corner seat and his gloom was broken by his sudden smile.

"I'm running the joint while Julia does an errand," he said. He pulled a raw-hide chair where I wanted it, facing the window on the plaza, gave me a ciga-rette, lighted it and sat down again. He wore his working clothes. His weather-stained dog-eared Stetson was in the seat beside him.

He said, "I forgot to ask if there was anything I could do? Or whatever it is Julia would say."

I laughed, because nobody ever knew what Julia might say, at any time.

"You can talk," I said. "That's why I come here."

Hugh's gloom descended over him, and me too, like a black fog, as he said, "I'm afraid I'm not very good at talking."

Oh, my, I thought, how dismal he is! Surely he isn't always like this, or Karen wouldn't want him, though of course you never can tell who people will fall in love with. But at that moment Hugh seemed pretty heavy for my taste. I remem-bered Julia's saying once about somebody or other that he would be a bore to marry because he was too correct. A boy ought to whistle after the girls at least once in his life, Julia said, and so, at this moment, I saw Hugh as too ponderous, too cautious, in short, not enough fun.

But what about that business with Edwina? Meeting her in the hall like that? You couldn't call that cautious.

No, dumb was the word for that, which wasn't attractive, either.

His expression changed.

"I was thinking about you when you came in, Mrs. Abbott." His face had got somber again. "Or rather about Pat. I was just wondering if he was well enough to be bothered with something—well, kind of serious?"

"Jean to you, Hugh. You got rustlers?"

"Rustlers? What made you think of them?"

"I can't think of anything more serious to a cowman than rustlers, and they've had them around here, they say."

Hugh grinned, and for a few seconds his face was all sunshine, and he was different entirely.

"We're not much worried about rustlers up in Sky Valley. Too hard for them to get in and out," he said, and sobering, he continued, "No—it has to do with a friend. I'm worried for someone. I would like to have Pat's advice."

Oh-oh, I thought, and no you don't. I am not going to have my Patrick wasting his energy doing service for Edwina, if she's the one you've got on your mind. If he wanted to do something for Maurice and get properly paid and it wasn't too strenuous, that was all right. But I didn't want him working to help Edwina.

"Hugh," I said, "he mustn't. He shouldn't have things on his mind, you see."

Hugh took me at my word.

"Thanks for saying so, Jean. I'm sorry."

There was an interval, and I began to regret my haste, thinking that it might have been something else Hugh wanted Pat for, not Edwina's troubles at all. Anyway, I might as well know what he wanted. But I hardly knew how to get back to it.

Hugh looked at his watch.

"I may have to turn this joint over to you," he said. "Julia said three minutes. It's been twenty."

"All right, Hugh." He didn't go, however, so I said, "Have you got a lot of cows, Hugh?" I asked it to make talk. I meant to get back to whatever he wanted with Patrick.

"Cows?" Hugh looked astonished. "Oh, yes. Yes, of course. You never know just how many until a round-up, though."

"That's what makes it easy for the rustlers."

"Rustlers? Oh, yes," Hugh said, vaguely.

"You like ranching?"

"Like it? Nuts about it." He came out of his abstraction and his face brightened. "You think you can't live unless you can do something, and they won't let you. I wanted to fly. You die inside when you're told you must do something else. You wind up crazy about what you didn't want to do. Does that make sense?"

"You mean ranching, Hugh?" He nodded. "Well, I can imagine myself liking that all right. I wish we could have a ranch when the war's all finished up. I wish Patrick could see your place."

His dark eyes shone. "Well, why not? Any time you say." He looked doubtful. "It's only a cow-camp, though."

"That's the kind we like, Hugh."

"It's pretty rough. Karen and Bee like the set-up, but Edwina thinks it's pretty crude. It is, of course. The boys have their own bunkhouse but they chow at my place. I don't know if you would want to come to eat—you'll have to eat with the hands . . ."

"When?"

Hugh was pleased. "How about tomorrow night?"

"Some time next week would be better. I don't know about that altitude yet, for Pat."

"Any time you like. I'll ask Karen and Bee when you come."

"How nice! Karen has got to be so stunning, Hugh."

"Stunning? Well, I don't know. She's a lot of fun."

"She's wonderful looking, Hugh. She's like Bee. You never get tired looking at their faces because they're different every time."

Hugh looked baffled, then he said, "She's a very swell kid, but I don't understand her exactly. She's not at all like Edwina."

He looked at his watch. He unfolded himself and stood up. "Here comes Julia," he said. He smiled at her as she sailed into the shop. "About time!" he chided her, amiably.

Julia was talking breathlessly as she stalked and jangled.

"*Madre di Dios,* kids! What trouble! Maurice Ames is dying, they say. Murdered, maybe."

Hugh's smile on seeing Julia changed to a dark cynical stare. He stood without moving. A little spiral of smoke curled from the cigarette between his fingers.

Julia had stopped beside us. Her stretched eyes went up and down, between Hugh and myself.

"He's been poisoned. He thinks somebody did it on purpose. Doc Johnson's been out there for hours. Maurice himself demanded that Jim Trask come out, and he told him to have a post-mortem. Isn't that horrible? A post-mortem on yourself!"

Hugh's cigarette scorched his fingers. There was a tiny odor, like burned hair. He tossed the stub at the fireplace. He looked blankly at the burn, rubbing it, and not as if he comprehended what it was exactly. Nobody spoke for what seemed quite a long time.

"Think of ordering your own stomach to be removed and sent to a laboratory!" Julia wailed, and all her jewelry clinked and chittered.

"I don't believe that!" Hugh said.

"Oh, Hugh!" Julia reproached, sadly. "Jeanie, you must know what it's all about. With Patrick out there, too?"

Hugh turned on me. "Why didn't you tell me?" he cried. "I could have been halfway out there by now. Somebody's got to look after Edwina."

"You stay away from there, Hugh Kennicott!" Julia said. "You needn't worry about Edwina."

Hugh swooped to pick up his hat. He avoided our glances. He was again the obstinate dismal young man he had been when I entered the shop. I was filled with impatience, as you are for people who look bright and handsome and are, after all, merely stupid.

"Don't be a damn fool, Hugh," Julia said, and imploring him, she said, "That's the very last place you should go. You stay away. Edwina can look after herself. I shouldn't be surprised if she didn't have a finger in this."

"My God Almighty, Julia!" Hugh shouted, and he rushed out of the shop.

Julia sank into the seat he had left, and I gave her a cigarette. "Now, I've done it," she lamented. "Now, I've not only hurt his feelings, but I've made him think he has to be a hero and rescue that slut. You can't do anything about that kind of women, Jeanie. They win every time. Listen, why on earth did you let Pat go out there with Trask?"

"How did you know that, Julia?"

"Everybody knows everything," Julia said. "Don't you remember the Santa Maria grapevine? To start with, the telephone operator listened in when Maurice got hold of Trask and told him to bring Patrick. She heard him offer a hundred grand if Pat could find out who dunnit—is that true, Jean?"

I nodded. It sounded very fishy now. It was too much money. I said so. Julia said that it certainly pinned the rap on Edwina, because Maurice would do it to cheat her out of what she hoped to receive by polishing him off. I said I couldn't see why she would want his money if she was going to marry Hugh and the Kennicotts were supposed to have so much. Julia said that, money or no money, Maurice would be such a nuisance if she tried to unload him that murder would look simpler than a divorce.

"Poison is exactly the method she would use," Julia said. "Wait till I tell you the rest. That's a party line. Dorrie Thayer also listened on the phone when Maurice called the sheriff. Dorrie then phoned Scott Davies at the Public-Health Office. The operator also heard that, and passed it along. Meanwhile one of the Ames' servants used the line when the others weren't on it and reported that after Maurice got sick Edwina only stayed at home long enough to see that everything in the way of food in the icebox was put in the incinerator and then she lit out for the Kennicott ranch in Sky Valley."

"Oh. In that case maybe Hugh might as well have gone out to Ames' first. Pat's there. He may advise Hugh what to do."

"Hugh's a mule," Julia said. "He thinks Edwina is an angel. He will take her in, of course, give her his room and bunk out with the cowboys. It's a mess." Julia jumped up. I'm going out and talk to Bee. She's the one. She can handle Edwina, and Hugh, too. Hell, why hasn't she a phone? What's the matter with people, anyway? Why haven't people got telephones? Oh, it's the war, of course. Jeanie, you come with me.

"Nope. I'll hang around the plaza and wait for Pat. Want me to lock this place up?"

Julia put on her peaked Mexican sombrero and got her jacket.

"Thanks, Jeanie. Leave the key for me at the desk in the Castillo." Julia turned at the door and said, "I can't remember when I've gone to such a lot of trouble for an idiot. I mean Hugh. I like that boy, but he is a complete fool!"

6

I stopped at the Plaza Pharmacy for aspirin, on my way to the Castillo.

Bee and Karen Chandler were perched on high stools at the fountain, drinking cokes. They wore levis, work-shirts, bandannas, and their wide-brimmed hats and windbreakers were piled on an extra stool. Brown horn-rimmed spectacles jutted from the pocket of each wool shirt.

On seeing me their mobile red mouths smiled welcome and Bee wanted to buy me a drink. I didn't want a soft drink, but a cocktail. However, considering the drama in the air, and their apparent nonchalance about it, I said yes and hitched myself onto another stool, and when the boy had made the drink and had gone off into the back of the store for reasons of his own, I said, "Julia's just gone out to your place, Bee."

"Oh," Bee said. "Well, hurry up, Karen, and maybe we'll get there before she leaves. Or maybe before she arrives." Bee and I grinned because she was referring to Julia's ability to be sidetracked anywhere and at any time. But Karen didn't grin. She looked straight down into her glass.

She said, "Julia probably went out to break the news to us gently, Bee."

"Oh," I said. "Then you know?"

"People are funny," Karen said.

"Julia's all right," Bee said.

"I didn't say she wasn't," Karen said. "Only why get hot and bothered because Maurice takes to his bed and starts screaming murder? Maybe it's a trick. Maybe he's just trying to interest Edwina?"

"Well, he might not be, either," Bee said tartly. "You ought not say things like that. Maurice might die."

"Then I would be sorry," Karen said.

She didn't sound sorry. She sounded unfeeling.

"I would like to know if he uses that British accent when in agony," Karen said.

"I kind of like Maurice," I said.

"Maurice is all right," Bee laughed. "Look, Jeanie, I think instead of going home and trying to catch Julia I had better run along and be with Edwina. She's probably upset."

"Now Bee's getting reactionary," Karen said. "Let Maurice pull the feudal stuff, chum. You keep out—hear?"

"Listen to her, Jeanie," Bee said. She said to Karen, "Feudal or not, darling, I'm going out to Edwina's. You'd better come too."

"Nope," Karen said.

"Suit yourself, Baby. But you may have to hoof it home."

"I'll drive Karen home, Bee," I said, and, after hesitating to say it, I said, "I don't think Edwina is at home. The grapevine has it that she's gone to Sky Valley."

"That's probably just talk," Bee said. Her tone was matter-of-fact. She laid the money for the drinks on the fountain. She slid off the stool and put on her hat and jacket. "I won't be too late, Karen," she said.

We all said so long. Though they argued, there was no heat in it, and Bee made no effort to persuade Karen to accompany her. "Bee isn't very feudal," I said, "You ought to be grateful for that, Karen."

Karen smiled. "She's well, but she's wasting good energy getting mixed up in this. Do you know anything special about Maurice? We only heard the gossip. At the post office. We thought if he was as sick as all that Edwina would have let us know."

"Pat went out there," I said. Karen nodded. They knew that, then. "I won't know anything definite till he comes in."

And maybe not then, I thought. Maybe he wouldn't want to talk.

"I like Maurice better than Edwina at that," Karen said. "I suppose it's awful of me, but I don't like Edwina at all. I never have. There is something decent in Maurice. He bores me talking about only what he's interested in and I don't approve of the way he runs after power and money and seems to think that any means of adding to what he's got is legitimate, and all that sort of thing, but he's got something—something deep inside—that I can't help but like. We quarrel. He spats with me, the way he did last night because I didn't dress up, but I understand it. Hugh doesn't. Hugh has a frightful temper. I was afraid they would have a real fight when Maurice kept griping about our not being dressed up for his party."

"Will you come along to the Castillo for a cocktail, Karen?"

She shook her head.

"No. I've got to shove along home in a minute. The chickens have to be shut in, and the sheep."

"You got sheep?"

Karen grinned, "Four. It's only a *rancherito*, you know. I love that darn place. I took bacteriology at school and I ought to get out of here and get to work, but Bee says I'm doing just as much good working on the rancho, and maybe she's right. Only I like it so much I feel guilty. But later—soon, maybe—I'll go to New York and go to work."

"I shouldn't think a rootin'-tootin'-shootin' gal like you would like New York, Karen?"

"It's a good place to work."

I said, "You wouldn't be bolting, by any chance?"

Karen's face crumpled, for a split second she looked as if she were going to cry, then she stiffened and said, "Why should I bolt? What a question!"

As we walked out of the drugstore we ran into Scott Davies. His face was twisted with worry.

"Have you heard anything?" he asked Karen. "Is it true that he's dying, do you think?"

Karen said, "We don't know much, Scott. We heard the news at the post office and Bee called up and got the cook on the phone. Geronima wouldn't tell us anything at all and she wouldn't let Bee talk to anybody else."

"I'm going out there," Scott said. "I started out half an hour ago. I had a blowout—the edge of town—the tire is being fixed. I haven't got any spare."

"I'll drive you out," I said.

"Go ahead," Karen said. "I'll hitch a ride home, Jeanie."

"We can take you home first," I said.

"If you're taking Karen home I'll ride out and back with you," Scott said. "By that time my car should be ready."

It seemed later than it was driving east against the dark mountains. Driving back, there was still a brightness in the western sky, with the faraway peaks rising mysteriously against it. It was a lovely time of day. Everything seems new, as if seen for the first time ever, when the headlights pick it up at twilight.

We had dropped Karen and were back at the garage where Scott's tire was being worked on within fifteen minutes. The tire wasn't ready yet.

Patrick was standing outside the Castillo.

"I don't think there's any rush, Scott," Patrick said, when we parked and Scott insisted he'd got to dash on out to Ames' somehow. "There's nothing anyone can do. The doctor gave Maurice a hypo and he was asleep when we left. If you want us to drive you out there right away, okay, but you can't do anything and you would have to come back for your car."

"What does the doctor think it is, Pat?"

"Come on in and have a drink and I'll tell you all I know," Patrick said.

Scott hung back. "What about Edwina? How is she taking it?" he asked.

"Edwina isn't there," Patrick said. He didn't spare Scott, but after all he wasn't as conscious of his obsession for Edwina as the rest of us. "She went up to the Kennicott ranch."

"After—after Maurice got sick?"

"Everybody knows it, Scott," I said.

Patrick said, "She went even after the doctor told her Maurice was fatally sick."

"She didn't think," Scott said. "It was such a shock. She didn't consider how it would look." He seemed devastated. "Well, if I can't do anything, I suppose I might as well wait here with you. If you don't mind. I expect you're hungry."

"I expect you are too," Patrick said. "Have dinner with us, Scott. Seriously, you can't be of any use out there at all. The doctor had got one trained nurse and he was staying on the job till she got there. There are servants enough, everything."

"I'm thinking about Edwina," Scott persisted.

I said, "Bee went to Edwina. Did she come out to the Ames', Pat?"

"Not while I was there."

"Then she went to Sky Valley," I said. "Trust Bee, Scott. She'll look after Edwina."

"Bee's wonderful," Scott said, after we had gone in and sat down. Scott wouldn't have a cocktail, but he accepted a glass of sherry. "They all are. They are the most remarkable women we've ever had in Santa Maria." He was so sincere that you couldn't have disputed him even if you didn't entirely agree, as I did. He sat a little forward in his chair, his wrist resting on the table and his fingers clasped around the sherry glass, and his eyes warm with enthusiasm.

"People tell such lies about Edwina," Scott said. "It's because they're jealous. All women are jealous of Edwina."

I held myself in, then I gazed inside myself, and I knew that he had spoken the truth. I was jealous of Edwina. And how.

"There might be something in that," Patrick said.

That made me cross. I said, "Edwina makes people mad. Also, she ought to watch her step, Scott. She's too crazy about Hugh Kennicott."

"No, she isn't, Jeanie," Scott said gently. "She's fond of him, of course, but she's dying to have him marry Karen. You know how those things are. I mean, she can't say so, but she is as nice as possible to Hugh, has him round, does what she can in a quiet sort of way to further the match." Very quiet sort of way, I thought, thinking of their two silhouettes in the shadowy hall last night, meeting by prearrangement, very sneaky—a very nice way, indeed, to promote romance for your kid sister! "Hugh was terribly knocked out when he first came out here, Jeanie. He thought his whole life was ruined because he couldn't kill Japs the way he had trained to do—and a lot of people around here were bored with him because, after all, it looked to them as though Hugh had pretty much everything anyway. I think I can understand how Hugh felt. He was young. His life lay ahead of him and he had been cut off from what he expected to do." Yes, Scott could understand that, because it had happened to himself, but he was different, he hadn't everything, he couldn't retreat to a ten-thousand-acre ranch in an idyllic valley. "Edwina met him somewhere and she sympathized. Maurice was nice to him, too, still is, but Maurice grates on people. Maurice takes a lot of understanding. You know that, Jeanie. But Maurice *does* a lot of understanding, too. It works both ways. Maurice understands Edwina."

Who didn't, I thought, coldly, but I kept it out of my face, and, glancing at Patrick, I saw that he was taking it as Scott meant it, agreeing with him in every way.

"Maurice is swell about Edwina," Scott said. "He realizes that she needs people her own age. He knows how lovely she is. He doesn't expect her to be a cut-and-dried housewife. Maurice realizes that Hugh is half in love with her, but he knows that that will pass."

"What if it doesn't?" I asked, thinking of Edwina having all the food from the icebox destroyed before she ran away up to Hugh's ranch. Now, why?

"But it will," Scott said. "Hugh will marry Karen."

"I wish I thought so," I said.

Little lines tangled between Scott's sky-blue eyes. "If he doesn't, it will be Karen's fault. She is too impulsive. Karen is so jealous of Edwina. It is the one real flaw in her character, I think. I wish—I wish you would tell her that, Jeanie. A man can't."

"Neither can I," I said. "Besides, I don't believe it."

Scott did not argue it. He waited a moment, then asked, "Just what does Dr. Johnson think about Maurice, Pat?"

Patrick said, "He says he has encephalitis, Scott."

"What's that?"

"Inflammation of the brain. When we got there Maurice was out of his head. He had a lucid interval or two, but they didn't last. The doctor gave him a hypo then and he dozed off. He may come through it all right." The worry lines went out of Scott's forehead. "And then he may not," Patrick said, and Scott drooped again. "Johnson seemed pretty worried, Scott. He's staying right on the job."

After dinner we dropped Scott at the garage and drove on home. We built up our fire. Patrick stretched out on the sofa. I pulled up a stool and leaned my head against his knees. The Venetian blinds were open. Once before, one of the first times Patrick had been in this house, somebody had tried to shoot him through that window. I should close the slats, I thought. I would, in a minute. I wasn't worried. History never repeats itself.

"Tell me every little thing," I said.

Patrick said, "Well, I told you every little thing, really, except some of my own imaginings, which I didn't want to tell Scott. He's pretty intimate with the Ameses and the Chandlers and I didn't want to be quoted. The thing that made me suspicious was the way the doctor behaved. He didn't want us to go into the room. When we did, he kept hanging around. Ames was lying in the middle of an enormous old rosewood bed."

I knew the bed. Maurice had found it in Mexico City. It was made of Central American rosewood, and it was big enough for three or four people. Maurice must look odd in such a big bed.

"God, he did look terrible, Jeanie. I felt scared. When Johnson wouldn't go out of the room, though, he lost his temper and raved. He said he would prosecute him as an accessory before the fact. The doc got nervous then and left, but he snooped at the door. He oughn't've left the room, Jeanie. I hate a weak-willed doctor."

"What did Johnson say to you? Frolicking around like that?"

"He didn't say anything. He was too worried about Ames. He said his pulse was failing rapidly. Ames kept wanting water. . . ."

"Why?"

"He was thirsty, I suppose. Anyway, he really did have only a couple of really clear intervals after Johnson left the room. Ames said in one of them that he meant what he said about the hundred thousand bucks, and I said to forget that and to go ahead and say what he wanted to tell us. He said he had been poisoned. Then he said to forget what he had said last night about shadowing his wife."

"Oh, oh."

"He said Edwina was not guilty, in any way, of what was happening to him. It was something else entirely, he said. Then his throat was paralyzed. He couldn't speak. Then his eyesight went. That did it. He screamed with terror, and back came Johnson on the run, and stuck him with a hypo of morphine. He wasn't really conscious again after that."

"Funny that he remembered about the money, Pat? If his brain was inflamed."

"Maybe that part of his brain wasn't inflamed."

"Is that supposed to be funny?"

"No. Not in the least."

"Oh. Did he speak with his British accent?"

"Good God!" Patrick said.

"Karen gave me that idea," I said. "Well, go on."

"Well—that's all. I prowled around the house some. The sheriff and the doctor stayed in the room with Ames. In the kitchen the Indian cook was in a temper. She wouldn't say why, but one of the girls told me . . ."

I put in, "That everything in the icebox had been thrown in the incinerator."

"How did you know that?"

"Everybody knows it. The girls gossiped."

"Not the cook."

"Nope." I glanced at the window, thought about the open slats. "Go on." I said.

"Well, I went back upstairs and asked Johnson why the food was destroyed. He said that Maurice told Edwina to have it done. He was there when Maurice said it. He followed Edwina out and told her not to bother, but she said that if she didn't Maurice would say she hadn't done what he asked. So Edwina made the cook destroy everything. So, you see, she wasn't to blame about the food."

"Dear, dear Edwina!"

"Do you think you're being fair, dear?"

"Yes, I do. Go on."

"That's about all. Oh, Hugh Kennicott came out. He does hate Ames. It was hard for him to ask after him civilly. He went away, right away."

"Because Edwina wasn't there?"

"He didn't say."

"Do you think Maurice will die?"

"I don't know enough about him to think. The doctor thinks he will."

I said dreamily, "A hundred thousand dollars!"

"Darling!"

"We could put it in war bonds," I said quickly.

Patrick snorted. "Maybe he hasn't got a hundred thousand bucks. And the doctor would testify he was out of his mind."

Patrick was stroking my hair, curling it around his fingers. I closed my eyes. The room was filled with a curious, dense quiet. The clock ticked on the wall. The fire sighed and rustled. There was nothing but stillness roundabout, no sounds of cars passing on the road at the foot of the hill, no footsteps in the lane. When there came a noise slight as the breaking of a twig and on the terrace perhaps, I opened my eyes automatically, and Pancho's glance caught mine, questioning me, and I smiled and shook my head. It would be a mutt, probably, from the throng that lived a sparse communal life in the Mexican section across a wide corral behind our house.

Pancho kept listening. He had his long ears up. He kept watching me.

I shut my eyes and turned my cheek so that it rested against my husband's hard muscular thigh. I felt comfortable and warm and content.

The dog's maniacal bark caught me off guard. I sat up. Patrick sat up. The dog dashed around the sofa and begin a frantic noisy leaping at the window.

I looked in time to see a hideous blue-glinting line of steel beyond the black windowpane. I heard the gunshot and the clicking cracking of the window. It was like nothing compared to the frenzied roaring of the dog, which filled the room with a blare of cacophonic sound.

I jumped up then and snatched the cord which closed the slats of the blind. I didn't realize that Patrick had been hit until I saw him then, lying pale and lifeless.

7

I reached for Patrick's wrist. His pulse seemed normal. His face looked pale. I tried to think what a First-Aider did when there was concussion. Was it concussion? Should I look at his eyes to see if the pupils were uneven? Well, I couldn't decide. I was too frightened.

The dog had run to the door and was barking like mad.

"Hush!" I said. Pancho stopped for a minute, then started it again. "Be quiet!"

He was quiet, and suddenly there seemed to be no noise in the world, none at all—and then I heard a car start up at the foot of the hill.

I had closed the slats. But the shot had broken out a windowpane. I could hear the engine as plainly as though I stood outside. There was an odd little tappet in one cylinder. It distorted the rhythm of the motor.

Patrick sat up.

"Darling!" I said. "Lie down!" You kept them lying down. I could remember that, anyway.

He went on sitting up. He gave his head a little shake and blinked and his fingers explored his crew cut. They found something. I looked, and saw a red welt. I felt faint.

"What happened?" Patrick asked.

"You got shot!"

He jumped up, and quickly sat down.

"Get me some whisky," he said.

"Nope," I said. You didn't give them stimulants anyway. "Lie down, darling. I'll get the ice-bag."

"An aspirin would be more like it. I'm getting a headache."

I got both. Patrick sat rubbing his head. He set the bag on the welt at a cocky angle and said, "Too bad it doesn't show."

"Don't joke about it, darling."

"Must have been a Nip."

"Darling! No humor, please."

He rearranged the ice-bag. "Somebody's taking Ames' interest in me pretty seriously," he said.

"Is that what it is, darling?"

"What else? And, the other night, after we were at The Rock, somebody lurked about this house. So there's a connection!"

"What kind of a connection, darling?"

"Between Ames' illness and Ray Thayer's death."

"Pat! Be sensible, really! Maurice has inflammation of the brain. The doctor said so."

Patrick paid it no notice. "Subconsciously, sick people often know what ails them," he said. "They can't diagnose their sickness specifically, and they don't know the name for it, but there is something, some nerve sense, that warns them of the cause. Ames thought he was poisoned. I think now he was right."

I couldn't argue him out of it. All I could do, finally, was to give him a sleeping tablet—saying it was another aspirin—and persuade him to go to bed.

I woke first.

Mr. Trask's Buick was roaring up our hill.

I swung my feet onto the rug and slipped them into my leopard-skin mules and snatched up my bathrobe. It was a soft green wool between an emerald and jade, very tailored, with a long sweeping skirt which entirely covered up my yellow-satin nightgown. In a jiffy I was ready to step to the casement window which opened on the lane and without more to-do put a finger on my lips. The sheriff would understand that Patrick was still sleeping. He mustn't be bothered after his narrow escape last night.

I was mistaken, for Patrick sat up and reached for a cigarette and was at the window, in his pajamas, as soon as I.

"Not a word about last night, mind!" he warned me.

When Mr. Trask stopped the noisy motor the morning seemed amazingly still, as the night had, last night, when Pancho stopped barking.

"Morning, ma'am," he said, remaining in the car, as if he were in a great hurry. Now what? I felt breathless, wondering what he had come to tell Patrick. "Howdy, Pat."

"Hi, Jim," Patrick said.

"Sorry to get you out of bed, folks."

"That's all right, Mr. Trask," I said.

"Time we were out," Patrick said.

"Nice morning," Mr. Trask said.

For heaven's sake, I thought, do get on with what you've come for! What is it! What has happened?

"Looks darn nice," Patrick said. He sniffed. He remarked, "Must have rained in the night."

"We had a nice little shower along about four o'clock," Mr. Trask said. "Too bad rain cain't be rationed. If we had half as much rain every month the year round as we have in the spring and early summer I reckon we wouldn't have any desert around here. Well, it's a pretty country. You cain't have everything."

Patrick blew a smoke ring.

"You said it, Jim," he said.

There was one of those silences, and I thought, "The hell with these Westerners! Why doesn't he get on with what he came about?" Maybe they wanted me to leave. Well, I wouldn't. I myself wanted to know what had brought the sheriff and his snorting old Buick up the hill, so I took action.

"Have you heard from Maurice Ames this morning, Mr. Trask?" I asked.

"That's what I come about, thank you, ma'am," Mr. Trask said. He smiled pleasantly. "He pulled through the night, ma'am."

"I'll be damned!" Patrick said.

"Never thought he would make it, did you, Pat?" The sheriff was making himself a cigarette. He kept his eyes on Patrick, however, and there was a queer gleam in their blueness, as he said, "Doc Johnson stopped by my house as I was eating breakfast. Said he thought Ames was out of immediate danger." The sheriff fixed his eyes on the cigarette. "Said Ames cain't remember a thing that went on last night, Pat."

Patrick chuckled. "What do you know!"

Trask said, "A man's memory can be as handy as a pocket on a shirt, I reckon. Maurice Ames is tighter'n the bark on a tree. I wouldn't be surprised if he started worrying in his mind about that money he offered you, Pat, and maybe he decided that checking out would cost him too much."

Patrick grinned.

"Good thing it wasn't spent yet, Jim. Well, I'm glad he made it. Johnson give you any details?"

"Nope. He looked petered out, couldn't wait to hit the hay, I reckon. Wouldn't be surprised if his memory fails him, too. Think we ought to drop out and make a polite little call on the sick man, Pat?"

"Might be a good idea."

"*Darling!*" I said. I looked at his head. Maybe there was a concussion or something. He ought to take care.

"If you don't feel up to it . . ." the sheriff began.

"I feel fine, Jim. I'll get dressed and get some breakfast and stop over at your office. How's that? Say in half an hour."

"Okay, Pat. Good-bye now, Mrs. Abbott, ma'am."

Patrick went along in about an hour. After he was gone I had a bath and fiddled around doing my nails and straightening up the bureau drawers and things like that. I felt lonely. I felt lonely in a way I had never felt lonely in all my life. I had got used to having Patrick around all the time in just these few weeks and now here he was running out and doing things and leaving me behind. It would be like this all my life, I thought. It had been like this before he went to the war, of course, but at that time I hadn't got used to having him around, so I didn't mind it, at least, not like this. Finally I went to the kitchen and bothered Mrs. Dominguez. She sensed right off what was wrong and she said what I needed was kids. I said this was no time to have kids when you couldn't buy so much as a diaper or a baby buggy and she eyed me superiorly and said what had that to do with it. People ought to have kids, she said. I said maybe you had the kids and then your husband got killed in the war and she said well, then, you had the kids. Mrs. Dominguez was a fine flourishing brown woman with a lot of fine brown kids. She was specially proud because she had children younger than some of her grandchildren. I never remembered having even seen Mr. Dominguez, and I knew no one who had ever set eyes on him, but he was around somewhere because every so often Mrs. Dominguez would produce another neat brown little baby. The event hardly interrupted her in her work.

She was polishing silver and talking on about kids when the door knocker sounded.

"I'll go," I said. I was glad to have that much to do.

I opened the door to Dorrie Thayer.

Dorrie Thayer stepped in without being asked.

"I want to see Detective Abbott," she said.

She had one of those thin flat voices without any overtones.

For a moment I couldn't speak. My goodness, I was thinking, oh, my goodness, no wonder everybody was shocked.

She was a thin-legged blonde, not more than five feet high without her high heels, and she had a persimmon-shaped face.

She wore a navy-blue coat, a red hat, red gloves, red pumps, and red fox furs. She carried a red bag swung by a strap over one shoulder. None of the reds matched.

Her hair was too kinky from a new perm, and above her round blue eyes her brows had been plucked out and painted back on a fine shiny brown. Her rouge was pink, her lipstick was garnet red and her little round fingernails, when she took off her gloves, were crimson. She was young and she hadn't a line of any kind, but she didn't look young.

"She looks like something preserved in a bottle," I thought. I said, "I'm sorry. Lieutenant Abbott isn't at home."

"Are you Mrs. Detective Abbott?" Dorrie asked. I nodded. She minced, "Pleased to meet you. I'm Mrs. Raymond Thayer."

"Oh," I said. "How do you do?" No wonder everybody was shocked, I was thinking. Why on earth? "I'm sorry, Mrs. Thayer, but if you want to see my husband on business it's no use. He isn't making any private investigations now."

Dorrie's round blue eyes were roving the room and in spite of the expressionless character of her persimmon face she showed that she perceived that we hadn't much. Plainly her taste didn't run to adobe, and carefully collected old Hopi rugs, shelves of books, and really good pictures. Patrick had even brought along his three Renoirs, his greatest treasure. Dorrie wasn't impressed, maybe she didn't even see the Renoirs, since they were rather small.

"Okay, I'll wait," she decided.

My hand was still on the doorknob. "But . . ."

"That's all right. Go ahead with whatever you were doing, see. I got a little while, and maybe he'll show up."

Dorrie tripped along and sat down on a straight chair not far from the door.

I closed the door. I said. "Don't take that chair, Mrs. Thayer. Sit by the fire. Sit on the sofa, or one of the more comfortable chairs."

"What's the matter with this one?"

"Why, nothing. If you're comfortable."

"It's okay."

I sat down not far from her. I got up and picked up a cigarette box. She refused a cigarette as though the offer annoyed her. I sat down again. She kept looking around the room. Her furs kept slipping off her narrow shoulders and she would hitch them up and go on looking. She didn't like anything she saw, I thought.

"I'm afraid you're just wasting your time . . ." I began.

She turned on me. "I've got to hire a detective. They said he's the only one around here so I might as well wait here as long as I can. I got money to pay, if that's what's worrying you."

I could feel my temper coming up.

"That's not it. He's still in the Army. Navy, I mean. The Marine Corps."

"Won't he be sticking round here for some time?"

I said determinedly, "He's not free to do a private investigation. Besides, he's not able."

Dorrie shrugged that off. Also her furs, which she recouped.

"There won't be any hard work. Just a little snooping round, and that's all. I could do it myself only they'd get wise, see. I'll pay him for his work. It's on account I lost something." She made a face. "It wasn't lost, though. Somebody broke in my house and stole it."

My mind did a flashback to what Julia and the sheriff had said about Dorrie's thinking something was stolen. Dorrie had accused Maurice Ames. My curiosity got the better of my judgment.

"What was it, Mrs. Thayer?"

"I don't know."

"If you don't know what it is," I said, and very politely, "how do you expect to find it?"

Dorrie's expression was superior. "That's why I need a detective. I know who took it. What I don't know is what he took, see."

She hitched up her furs.

What had possessed her to mix up red fox with all those other reds? I could wring her neck, I thought, singling out reds, orange-red rouge, cherry-red, scarlet, burgundy, garnet, crimson, and finally those red foxes, which weren't red at all!

Oh, dear! I thought, suddenly. I wasn't being fair. I was antagonistic for the most superficial reasons, simply because her taste and mine clashed. I felt ashamed of myself. She was to be pitied, in this valley. She was a lost soul in the sophisticated neurotic society which had settled around and in Santa Maria. She was pathetic and was her being here her fault? Hardly. Ray Thayer was over thirty surely—and plenty worldly.

Only, why had he done it? How come? What had possessed him to make such a mistake? He must have been drunk. And he engaged to Karen!

Dorrie said, as if she read my thoughts, "I kind of thought maybe you wouldn't be against me like the rest of them around here. As you've just come back. Everyone around here is lined up solid against me. I never did anything to them, but that's how they are. They're snobs, see. And what have they got to be snobbish about? They're not even well off, except Maurice Ames, and a few others. You would think I had committed some crime. Nobody except Scott Davies has treated me even decent." Dorrie took a breath. "Maybe they're jealous. I'm a California girl. Everybody is jealous of a California girl, specially if you're from Hollywood." She elevated her brown-painted brows. "I guess people are different out there. More friendly. When they have a death in the family in Hollywood everybody runs in with something, a cake or something, and says they're sorry for your trouble. Why, if Raymond could know how I am treated here he would turn in his grave."

Raymond? I had never heard Ray Thayer called Raymond. Maybe he ditched the *mond*. Some people did. The name sounded primly wifely from Dorrie.

"Why do you stare at me like that?" Dorrie asked.

"I never heard Ray called Raymond," I said.

"Pardon," Dorrie apologized. "I should say Mr. Thayer."

There was a pause.

"In this place," said Dorrie, "instead of acting friendly they accuse you of committing murder." And her face looked like an infuriated Christmas-tree bauble.

"Do you think Ray was murdered, Mrs. Thayer?"

She screwed up her mouth. "I can't prove it. I think he was. But my lawyer, Mr. Ottoway, says not to say so. He says they can sue you for saying so. He also says like as not Raymond—pardon, Mr. Thayer—slipped off The Rock. Well, then, what was *she* doing out there?"

"She?"

"Karen Chandler. How come her glasses was in our car? Not that she cared her little finger! Hugh Kennicott was here by then and he's worth more than Mr. Thayer was. Why, he don't even have to work unless he wants to. I guess that Chandler family likes money. Look at the one who married Maurice Ames, an awful old man—now, what would she want of him except his money? I bet she don't even have to sleep with him, either."

Now, I would be dishonest if I said I had no interest in Edwina's or anybody else's love-life, but I didn't want to discuss it with Dorrie. Her remark roused the cautious Scot in me, and I stood up, and said, "Really, there's no knowing when Pat will come back, Mrs. Thayer. I don't think that . . ."

Dorrie was eyeing me shrewdly. "What's the matter? She a friend of yours?"

"They both are. And I don't think that Maurice is an awful old man, Mrs. Thayer."

"Well, he's over forty, ain't he? Excuse me. I wouldn't've said what I did if I had knowed they was your friends, Mrs. Abbott. He's treated me so bad, Maurice Ames has, but Mr. Ottoway told me that Mr. Thayer's death was over and done with and nothing could be done now to help that. Karen Chandler has left me be, too, and I'll do the same for her. All I want Detective Abbott for is to find out what was stole from my house the other night."

I sat down. "If you could tell me exactly what . . .?"

"I'll tell him, but not you. It's a strickly confidential matter." She consulted her dinky wrist watch. "I got to wait some place, see."

Thinking it would pass the time, I asked, "Will you have a cup of tea? Or coffee?"

"What makes you keep offering me things?" Dorrie asked. "No, I don't want tea or coffee or cigarettes. All I want is what's mine by rights. I guess if Detective Abbott is as smart as people seem to think, maybe whoever stole it will sneak it back when they find out he's working for me."

"When was it stolen?"

"That's none of your business."

I popped up. All intent to be kind had gone out of me. "See here!" I said. "You're wasting my time." I went to the door and opened it. "Good morning, Mrs. Thayer."

She drew back in the chair and sat there cringing as though I had slapped her. She began to cry. Tears curved down over her smooth painted cheeks.

I shut the door. I felt like a heel.

"I want to wait here," Dorrie wailed.

I went back to my chair.

"I'm scared," she wept. "I don't know what of, even. Somebody—some *thing*— has been hanging round my house. I ought to go away. I don't know what to do. If my lawyer was here maybe he could tell me. You don't think Maurice Ames is really sick, do you? I—well, I happened to get on the line when he called for the sheriff and I heard him tell him to bring Detective Abbott. Maurice Ames is alive and kicking this morning, you notice!"

I said, "Do you think Maurice Ames has been breaking into your house . . .?"

Dorrie sniffed.

"Would Maurice do what he could hire some man to do for ten dollars? Listen, they're all rotten, that whole bunch, Maurice and Edwina and Karen and that mother they call by her first name. Karen will marry money just like Edwina did. Nobody can ever say that about me. Because, when I married Mr. Thayer, I didn't even know he had money."

I gave her a very encouraging smile. It worked.

"I was the coatroom girl at a restaurant where Mr. Thayer used to eat. It was just off Hollywood Boulevard, see. It was a high-class place. I mean, they wouldn't hire just anybody to work there. The help wasn't allowed to date the customers—that's how it always is in a really high-class place, see. Mr. Thayer was always nice and friendly, but very much the gentleman, always. When he took his hat and coat he always had a few pleasant words to say and he always gave a good tip. He really took real interest in me. Sometimes if it was about closing time he would ask could he give me a lift. I had to say no. I knew his big blue car, which was always parked out front when he was eating, and I hated to refuse because I roomed a good piece away and I would have to hang on the corner, goodness knows how long, waiting for a bus. But it was against the rules, so I always declined the invitation. The night he was leaving to come here he was the last customer. He left just as I was putting on my coat. He gave me ten dollars as a tip. Gosh! Then he says couldn't he drop me at home, and I decided to risk it. I told him to go along and wait around the corner. He had never said the least thing sexy or anything like that, see. He was always the real gentleman. Well, when we got to my place he said wouldn't I like a sandwich at the drive-in along the block, and he did it so nice that I said okay, if he would wait till I got a sweater to go under my coat—the car top was down, see—and I went in and got it, and came down and got in the car, and when we parked I had a chicken-salad sandwich and a cup of chocolate and he had a seltzer and bourbon." Dorrie made a sarcastic grimace. "All he talked about was this place. He was leaving as soon as he dropped me for heaven, he said. Heaven! This awful place!"

"Don't you like Santa Maria?"

"I hate it!" she blazed. "I think it stinks."

Her eyes went to the watch.

"Say? My watch has stopped!" she exclaimed. "What time do you suppose it is?"

My glance consulted the wall clock above a bookshelf. Before I answered she followed my gaze and jumped up. "Is that clock right? Why, I've not got a minute to spare, then." Her furs had fallen on the floor. She collected the two joined fat foxskins and threw them around her neck. The tails swished. She rushed at the door.

"You tell Detective Abbott I'll be back here tonight sure. And tell him I'll pay."

She stumbled when one of her heels caught on the stoop. She righted herself and tripped along the terrace to the gate. She got in at the wheel. She sat forward, having to stretch to reach the starter. She raced the beautiful motor mercilessly. She crouched over the wheel, her arms akimbo, her round blue eyes straight ahead, and she crashed the gears as she backed up and turned, just as you were sure she would. She let the car roll down the rutted hill.

There was a glistening spot of fresh oil where her car had stood.

Patrick drove up the hill half an hour later.

"Anything happen?" he asked, when he kissed me.

I decided to hold out on him. Dorrie could find herself another detective.

"Nothing. What happened with you?"

"Nothing."

"How does Maurice look, after his ordeal?"

"We didn't go out."

"Did you talk with Dr. Johnson?"

"Nope. He was out somewhere on a baby case. I sat around his office and waited for a while and read some of his books."

"That must have been pleasant." I have seen doctors' books. They simply creep with things you'd rather not know. "What was Mr. Trask's opinion of the Ames' business, Pat?"

"Well, we didn't discuss it, Jeanie. I was telling him how I could have got at least two Nip snipers there in New Britain if I had happened to have a lariat, and a few other yarns you've heard over and over, and he talked some about his Texas Ranger days. We had a lot of fun."

I thought of Dorrie, and I was cross. "Meanwhile here I sat taking punishment from one of your would-be customers. The hell with you, Pat! Either you stay home or . . ."

Patrick kissed me. "You mean Mrs. Dorrie Thayer?"

"Why—how did you know?"

"She nabbed me on the plaza. She came out of the bank just as I walked past. She was carrying a big brown envelope. She stopped me and asked if I was Detective Abbott. She's a suspicious little thing, isn't she? She put the envelope in the glove compartment of that big car before she would say what she wanted to say to me, which was that she had to hire a detective and had picked me— inasmuch as there wasn't anybody else."

"Did she honestly say that?"

"Words to that effect. She informed me then that she would come to the house tonight when she got back from Santa Fe. And she told me what she'd pay."

"Oh," I said. I cheered up a little, thinking of all our expenses. "How much?"

"Fifty dollars."

"Darling!"

"What's wrong with fifty dollars?"

"Nothing," I said. I began to laugh. I felt hysterical. I laughed like a fool. Patrick pulled me over to the sofa and pulled me down on his lap. I put my head on his shoulder and laughed till I cried.

"There seems to be a vast difference in Santa Maria about the value of my services, Jeanie," he said.

"Rather," I laughed again. "You didn't take her seriously, I hope?"

Patrick's eyes narrowed and took on the green look they take when he is deadly serious. "I'm afraid," he said, "that I do. Also, I warned her to be careful."

8

Patrick was practicing with his rope. He stood on the terrace and lassoed chairs, stones, me, Mrs. Dominguez when she came to the door to ask a question, Toby the cat and Pancho the dachshund.

When it happened to him, Toby permitted himself to be released and then stuck up his fine bushy tail and with dignity walked off around the house out of range. Pancho was uncertain, he came over and sat beside me on the stoop, he kept watching the rope, then he would watch us to see if we would laugh. "This isn't a joke on my shape, or anything?" his eyes beseeched us.

I stood for it till Patrick accidentally snapped off three red tulips, and then I said, "Look, darling, wouldn't you like me to bring out your painting stuff?"

The rope snaked at the gatepost.

"I could get it if I wanted it, dear."

"But, darling—that's a little strenuous!"

Patrick slipped the noose from the gatepost, dropped it neatly around my shoulders, and dragged me toward him.

"Pat, this has gone on long enough."

He kissed me.

"Well, anyway, don't rope Pancho. It worries him. If you have to rope a dog, get yourself a mutt. Or one of those collies that don't think." Patrick had stopped roping and was feeling his head. "Does it still hurt, darling?"

"Not very much. I had hoped it would start my brain functioning, but nothing worth mentioning has come forth yet."

"Do you think Dorrie was the one that shot at you through the window night before last, darling? She did an awful lot of looking around when she was in this room yesterday morning."

"Your guess is as good as mine, dear."

"My goodness, aren't you even interested?"

"I'm damned interested! Give me time, woman! Stop nagging!"

"All right," I said. I always simply panted to clear everything up immediately. I never could wait the way Patrick could.

I felt now that Dorrie's behavior yesterday morning had been very queer. I had been so startled by what she was and looked like that it didn't occur to me while she was there that she had come to look our house over, and now, thinking back on her, I decided she probably had a diabolical sort of cunning and evil, and that she had come here purposely to examine the place so as not to miss next time. The Venetian blinds wouldn't stand wide open again—but she would probably use another method. Maybe she came to plant poison or something. Wasn't Maurice Ames poisoned? Patrick was being pretty silent about that.

We must take great care. Patrick was in danger. I was sorry I hadn't pried more about Dorrie out of Julia. I decided to breeze over to the shop now.

"I think I'll go to the post office, darling," I said, getting up from the stoop.

Patrick gave me a sidelong look. "The stage doesn't get in with the mail till eleven, dear."

"Right," I said. But I didn't sit down. "Look, I might as well own up that I want to talk to Julia about Dorrie Thayer." Patrick was coiling the rope, tossing it on one of the chairs. "I'm afraid of her, Pat. I was sorry for her when she came here yesterday, she looked like such a lonely little thing, but now I'm suspicious. Maybe she's a homicidal maniac."

"Think so?" Patrick said, taking out his cigarettes. "I've always wanted to meet one. Smoke?"

"No, thanks, and don't be so flip. Somebody is trying to kill you, darling. Now, why did she come here and sit so long in this house yesterday? If she wanted to see you so much why didn't she talk to you when she finally saw you? Why did she tell me such a sob story about herself, and then break off just at the point when . . .?"

Patrick put in, "When she was getting interesting, and about to tell you what everybody wants to know—in brief, how come Ray Thayer married her."

I shrugged. "Right. Well, she didn't come back here last night?"

Patrick lit his cigarette. "Maybe she thought my services weren't worth her fifty dollars."

"Oh, darling, why can't you be serious?" Patrick pulled me down on the stoop and held me tight. I moved away. I said, "I don't think you've got any of these people quite straight, Pat. There's something terrible going on, and you don't realize it. You ought to keep an eye on that Dorrie, and you ought to keep another eye on Maurice Ames. I don't think the sheriff understands Maurice Ames. For one thing, I don't think he's tight. He spends money like water on things he wants, on himself and Edwina and on his table. Julia told me that when he could no longer get real *pâté de foie gras*, because of the war, he bought special geese and fixed up a place for them and fattened them to make their livers special the way they do in Strasbourg. That's only an item, but it's typical of the bother and expense Maurice will go to when he wants something." Patrick didn't say anything. I said, "So, suppose little Dorrie did have something in that house Maurice wanted. Or suppose he thinks she knows something, and she knows he knows it—I mean, maybe Maurice was poisoned, and Dorrie knows it because she did it herself, and so she came here night before last and shot you through the window, because Maurice had sent for you, but the bullet just skimmed across your head and knocked you cold but didn't kill you, which she knew by yesterday morning, of course . . ."

"How?"

"Oh, darling, if you had really been killed everybody would have known it at once. Everybody knows everything here pronto. Anyway, maybe Dorrie came over when she knew you weren't at home, just to look at our house. I'm afraid of her, Pat. She probably killed Ray Thayer and planted Karen's specs in his car herself."

Patrick said, very casually, so I knew he was taking heed, at last, "Tell me every little thing about Mrs. Thayer's visit here yesterday morning, Jean."

I told everything, including how she had roused my sympathy. And I could see now that that had clouded my judgment.

"I think I'll go talk to the sheriff," Patrick said then.

"Can I go along?"

"If you like."

Mr. Trask wasn't in his office. A deputy with a peg-leg was sitting there with his good leg on Mr. Trask's desk. "Jim high-tailed it out of here half an hour ago," he said. "Seemed in a hurry. Didn't say why."

We came out and then walked around the plaza under the portales which covered the sidewalks. It was an interesting time of day. The Indian women were in town, and walking with their mincing steps from one shop to another, doing their marketing. They wore snow-white deerskin boots, gay calico dresses, and pink or blue silk shawls, and they didn't do any talking except when they had to. The Mexicans on the street were gay and noisy when in groups, and serious and dignified when they walked alone. There were a few cowboys about, modest and difficult, the way they are, and the ranchers' station wagons angled at the curbs, in town to get the groceries and the mail. We kept seeing people we knew.

When we got to the Turquoise Shop and Patrick saw Dr. Johnson standing by the jewelry counter talking to Julia he said we would go in.

The doctor seemed glad to see Patrick.

"I've just been telling Miss Price that Ames is coming along fine, Lieutenant," he said.

"That's wonderful," I said.

"Glad to hear it," Patrick said. "How about his eyes?"

The doctor seemed at once indefinite. "Well—we shall see about that," he said. "He's rational now, however, and resting."

"Suffering any pain?" Patrick asked.

"Yes and no," Dr. Johnson said. He stuck out his lower lip and his long sallow face stretched. "I don't mind telling you now that I was pretty worried when you and the sheriff got there the other night. It looked then like a job for a brain surgeon. That meant taking Maurice to Albuquerque or Colorado Springs, and Pete Martinez has the only ambulance short of Santa Fe and he was twenty miles up in the mountains bringing out a cowboy with a mashed thigh." The doctor blew out a long breath. "Boy, I was scared!"

"I don't wonder!" Julia said, from behind the jewelry case. The rest of us were standing in front of it. "I had a friend who had a brain tumor, Dr. Johnson. Her eyesight went, just like Maurice's. She died on the table."

The doctor wriggled.

Julia said, "Were you able to get any nurses?"

"I've been fortunate in getting one trained nurse. The family takes turns spelling her."

"Edwina?" I asked.

The doctor said, "Edwina's no good in the sickroom. The maids help out, and Bee and Karen are doing what they can."

He fidgeted with his black bag, said good-bye twice, and paused at the door.

"I hope I didn't sound too optimistic?" he said, as a farewell.

The doctor went out. Julia got off the stool and hustled us into the seats beside the fire. Patrick grabbed the corner seat with its view of the square. The sheriff's office was directly opposite, and I knew he was watching for Mr. Trask. "Listen, kids," Julia said, "Doc's all right, but he's not telling us the whole truth about Maurice. They've ordered him a wheelchair. My cook found that out. Now, why does he need a wheelchair?"

"Maybe he wants it in time for his old age," Patrick said.

That was a joke, because of it taking so long now for a civilian to get anything.

Julia flicked a wide brown glance at Patrick, and said, "Pat, darling, there's more behind that business than the doc is letting on. Listen, you keep out of it. Hear?"

"Okay, Julia," Patrick said.

He was watching the plaza. In a minute Julia said, in a low tone, for me only, "Edwina's making hay while the sun shines."

I lifted my eyebrows. "Hugh?"

Julia nodded. "She dashes up to Sky Valley morning, noon and night. It's a damn shame. Listen, did Dorrie Thayer come to your house yesterday morning?" I nodded. "She told me she was coming over there. If you had had a phone I would have warned you not to let her get inside."

"I think myself she bears watching," I said.

"You said it," Julia said. "What did she come for, Jeanie?"

I glanced at Patrick. He didn't seem to be listening.

"Well, she wanted to hire a detective."

"Oh, for God's sake!" Julia said. "She must be stark staring crazy. You know Ray's house. What on earth has it got in it that anybody would want to steal?"

"Well, she didn't seem to know what it was, either," I said. (Patrick wasn't stopping me, was he?) "Anyhow, she changed her mind. She said she was coming back last night, but she didn't."

"She went to Santa Fe," Julia said. "I asked her why, since she made a sort of mystery of it, but she gave me one of her looks and didn't answer. Pat, wake up! We're talking about Little Dorrie. I don't want you to get mixed up with her, hear?"

"Okay, Julia," Patrick said, very nonchalantly.

Julia flung her cigarette at the fire. "Now, listen to me, Patrick Abbott! I mean it! If you had been around here last fall when Ray was killed and had heard the way that awful woman screamed about Karen, until Karen waived Ray's property to her . . ."

"Why did she?" Patrick asked, softly.

"She had to, with Dorrie his widow," Julia snapped. "Karen didn't want Ray's money anyhow. But that woman wouldn't understand that. She's got a hide like a cow. If she could sense how people really feel about her she'd've got the hell out of here long ago."

"She knows people don't like her," I said. "She told me so. I felt sort of sorry for her."

"Good God!" Julia said.

"Well," I said. "I just tried to see her point of view. . . ."

"Don't!" Julia said, and I had never in my life seen her so decided about a thing. "She's horrible. She did everything she could to ruin Karen, a young girl, just because of those amethyst spectacles . . ."

Patrick said, "Could Karen's mother have gone out there to meet Thayer, Julia?"

Julia's mouth hung open.

"Bee? Take a hand in Karen's affairs? Hardly. Where did you get that idea?"

"They both wear the specs," Patrick said.

Julia said, slowly, "Bee was questioned. She was rather strange at the inquest, as if she knew more than she told, but you know how Bee is. You always think she knows a great deal she never puts into words. Maybe she does. Maybe she doesn't. But—well, I don't want to talk about that business, further than to warn you both that Little Dorrie's poisonous. Leave her be. There's something awful about her. Vile." Julia's chin trembled, as it did when she was worked up. She said, "Anyhow, Karen wouldn't kill a man in any such a horrible way as Ray was killed. There are lots of ways to do murder. Karen's a crack shot, for one thing, and she majored in science at school and knows all about all sorts of things, I should think, so if Ray stood her up at the altar and she planned murder, she wouldn't push him off The Rock, would she? Oh, Karen didn't do it. She was never in love with Ray. Dorrie did it herself. She married Ray for what he had and she finished the job by murdering him so as to have it all for herself."

I said, after a short interval, "She told me yesterday she didn't know he had any money, Julia, at the time they got married."

"Well," Julia snorted, "she knew he had that blue Cadillac, and that he wrote for the movies. See here, sweeties, leave her be! She's no good."

"Thanks, Julia," Patrick said. "I think maybe you're right. Partly right, anyway."

"Oh, I am!" Julia cried.

Patrick asked, "Was Thayer a drunk?"

Both Julia and I were amazed. "Ray?" Julia asked. "Oh, no. He wasn't a teetotaler of course and he drank more between jobs than when on one, but I never in my life saw him take too much."

"Did women like him?"

Julia said, "Why, yes. He wasn't exciting, Pat—he was easy-natured and generous. Would have made a good husband, I think, but I guess Karen isn't old enough to see a man the way I would."

"Would he be likely to take pity on some little woman and marry her to take care of her, Julia?"

"Pat—my angel! He was *engaged* to Karen!"

"We used to think it was Bee he was after," I said to Patrick. "Karen was just a kid and after all Bee isn't too much older than Ray to be attractive to him. They all went around together."

"Bee ever jealous of Karen?" Patrick asked.

Julia and I hooted again.

Then Julia said, "Well, while I'm about it, I might as well spill everything." She paused. I didn't speak, and Patrick sat listening. A log settled in the fireplace. Sparks flew upward.

Julia said, "I've never told this to a living soul, but Bee and Edwina had a quarrel here in the shop, at the time Ray came back with Dorrie. Bee was sitting where Pat is, and being quiet, the way she is, having a cigarette, and in walks Edwina, sidling along like a queen, and she announces pointblank that Ray is back from Hollywood with a blonde. I wish you could have seen Bee! I'd never seen her in a temper. I didn't know she had one. She tossed her bag at the fire and got up and she slapped Edwina. She gave her a real crack. She told her if she ran around town talking she'd kill her. It was only the way you talk when you're mad, but Bee looked as if she meant it, and Edwina was scared to death. Bee took her by the elbow and marched her out of the shop. Bee's car was outside and she made Edwina get in it and drove it away. Neither ever mentioned the episode to me again. I think Edwina might though—if I led up to it. But not Bee." Julia pushed back her hair. "I've talked like a damn fool, chums, but if it keeps you from getting mixed up with Little Dorrie maybe it's worth it."

"It won't go any further, anyway," I said.

"Right," Patrick said. He unscrambled himself and stood up. "I'll see if there's any news from Trask."

"Don't go anywhere without me," I said.

"He's a swell guy," Julia said, as we watched his long, lean, easy-walking figure crossing the plaza. "Much too swell to use up any good energy trying to help Dorrie. There isn't any helping Dorrie, Jean. The Lord didn't endow her with anything that can be helped."

Patrick was scarcely out of sight before Hugh Kennicott came in.

We said hello. Julia urged Hugh to sit. He hadn't time, he said. He'd come in to buy a concha belt. He even knew which one, he said, with his sudden grin, a very special one with expertly worked silver conchas set with azure turquoise— priced, he believed, at sixty dollars.

Julia went behind the counter. She put her lower teeth in her lip. She hesitated. Her big round brown eyes searched Hugh Kennicott's long brown eyes.

"That belt is reserved for—somebody," Julia said, at last.

Hugh laughed. "So I hear," he said.

When Hugh left carrying the box Julia said, all glowing, "He bought that belt for Karen. I put it aside for her a few days ago. She said she hadn't the cash and

I told her to take the thing and pay for it when she got the money, but Karen and Bee never will do that, Jeanie."

"I wonder how Hugh knew about it?"

"People in love have got ways," Julia said, and then she looked blissful and went off into one of her sentimental phases. "Isn't he the best-looking guy you ever set eyes on, Jeanie? Don't they make a lovely couple? Isn't it nice that he came in and bought the belt for Karen, dear? When she was so crazy about it, too. And doesn't having a nice thing like that happen clear the air, after the poisonous things I've been saying to you and Pat?"

In my mind it wasn't so simple as all that, for I was thinking that Karen wouldn't've told him about the belt, or Bee either, and that led me back to Bee, and what an inscrutable character she was, really, and I wondered how she felt when Karen's fiance came back married to Dorrie, and what she might have done about it, and I thought and thought about her having socked Edwina one. Whoever would imagine self-controlled Bee doing a thing like that?

Mr. Trask walked in while Julia was still raving on about young love.

The sheriff looked very grim.

"They told me Pat was in here?" he said.

"He just went to your office," I said.

"I'll get over there now," the sheriff said. "I went up to your house first, ma'am. Reckon I wasted time."

"What's the matter?" Julia asked.

The sheriff had started to the door, and he spoke over one shoulder. "It looks like that little widda Thayer drove her car off The Rock into the canyon last night." He stopped and said to me, "If I don't find Pat, ma'am, tell him I'd like to talk to him when I get back. I'm going with Pete Martinez and whoever we can get into the canyon to fetch out the body."

9

Last night there had been music in the Rio Grande Canyon. A radio had tinkled thinly in the night. An Indian passing by on one of his mysterious nocturnal treks had heard it and had waited on The Rock until morning to see what it was, and meanwhile the battery had run down and the music had stopped. To the sharp Indian eyes dawn revealed a mass of blue wreckage far below, a red dot which was a hat and a diminutive commasized crescent which was a high-heeled slipper. The Indian trudged into Santa Maria and reported the wreck to the sheriff. To others he said nothing at all and went about his business, if any, and whatever it was, and wherever, without more fuss.

But by the time the sheriff had collected Pete Martinez, the coroner—who, being also the undertaker, had available an ambulance and the proper basket—and a few able-bodied assistants, the news was all over town. People risked tires they had been coddling for two years to drive over the ugly trail to The Rock.

I left the shop at once and spotted Patrick as he came striding onto the plaza from somewhere and jumped into the car. Another minute and he would have been gone without me.

We drove to the house. He dashed in for his field-glasses and the magnifying glass he had always carried, in civilian life, in his coat pocket.

We were at The Rock within three quarters of an hour after the sheriff told us about Dorrie there in Julia's shop. A good many others were there ahead of us. People stood or squatted or lay on their stomachs on the rim and stared hundreds of feet down at the wreck. I made Patrick lie down before he looked. I lay down too. The car was upside down. Its tires stuck up in the air and looked foolish and futile. The car hadn't burned, and it didn't lie in the river. I saw the hat. I couldn't see the slipper with my naked eye the way the Indian could, but Patrick could see it and later I found it with his glasses. If Dorrie was there she was under the wreck.

She was there all right. Or somebody was. The hungry desert buzzards were already beginning to gather on the rim on the other side of the canyon. They lined up, waiting.

"You would think she'd've been thrown out of the car," I said.

Patrick didn't answer. He eyed the area around the wreck bit by bit. Then he got up and examined the surface of The Rock. Nobody paid him any attention. All were staring down at the wreck. The crowd was awed and quiet.

Patrick halted when he came on a round fresh oil spot on the surface of The Rock, the length of a long car above the usual parking space. I remembered the same sort of spot outside our gate yesterday.

"Her crankcase was spilling oil," I said.

Patrick didn't reply. He noted the position of the oil and looked for and found smaller oil spots between it and the rim. They made a beeline.

I said, "She was a lousy driver."

"I noticed that," Patrick said. I asked when. "On the plaza," he said, briefly. He noted again the incline of The Rock, how it rose very gradually from the parking place to the rim.

"It couldn't have rolled over by itself," I said. He paid no attention. "It had to go over under power, darling. It didn't go off by mistake, I mean because of her clumsy way of driving. She wasn't trying to turn around. She did it on purpose, Pat."

More of those rusty-black naked-headed birds flew over us. They joined their lugubrious brethren on the other rim.

"Do you believe the radio kept playing, Pat?"

"Why not? I saw a car smashed by a train once. The dead lay all around. The car looked like pulp and the radio was going like hell."

"It's macabre just the same. It's as if the radio was a live thing, screaming for help, or something. Let's scram out of here, Pat."

"Okay."

I was glad to get away, to leave the thickening crowd to its peering, to turn my back once more on the cancerous colors of the canyon. "I'm getting neurotic about this place," I said.

What I didn't anticipate was Patrick's turning south when we got to the highway and, half a mile on, he turned left up the Silver River road.

I assumed we were going to the Ames'. Scott Davies wouldn't be home at this hour. There was no one, of course, at the Thayer place. I felt pleased, in a pathological sort of way, to be calling on Maurice. The doctor had certainly been very vague, there in the shop, this morning.

When Pat braked to make the turn into the Thayer place I was caught by surprise.

"Look, darling, what are you up to?" I said.

"What do you think?"

"Yes, what?" I said, as I followed Patrick from locked door to locked door, "What are you trying to do?"

"I'm trying to get into this house."

"But, darling . . ."

Patrick gets bored when I follow him around on a case.

"Pipe down, Jean. Go and sit in the car. Dorrie is suddenly very much my client. I hope to get a look through this house before anybody else has the same idea."

"But maybe she isn't under that car, Pat?"

"Give you a hundred to your one that she's there, Jean."

All doors were locked. The kitchen door had an old-fashioned lock. Patrick produced the skeleton key he carried on his key ring. It wouldn't work because the key was in the lock on the inside. We got in finally through an unfastened window on the kitchen porch.

I knew the house. The kitchen and pantry and dining room were on the side toward the road. The living room and the best bedroom opened on a terrace facing the Silver River valley. There was a private bath off that bedroom, and off the bath and making an ell with the built-on garage was a study with three windows in a row looking east toward the mountains and the Ames ranch. On the west side of the house and off the hall between the living room and the kitchen was another bedroom and another bath.

Patrick closed the window after we entered and locked it.

He pulled a pair of gloves from his jacket and put them on. "Don't touch anything," he reminded me.

"My God!" I said. "How it smells!"

It was the kitchen, and it stank. It was the stench of filth, a mixture of the odors of stale grease, mice, cockroaches, decayed food, stopped-up drains, and an open garbage pail badly in need of emptying.

Patrick went about poking into everything. In due course he opened the door of the icebox. Its misty light came on, disclosing a festering interior. Patrick poked at a coil of liver sausage and sniffed at the contents of dirty dishes. Smells fascinating for their horror floated out to mingle with the rest. He shut the box. He stalked into the hall. He opened the door of the dining room. The table and chairs and sideboard lay under layers of adobe dust.

"I'll bet she never used this," I said.

There was a door at one side of the dining room leading into the garage. Patrick walked over and turned the knob. It was locked.

"We'll look at the garage later," he said.

The next room was the bath that Dorrie had used. There were more rings in the bathtub than you could have imagined Dorrie had ever taken baths.

Dirt had encrusted on the basin and the toilet. I turned up my nose and watched Patrick from the door as he examined the contents of the medicine cabinet. He put one bottle, after sniffing at it, into his shirt pocket.

"What is that?" I asked.

"$CCl_3 \cdot CH (OH)_2$," he said.

"Don't show off, darling."

"Don't ask questions when I'm busy, dear."

Dorrie's bedroom was next. It had been Ray's spare bedroom. Dorrie had done this room over in her own taste. It had shiny rayon cerise curtains. The bedspread matched. A new linoleum rug was unctuous with cerise roses. The bed was unmade. The sheets were gray from needed washing. The smell in this room puzzled me for a moment, and then I wondered why I hadn't immediately recognized it. It was the slum smell, the smell of poverty plus dirt. It was the sweetish nauseating smell which lingers over the depressed areas in cities.

My imagination reached out, trying to picture what Dorrie's childhood had really been, if she did not even know that her room had this smell. She didn't smell it, I imagined, because she was inured to it.

Patrick examined this room meticulously. Next we went to the living room. Dorrie had used this long room, but had left it as Ray had had it. It was a man's room with dark furniture and tweedy-looking chairs and sofas. It was not clean. The fireplace was glutted with dead ashes. There were spider webs on the *vigas*— those of black widows, like as not, or at least the dirty-looking little webs like those that vicious little spider fashions. The windows were smoke-gray from dirt. The adobe walls were peeling and covered with the moldy-looking spots adobe gets when neglected.

Patrick opened the door from the living room into the master bedroom.

This had been Ray's room. It was immaculately clean! His things were in the dresser drawers. They were clean and neatly folded. His clothes hung on hangers in the closet. Some were in mothproof cellophane bags. In his private bathroom his shaving soaps and lotions were neatly drying up from age and disuse.

"Superstitious, wasn't she?" I asked.

"Maybe."

"Funny the impression you get about a person from a house."

"Is it so different from your impression of Dorrie?"

"Well, no. It's just more complete."

Patrick opened the door from the bathroom into the study. He whistled, and stepped inside carefully. I stood in the open door.

The room was in great disorder. The drawers of a double tier of olive-green steel files which stood to the right of the three windows had been pulled out and left out and papers and folders lay around the room in utter confusion. The windows had Venetian blinds. The slats of the blind nearest the files stood open. The others were closed.

Patrick went to work. This was what he had come for, I supposed. It was from this room that something had been stolen, and Dorrie didn't know what.

I knew what Patrick would do. In his quick, thorough, precise fashion he would leaf through all those papers, he would see everything, and he would remember it after we had gone. The room would look exactly as it did now when we left. No clue would be disturbed, merely noted, unless he found something he chose to take away with him.

He would be quick because he was professional, but even so it would take time. In advance, I felt bored.

"I'll wait on the terrace," I said.

"All right. But don't poke about the kitchen. I'm not done out there yet."

"Darling, you needn't worry. I'm anything but enamored of that kitchen," I said.

"Be careful," Patrick warned me. "Don't do anything dumb."

There were double doors, bolted inside, leading from the living room onto the terrace. I opened the doors, and leaving them open, I stepped outside.

The air outdoors seemed lovely. I hadn't noticed it specially till I came out of that revolting house. What a beautiful day! The sky was very blue. In the wide flood plain below the bluff, which made an arbitrary edge to Ray's front yard, fifty feet or so from the terrace, and where steps led down to the fields and orchards, the alfalfa was green and the late fruit trees stood in bloom. The air was scented, however, by the evergreens which grew in a clump at the west end of the terrace.

There was a bench near the evergreens and I walked across the flags to sit down. I was wearing a short green jacket, a flannel shirt, and wool slacks. In the sunshine pooled on the terrace my jacket was too warm. I took it off and hung it over the arm of the bench nearest the edge of the lawn. I sat down.

I wished then that I had a cigarette. I had left my own in my bag in the car. I thought of going for them. I thought it would be easier to bother Partick.

I decided doing either wasn't worth the effort.

It was warm and snug in the sun. I relaxed on the bench. I stretched out my legs and rested my head on the back of the bench and listened to the bees and the redwings and the meadowlarks. I closed my eyes so as to hear them the better.

I opened my eyes when I heard a flat hollow sound deep inside the house.

Now, what was that? I listened, my ears traversing the house, trying to isolate that single arbitrary sound, define it.

I got logical. Patrick probably made the noise. It could have been the dry hollow sound made by one of the drawers of the files, closed gently.

I was well away from the study at this point on the terrace, and there was the living room, the bedroom, and the bath between me and Patrick. Even with all the doors open he would be at a distance. It was odd, indeed, that I had heard him at all. When working he was quiet as a cat. And as inscrutable . . . I yawned, and settled back comfortably on the bench. It was a nice bench. It had been designed by somebody who understood the contours of the human shape, very rare in a bench, I thought, with admiration. Whoever made this bench deserved a medal. I relaxed blissfully.

The sunshine, the sheltered wall, the bank of evergreens gave my bench a delicious spicy isolation from the house. I went off in a drift of thought. What a queer business this was! All of it. Dorrie's being here at all was extraordinary to start with. And in possession of this house? A girl like that! How come? If Ray had been the impulsive kind, or hot-blooded—but he wasn't! Why had she looked after his private quarters in the house so scrupuously? When the rooms she herself used were so very filthy? Was she afraid? Did she believe in ghosts? Why did she stay in the house at all, then?

What had Ray Thayer been to Little Dorrie?

Would we ever know the real truth?

She was a delicatessen-feeder, if the contents of that icebox was a sample of her fare. I had seen potato salad and that strange-looking cole slaw they exhibit in those places, there was that sausage, and pickles, and vague things swathed with waxed paper.

I considered the clothes in her closet. They were cheap, fancy things. One bureau drawer had been full of "accessories."

I thought of the cerise curtains, the cerise counterpane. I winced, remembering the grayish sheets.

"Oh, the poor thing!" I reminded myself. But with difficulty, now that I had seen how she lived.

Well, she was tragic, no matter what, she had got herself into a spot, no matter how, she simply didn't belong in this valley or in this house. I would not think of her. I would leave the brainwork to Patrick. I would settle down on this bench and enjoy the sun and the songs of the birds and the smell of the fir trees.

I stretched out with my head resting on my green coat on the arm of the bench. I drowsed off.

Then I heard something move. It was a sly, cautious, deliberate movement. It sounded like a snake.

Everything inside me stopped. I listened. My eyes were wide open. I saw the white wall of the house and the hard blue sky.

I heard the sound again and knew then that it was a creeping sound and that it came from behind the evergreens. They grew flush against the earth and close against the end of the flags. There was no wall. The flagstones ended and firs began. They needed pruning. They had overgrown their allotment of space. I put my feet on the other area of the bench and fixed my eyes on the place where the fir trees covered the stones. I lay listening for another cautious reptilian sound. A sudden shadow fell on my face. I was aware of a Mexican hat. I felt long fingers, on my throat.

The next I knew I was lying face down on the terrace. I opened my eyes to a sort of green twilight. I had trouble breathing, because my head was in a sort of noose and there was a ropey something round my neck. Patrick said later that the pliancy of the jersey in my coat saved my life, for the noose was my own coat with the sleeves strangling my neck. I tried to yell. No sound came. I sat up after a while and struggled with the coat. When it was loose and my eyes were free the sunlight seemed dazzling. I got up and started along the terrace. I had to brace myself against the wall. I worked my way through the living room, bedroom and the bath and across the bath to the door of the study.

Patrick spoke up when he heard me. He was standing at the open blind with his field glasses trained on the Ames house. "Ames is standing on the second-floor veranda," he said. "He is watching this house through a telescope. His eyesight must be improving."

"Dar-ling!" I croaked.

Patrick whirled about. The glasses clanked as he slapped them down on the files.

He reached me in two steps. His arms went round me. "What happened?"

"Somebody bopped me," I croaked.

"Somebody choked you," Patrick said. He picked me up and laid me on Ray Thayer's bed. He examined my throat. "Jesus!" he said.

"Don't go on the terrace," I said.

Patrick didn't go anywhere. He stayed with me. "I must be slipping," he said. "I shouldn't've let you prowl around alone."

"Me, I asked for it," I said, in a voice which was now a caw. "I had warning. I heard something a good while before it happened—I know, it was a door! It might have been the kitchen door, Pat. It could have been, if closed softly."

Patrick consulted the time. We had been in the house thirty-four minutes. We figured that I had spent about ten unconscious on the terrace.

"It isn't likely," Patrick said, "that he's still hanging around." His face looked hard. The up-and-down lines in his cheeks were deep.

He didn't let me out of his sight while he made a thorough search of the house, first locking the doors onto the terrace and making sure that all the front windows were latched.

The hall door into the dining room was slightly ajar. The door from the dining room into the garage stood open. The kitchen door onto the porch was closed, but it was no longer locked.

"He was hiding in the garage," I said.

"Yep. I certainly am slipping."

"What made him come through the house?" Patrick asked himself. "Why didn't he leave the garage directly?" he wanted to know, when he saw that would have been easy.

"He?"

Patrick's grin was rather wan. "You've got to be chivalrous and call criminals he, till you know otherwise."

"Who was it, darling?"

"If I hadn't got a single-track mind which made me head into that study and stay there, I would know. And you wouldn't have got hurt. How do you feel, darling?"

"I've got a real pain in the neck, Pat."

"You poor child," Patrick said, tenderly. "You married a dope."

In the kitchen Patrick made a queer discovery. The sausage had been removed from the icebox.

Patrick was so furious with himself he was glum. I followed him around as he locked up. We went out by one of the living-room doors, which had a night lock. Patrick took a few minutes then to examine the premises. A flagged path led across the unkempt grass-plot to the edge of the cliff. A flight of stone steps led down to an orchard and a garden. The headwaters of the little Silver were controlled by a crude series of dams in the mountains. The valley seldom overflowed. It had been under cultivation for generations. It belonged almost entirely to small Mexican farmers, and their feet had made a path hundreds of years old along the base of the cliff. Ray and Scott had been lucky in getting hold of enough of this land to furnish them with room for gardens and a few fruit trees. Maurice Ames, for all his thousands of acres of grazing land, had never been able to buy even a foothold on the fertile plain.

It was now the long midday siesta period and there was not a Mexican *paisano* in sight in any of the fields.

As we walked back around the house to get into the car I borrowed Patrick's glasses.

"Maurice isn't on his veranda now, darling."

"No?"

"Was he in a wheelchair?"

"He was not."

"Did he have his eyes bandaged?"

Patrick put up one eyebrow.

"You can look through a telescope with only one eye, darling. Maybe only one eye is blinded. What did he have on?"

"He wore a white bathrobe of some kind. There was a white terry-cloth robe on a chair by his bed the night I went there with the sheriff."

"Darling, he was watching us!" I felt creepy. Maybe he was still doing it, from inside the house. "He had somebody here in this house, Pat. Somebody doing something for him!"

We had go to the car. It was Lulu Murphy's Ford coupe. She had lent it to us for this visit. Lulu was Patrick's ex-secretary. She was now building battleships for Kaiser, which was why, Patrick said, Kaiser was such a whiz. Patrick had sold our Mercury convertible when he joined the Marine Corps.

"Pat, what would Maurice want with a sausage?"

Patrick wrinkled his nose.

"Specially such a sausage?" he said.

"Another thing—why did the person who took the sausage leave the house the way he did? He must have known where we were. Why didn't he use the main road?"

Patrick waved the cigarette he was lighting at the landscape, an open book, many miles wide between the mountains and the canyon of the Rio Grande. I had asked a useless question. The cliff and the flood plain on the other side of the house offered cover.

Patrick got into the car. "How do you feel now?" he asked.

"All right. Nothing wrong that a lipstick and a compact can't fix."

"Headache?"

"Nope. I must be pretty tough."

"You've got blue marks on your throat," Patrick said.

I took out my mirror and looked at them. There were two small blue bruises, one on each side, under the jaw, where thumbs had pressed upon the carotid arteries until I lost consciousness.

Patrick started cursing himself, under his breath.

"Stop it, darling! I asked for it, didn't I? Look, you didn't come here to look for a sausage, did you, Pat? Besides, that *wasn't* what Dorrie wanted you to find. You found what you came for, didn't you, Pat?"

"I'm afraid not."

"Didn't you find any clues?"

He looked at me. "Can you keep your trap shut, Jeanie? No blabbing to Julia, or anyone?"

"You know I won't, Pat."

He took from his inside jacket pocket something folded in one of his linen handkerchiefs, and unfolded the linen for me to see a pair of purple-blue specs.

"I found these back of the files," he said.

He returned them to his pocket. I said, "Had Karen been there, Pat?"

"Maybe Bee left them," Patrick said.

10

Patrick thought it would save time to lunch at the Castillo. I persuaded him that, with luncheon no doubt ready and waiting, we could have it more quickly at home. Also I felt worse than I let on. I could do with a hot bath, which fixes me up from almost anything, maybe even from an escape from sudden and horrid death.

We were driving round the plaza when we saw Scott Davies coming out of the Castillo. He signaled us.

Patrick pulled out of the way of traffic.

"Have you heard the ghastly news about Dorrie?" Scott asked. We nodded. "Did you go out to The Rock, by any chance?" We nodded again. "Do you think she's under the car? I couldn't get away from the office all morning so didn't go myself, but people say that all you can see is her hat."

"And a shoe," I said. "You can see a shoe if you've got eyes like Patrick's, or the Indian's but it isn't on a foot."

"My God!" Scott said. "How did it happen, do you think? She was a terrible driver. The car was too big for her to handle, I think. Maybe it got out of control?"

"If it did, it headed straight over," Patrick said. He put his hand on the gear shift, and, sensing his haste, I asked Scott to come with us for lunch.

Scott shook his head. "I can't. I've had mine and I have to get back to the office so that the nurse who's there now can go to lunch. I've been wondering what ought to be done about Ray's house. Should it be locked up, or watched over, or anything? Trask is out of town, so's Ottoway—he's the state's attorney—and Trask's deputy doesn't seem to know what ought to be done. Maurice Ames is sick, I can't reach Edwina, and Bee and Karen haven't any phone, and I don't suppose they would want to be called on anyway."

Patrick took his hand off the gear shift. "We've just come from there, Scott. We locked the house up."

Scott breathed relief. "Well, that was thoughtful of you," he said. "I don't know how much you know about Mexicans, but sometimes they'll pilfer, that is, if they don't feel kindly or loyal toward a householder. I never lock up, and I know Jeanie didn't used to, but Dorrie dismissed Ray's couple in a nasty kind of way, and they've got it in for her. Well, you know what might happen, Jeanie."

I said I did, and I said, "The house is in a horrible mess, Scott. Simply filthy."

"It is? I've never been there, since Ray died. I—well, it's like looking at the dead to go into their house when they are no longer there, and can't be. It's sort of an offense to their privacy. I just couldn't go there. Ray was my best friend. I've tried to—to be detached—to be fair—but . . ."

He broke off. The sentence hung in the air, but there was no need to finish it, really.

"Did Thayer ever tell you why he married the way he did, Scott?" Patrick asked.

Scott shook his head. "He would have, I think. I wish he had." His hands finished the idea with a gesture expressing futility and regret.

"Did she tell you her side of the story?"

Scott hesitated, then nodded his head. "She told me *a* story."

"Will you tell me what she said, Scott?" Patrick asked. "She came to me yesterday, you know. Wanted to hire my services. She was to come back last night. Under the circumstances, I think it's my job to get at the bottom of this— this accident."

Scott looked at his watch, and said, "Look, come to the office after you lunch, if you can manage it. By that time they may know if she was under the car. I've got to get back. We're so short-handed, and the nurses work like hell. The least I can do is get back when I say I will."

"How about three-thirty?" Patrick asked.

"Any time's okay. I'll be in all afternoon, Pat."

I was glad that Patrick would rest till half-past three, and I felt all right myself after getting a shower and changing to a tweed suit, and after Mrs. Dominguez had fed us her excellent chili, a hearts-of-lettuce salad and apple pie.

Patrick was uncommonly silent.

"Do you feel all right?" I asked, over our coffee.

He jumped on me. "Hell, yes! Will you kindly refrain . . ."

"Sorry!"

"Good God! All I need is to build up resistance. You can't do that lying round and thinking about yourself, can you?"

"Well, if . . ."

"Okay, dear. Lay off!" Patrick suddenly changed. "How do *you* feel?" he asked, in a sympathetic tone.

"Me?" I sniffed. "I feel wonderful. Why shouldn't I? Don't ask me again, please. It bores me."

He grinned. "Okay, Jeanie. We'll both lay off, shall we? Want to come with me to talk to the Chandler gals?"

I breathed deep, getting ready to buck it, and then I said, "Oh. All right. Must we go right away?"

"We wouldn't've stopped for lunch if you hadn't got your neck hurt," Patrick said.

Bee Chandler's *rancherito* was a year-round oasis of green. She had transplanted from the mountains the native spruces, tamarisks, pinons and junipers. For leaf trees she had white-trunked aspens and the beloved cottonwoods. She had alfalfa in her neat small meadows, and two saddle-horses used her adobe stable, and a great many white hens had an up-to-date hen yard. Bee had turned rancher in a practical sense within the past three years. She apparently did it well.

"She must have had foresight," I said to Patrick, as we turned off the highway into her lane. "Also, some luck, I shouldn't wonder. It's practically impossible to buy land in this part of the valley, but Bee snared these forty acres somehow." It was hard to get just here because it was close to the mountains, and water was plentiful during dry spells. The Mexican families had had a corner on land like that for generations. "Funny she's so good at farming, when she had always lived in cities."

"Always?" Patrick asked. He had slowed the car down.

I said, "Honestly, that's just a guess. All I know about Bee is that I like her a lot, and that the girls' father was named Edwin Chandler and Bee married him in Paris. You know how people flocked to Paris right after the last war? It must have been about then. I heard her say once that she was very happily married. Mr. Chandler died suddenly in Paris—let's see—ten years ago. I know that, because I've heard her say that Karen was nine and Edwina was fourteen. He died from pneumonia at the American hospital in—what was the name of that suburb of Paris?"

"Neuilly," Patrick said.

Bee was in the kitchen garden. We caught sight of her as we got near the house. She wore jeans, a gray shirt and a broad-brimmed felt hat. A rifle was swung over one shoulder. Nearby a Mexican workman was transplanting lettuces.

When she saw us she took her horn-rims from her pocket and held them before her eyes without putting them on. When she recognized us she waved gaily. She said something to the man and tucked the gun under her left arm and came over a stile from the garden and on through a blue gate in the white adobe wall which enclosed the lawn.

I stuck up both arms, because of the gun. Bee laughed.

"I'm gunning for a real enemy—a chicken hawk," she said. "Pass, friends."

We shook hands. Patrick said, "I thought maybe that was one way to keep a hired hand these days, Mrs. Chandler."

Bee laughed again.

"I'm very fortunate. Pedro is not ambitious."

I said, "Look, Bee darling, keep it pointed at the sky or some place, will you? I hate the things."

"I'll hang it up on the terrace," Bee said. "This is simply wonderful, really. I love unexpected visits. I hope you'll spend the afternoon? I'm so delighted. I've been wanting to have you out."

"I'm afraid we can't stay very long," Patrick said.

Bee's violet-blue eyes looked past their black lashes directly into Patrick's, "Oh, I'm sorry," she said, without arguing. "Anyway, come in."

She led the way along the flagged walk. She walked as always, very straightbacked. She had to have a darn good figure to look like that in jeans. Having babies didn't hurt your shape, I thought, if you were properly looked after. Bee probably had good care. Edwina had once said that they thought they were rich till her father died. Then there wasn't much. I never want to see Europe again, Edwina had said. It was no fun living over there, she said, if you hadn't any money. You live just like they do, if you haven't money, and that's damn dreary, Edwina had complained. But Bee had never said so. Bee never complained. Bee never wore herself down with vain regrets or futile backward hankerings. She lived in the present and whatever she had promptly looked like paydirt. *Regardez* this rancherito. It was just a dump and a scraggly splash of sagebrush when she bought it. The house was the usual shapeless adobe, but now it was very white and fresh-looking and the planting gave it beauty, too. Bee had started by getting the irrigation ditches fixed up. The grass lawn was flat as a putting green and as thickly verdant. The irrigation ditch diagonally crossing the yard made me think of that little river at Cambridge University in England, because it had been made, with loving care, a waterway banked in beauty. Purple iris and tulips bloomed on both banks of the ditch and as summer progressed these would give way to a procession of perennials. The house had a blue door. It was the horizon blue beloved by the Indians, and our door was that same blue. I would like Bee for that blue door if for no other reason, I thought. All the people I really loved in this valley had blue doors.

The door opened flush off the stoop. The iron lantern which hung on the right of the door had come from Florence, Italy, and it looked entirely at home with adobe.

We entered directly into the living room, furnished much like ours with old soft-colored Indian rugs and dark furniture, but the little things here and there, the vases and pictures and the thises and thats, which gave the house a special character, reminded you that Bee had lived much abroad.

"Shall we sit outside? In the sun?" Bee asked.

"Let's," I said. She led the way.

Here was another flagstone terrace. It was enclosed on three sides by the house, this terrace. The kitchen opened from one end and Karen's bedroom from the other and the living room flanked the middle. Bee hung the rifle on the wall and, asking us to sit, went off to the kitchen.

I knew she had gone to put on the kettle. We should stop her, I thought. Not only because we hadn't time, but what Patrick had come about wasn't exactly social. You didn't drink people's tea, did you, when you had come to ask them why their glasses had been left in the house of a man and woman who had died under mysterious circumstances?

I sat down on the edge of a chair and tried to catch Patrick's eye. He had gone over and was examining the rifle.

"Isn't it a pet?" Bee called the length of the terrace as she came out with a tea-tray. She always kept the tray set and ready in the kitchen. She placed it on a low table and stood with her hands linked at the small of her back and her chin tilted up toward Patrick. "I'm lucky to have it. You can't buy them now, of course."

"Can you shoot?" Patrick asked.

"So so," Bee said. "I learned. I was terrified of living out here when we first came. I imagined there would be desperadoes and wolves and wildcats and rattlesnakes." She laughed merrily. "I have yet to see one of any, but I've shot some coyotes and chicken hawks. The ration board gives you a few cartridges."

"I'm awed," I said. "I'm terrified of guns, Bee."

"Bless you, so am I," Bee said. "Shooting's a natural for Karen, but not to me."

"Hear, hear!" Karen said. She stood in the living-room door. She wore jodhpurs and a checkered shirt. Her wide-brimmed hat was hanging down her back, held by its chin-strap. There was a riding crop under one arm, and she was stripping off her gloves. As she came out she gave off a whiff of horse. "Is it a party? Am I in time?"

"Hello, darling," Bee said. We all said hello. "You're in time to make the tea, dear. Or coffee?"

I looked at Patrick. He looked at me. I said meekly, "Tea, thanks."

"Good. I love tea-hounds," Bee said. "Sit down. The kettle ought to be boiling, Karen."

Violet-blue glances met. Did they speak to each other in a language we couldn't understand? I could not tell.

"Don't forget to wash your hands, dear," Bee said, as Karen started toward the kitchen.

Karen's wide lovely mouth opened, laughing, showing her white teeth. "Okay, Butch. What are you afraid of? Tetanus?"

"Tetanus?" I said. Karen had gone into the kitchen.

"Don't pay attention to her, Jeanie," Bee said. "She's always showing off how much she knows about germs and things. Tetanus has some connection with a horse."

She had sat down behind the tea-table. Patrick sat down on my right. I wondered when he would exhibit the glasses.

He waited until we had had the tea. Karen had pulled up a canvas chair between Bee and Patrick and nearer to Bee. Her back was half turned toward the
lawn. We were smoking, except Karen, who didn't smoke.

Then he did it. He took out the handkerchief and opened it up and without
touching the spectacles slipped them onto the tea-table.

There was a crisp interval of silence, broken by a flat diminutive plop. Bee
dropped her cigarette.

Her foot reached out automatically and crushed it.

Their faces looked masked, one older than the other, but save for that no
difference.

Patrick said, "Which one of you owns these spectacles?"

"I do!" Both said. Together.

Bee laughed an odd little laugh. "They're mine, really. I let Karen wear them
sometimes and I've left them to her in my will, but they really belong to me.
Why?"

"Darling?" Karen said. "You're lying through your teeth. You know darn well
you gave me those specs. Don't act like an Indian! What sort of example is that
for your sprout?"

She spoke mockingly, and with affection.

Bee was lighting herself another cigarette, holding her wrists stiff, as if that
could keep her fingers from showing their agitation.

"Where did you get the glasses, Pat?" Karen asked.

"I was about to ask you where you left them?" Patrick asked back.

Karen picked up the specs.

"I left them at Edwina's," she said. She opened the hinged side pieces, and
closed them. "The night we were all there for dinner."

"Don't be silly," Bee said. "It was I who left them at Edwina's. Where *did* you
find them, Pat?"

"Behind the files in Ray Thayer's study," Patrick answered, casually.

"How very odd!" Bee said. It was too glib, too bright, as if she had thought it
up, on purpose.

"How come *you* went there?" Karen asked, and her voice was deeply angry.
"What business had you . . ."

Patrick cut in sharply. "Mrs. Thayer was my client. It was my business to go to
her house after she was found dead."

Bee's hand flew to her heart, her eyes to Karen's, and there was another of
those violet-blue exchanges, which were sheer enigma to the outsider.

Karen said, "I just heard it in the village. Bee didn't know, yet."

Then something happened, and it was over so quickly, that it left even Patrick
breathless with admiration. Bee suddenly grabbed the rifle, snatched the glasses
from Karen, popped them on, took aim, and fired. I saw the chicken-hawk fall-

ing before I knew what she was up to. She gave a little sigh of satisfaction, and laid the specs down before she hung up the gun.

Karen got up, released the cartridge shell from the rifle, and dropped it into her shirt pocket. "Want me to reload it?" she asked Bee.

"I don't think there's any rush now," Bee said.

Patrick picked up the glasses and put them back in the handkerchief and, returning them to his pocket, said, "Well done, Mrs. Chandler!"

"Thank you," Bee said.

Karen grinned at her mother, and sat down again. "I couldn't have done better myself," she said.

I said, "But if you *can't* see things far away, Bee, how did you know it was there?"

"I can answer that," Karen laughed. "We've got special ears, we visually handicapped women. We heard the chickens chittering."

"If I had orbs like you two," I said with admiration, "I wouldn't call myself handicapped."

"It is a handicap, however," Bee said. "I can see anything at close range perfectly, and Karen can too. Karen sees better than I ever did, thank goodness, so may be in another generation the defect will disappear. I can see you distinctly, Jeanie. I can even see blue marks on your throat."

I felt a hush inside, a fluttering of my heart.

"I was wondering about those," Karen said.

"I did it," Patrick said. "I was trying to wring her little neck."

"I bruise easily," I said. "And I married a big brute!"

"I like them masterful myself," Bee said. She blew an elegant smoke ring. Karen laughed, lightly.

I took out my compact. It was a plastic trinket like a mirror with a handle. The round part had mirrors on both sides. These opened to the disc of hardened powder and the puff. I looked at my throat. It didn't look any worse. But the bruises did show.

"What a cute trick!" Karen said. "May I see it?" She reached for the compact and looked it over. As she was handing it back, Bee practically snatched it from her hand. She fingered it thoroughly.

The talk went off to other things. It snapped and crackled with fun. They never have a dull moment, I thought.

What a pair? Only, where did Edwina come in?

"Does Edwina look like her father, Bee?" I asked.

A tiny spasm of pain flashed across Bee's mobile lips, as it always had when her husband was mentioned, and then she smiled, and said, "No, Edwin was fair, with very pale hair and very blue eyes. Edwina is a throwback to a Spanish ancestor. On my side of the family, probably."

Patrick took note of the time.

"Do you have to keep the specs, Pat?" Bee asked.

"I'm afraid so. For the moment."

"Well, don't forget to return them when you're through with them. They're mine, remember!" Karen said.

We went soon after that, and as we walked around the house, the four of us strolling along together—and not one more word spoken about Dorrie, or the spectacles, either—Edwina turned into the lane, driving Maurice's station wagon.

Patrick discovered he had left his keys. He went back for them and caught up with us before we got to the gate.

Edwina got out and met us outside the gate. She wore a red bandanna tied around her raven-black hair, a blue jersey dress, and no coat. Girdling her tiny waist, which looked the smaller because of her full breasts and thighs, and with its azure turquoise winking softly from the heart of every silver shell, was the concha belt Hugh Kennicott had bought in Julia's shop.

"Look!" she cried, whirling about to show it off. "Isn't it sweet?" Her plump fingertips caressed it. "Hugh gave it to me," she said.

I glanced sideways at Karen. Her eyes were on the belt. They looked hot with outrage and hate.

11

The Public-Health Office looked utilitarian but not clinical, largely because anything Scott Davies had anything to do with had the right look. There were the usual desks, files, charts, hard chairs and such. A linoleum covered the floor, for sanitary reasons. But the windows were spotlessly clean and the walls were freshly calcimined and the haphazard furnishings were kept waxed and dusted, and thus, the place was not unattractive, as such offices frequently are.

Scott had apparently made no attempt to change the office when he had taken over. He just had it cleaned and freshened.

There were three flat-topped oak desks. Two were for the two visiting nurses. The third was Scott's. They were all alike. They had similar equipment. They were set as far apart as possible, to insure a small measure of privacy for those who came, reluctantly like as not, to be talked to about their cows, their wells and their outhouses.

When we entered, Scott was alone in the office. We sat down in chairs beside his desk.

"Any more word from Dorrie?" he asked us, at once.

"Not that I've heard," Patrick said. "You?"

Scott shook his fair head. "She was under the car, or someone was. Half a dozen people have come in to tell us that. I don't think they know if it's actually Dorrie. People watching from The Rock saw the sheriff and the coroner and their men uncovering a body, so they assume it's Dorrie."

Patrick said, "What was she taking from the bank yesterday, Scott? In a brown envelope?"

Scott said, after a short pause, "Well, I can tell you, I think. It can be checked later, if she's dead. If she isn't, don't let it go any further, will you not? She was moving the contents of her safety deposit box to a bank in Santa Fe."

"Why?"

Scott stirred uncomfortably. "I feel like a heel telling what she told me, Pat. I mean, it was confidential, after all. She made up her mind that this bank wasn't safe. It was silly, but Dorrie was used to Los Angeles and she was suspicious of our bank because Santa Maria is so small. Santa Fe is no metropolis but it looked like a better bet to Dorrie. I pointed out the federal guarantees all over our bank and reminded her that Santa Maria is the country seat of a huge and fairly fertile county and told her that the bank carries some pretty big accounts—such as Hugh Kennicott's and Maurice Ames' and so on—but Dorrie wasn't convinced. She hadn't had much experience with banks, I think." His smile took on a grim cast. "She was afraid of more darn things," he said.

"Thayer have his money in bonds?" Patrick asked.

Scott nodded. "Almost entirely. He wasn't a very rich man, you know. He wasn't interested much in investments. He parked what the income tax left him in government bonds because he thought they were safe."

"How much property did he leave?"

"I don't know exactly. Max Ottoway can tell you, though. He's Dorrie's lawyer. He's supposed to get back tonight."

"It may not be important," Patrick said. "Did anybody know she was moving the bonds? Anybody except you?"

Scott said, "I don't know. I told her to have the bank handle it. That would be a lot safer, I told her, but she didn't believe me." He frowned and said, "You think she may have been robbed?" Patrick said it was possible. Scott said, "Dorrie is not very discreet. She would call up Ottoway's office and talk about her business on the phone. To the office girl, even, if Max wasn't in. She may have talked to hangers-on at the bank. Or anybody who saw her go into the vault and come out with a manila envelope might suspect it contained something valuable. Why would she go out to The Rock, though?"

Patrick said, "If she was in as much of a rush as she said when I saw her leaving the bank she probably didn't go there till she got back. The car didn't burn, you know. If the brown envelope's still there, Trask will find it. Do you think Thayer killed himself, Scott?"

The question was abrupt. Scott frowned. "I don't like to say it, Pat—but—oh,

I don't know. I don't want to say anything because I can't prove anything. I said so to Trask at the time."

"You knew him better than anyone else, they say."

"Yes. He was the best friend I ever had. I think in the course of a number of years we talked about everything on earth there is to talk about including death and suicide along with it. We even discussed how we'd bump ourselves off if we ever got to the point where it made sense. I can assure you that we didn't consider jumping off a precipice one of the—the pleasant ways of doing it. I am positive that his death was due either to murder or accident. I prefer to think it was an accident."

"Maybe it was his heart," I said. "People nowadays are always dying from hearts they imagined were perfectly good till they suddenly up and stop."

Scott smiled at me and said, "It wasn't his heart. He had a proper check-up—Johnson will tell you—just before he started west. He was in fine shape. He must have slipped, or stumbled. It's the only way it makes sense."

"Lots of coronaries come on without any precedent," Patrick said. "What did Dorrie think?"

Scott was quiet for a minute. "Dorrie thought first one thing, then another. I never asked her, but she had a way of inflicting her opinions on anybody who would listen. My private opinion is that she either didn't know a damn thing or—or was smarter than she got credit for being. She didn't behave very well, to be brutally frank."

"I understand she accused Karen Chandler, until Karen waived any claim."

Scott said, "Dorrie was a pretty thorough heel, Pat."

"You don't think Karen killed him?" Patrick asked, in an innocent tone that was so sudden that it shocked me, and Scott, too.

"God, no!" Scott snapped. "Nobody in their right mind could think that. Dorrie just behaved according to her type. You come into contact with the rustic versions of Dorrie in an office like this, and the first thing they do when in a spot is accuse someone else of the dirty work. Maybe no one is to blame for whatever it might be, but they have to fasten the blame concretely on some other person. Dorrie found out that Karen and Ray were engaged before she appeard on the scene and naturally she decided that Karen murdered him. It's the way Dorrie's mind works. Karen never did care about Ray the way he did about her, or the way she cares about Hugh, now. It was the other way round. Ray knew it. I honestly don't think he ever really expected to marry Karen. She went as far as Albuquerque with him, you know, the day he left here for Hollywood, last September. It was the fifth of September—that all came out in the enquiry after Ray was killed, which is how I remember the date. Ray dropped her at the university and went straight on. She said he was in unusually good form—you know how funny he could be, in his lazy sort of way, Jeanie?" I nodded. "He always drove straight through from Santa Maria to Hollywood, left here very early in the morning and did the hot stretch across the desert at night."

"It's a thousand miles," I said. "He must have been pretty fit."

"He was, according to Johnson. He had a bum knee joint, and that was absolutely all that ailed him, according to Johnson."

"Did Dorrie murder him, Scott?" Patrick asked, with that appalling, deadly casualness.

I waited. Scott's eyes met Patrick's with a funny little quirk. He said, "I've asked myself that question a couple of million times, Pat, and, honestly, it has run through my mind every time I've been with Dorrie, and, for the life of me I just can't think she did."

"Why not?"

"Well, I don't think she had the nerve. People like Dorrie don't feel about things the way we do, you know. She was brought up thinking everybody was against her. Whatever she could get for herself, by hook or crook, was hers, by God, and also it was all she could hope for. She had a queer, awful point of view. There was no kindness in her world. It was full of hate. She thought everybody had it in for her."

"Maybe she went a little crazy for a minute," Patrick said. "Maybe she did kill Thayer."

"Nope," Scott argued, and he shook his head. "At least, I don't think so. I'll tell you why. She would be afraid to do murder. She was afraid of policemen, the devil, ghosts, everything. Incidentally, she was terrified of Trask. He made her feel he suspected her of killing Ray last fall, when it happened. She'll go miles out of her way to avoid even meeting Trask, because she thinks he's still after her." Scott said, "I seem to be mixing up my tenses. One minute I use the past, the other the present. I frankly will believe that Dorrie is under that car when they bring in the real proof, and not before. If she's alive, for God's sake, don't quote me, Pat."

"Of course not, Scott. What did she think was stolen from that house? Did she tell you?"

Scott shook his head. "She didn't know. It was all part of the same pattern. She was just generally suspicious. There might not have been anything at all. Or somebody may have pilfered—after food or something."

"Would Dorrie go into Thayer's study, do you think? And spill a lot of papers about?"

"She would not!" Scott declared. "She hired one of our Mexican neighbor women to take care of Ray's private part of the house. I doubt if she ever went in there. She was afraid. I told you she was superstitious. What made you ask that?"

"The study is in a mess," Patrick said. "It would be quite easy, I should think, for anybody acquainted with that house, if he had some means of access, to get in at night without her knowing it. Her bedroom is separated from Thayer's study by a bath, bedroom, living room and hall. Did Thayer have any valuable manuscripts?"

Scott shook his head again.

"Not that I ever heard of. I think he would have told me, if he had. He had no illusions about his stuff. It wasn't art, and he didn't think it was. It paid well and was his way of making his living, and that was that. He went to Hollywood twice a year, for six or eight weeks each time. If he left anything unfinished he put it in his safety-deposit box. He worked like a dog, you know, but you'd never get it from him. He always managed to seem poky and relaxed." Scott's face was suddenly illumined. "I loved him. Ray was what you call a right guy. There will never be anybody else like him."

"Everybody liked him," I said. I was dying to know more about Ray and Karen. "Was he much in love with Karen?"

"Terribly," Scott said.

"But why did he marry *that* Dorrie?"

Scott put his hands together, linking the fingers gently. He made no answer.

"Do you know why, Scott?" Patrick said.

"Yes," Scott said. "I think I do. But I'll be god-damned if anybody is going to drag it out of me. It is just one of those things you don't blab."

"Sounds pretty lurid," Patrick said.

"I don't want to discuss it," Scott said, a little stiffly. "But not on Dorrie's account. If she's dead, I'm sorry—but I would repeat anything she told me with pleasure, if it weren't that I can't do it without involving Ray. He was my friend. They can line me up and shoot me," Scott said, stubbornly, "before I'll let the gossips in for a feast of Ray's private affairs. Sorry!"

"I think you're quite right," Patrick said. "I hope you understand that I'm not prying into this business out of idle curiosity, Scott. I just happen to hate murder like hell, even if it is somebody like Dorrie. If she was murdered, chances are your friend Thayer was, too. He was your friend. He wasn't mine, for I only met him once or twice, but it happens that he was a United States Marine. We like to believe that we never let each other down."

"That's pretty swell," Scott said, and his voice was a little husky. "But why do the two deaths have to have any connection? Maybe Dorrie was murdered for whatever she had in the envelope, as you suggested yourself."

"Could be," Patrick said. "If she was as scared of ghosts and such as you seem to think, she wouldn't go alone at night to the place where her husband was killed, whether that was murder or accident or suicide or what. Somebody went with her. Maybe that person killed her for the bonds or whatever she carried. There'll be an autopsy, which will determine the approximate time of her death. Maybe the car had a clock. . . ."

"It did have a clock," Scott said. "It kept good time, too."

"Maybe the clock stopped when the car struck the bottom of the canyon. The radio went right on, you know, and attracted an Indian, and thereby gave us a little start on this business we mightn't've had. Tell me, what do you think of Bee Chandler?"

Scott looked amazed at another sudden shift of focus. So did I. I never could get used to Patrick's doing it. "Bee? Why, she's swell. Why?"

"How well do you know her, really?"

"Oh, very well, Pat. I've always seen a lot of Bee and Karen and Edwina. Jeanie can tell you that. We were a crowd. Maurice and Ray and I, and the Chandlers."

"She strikes me," Patrick said, "as a very peculiar and very secretive woman."

Scott said, "Well, she's rather laconic, and all that, but it doesn't mean anything. She's solid gold, really. I guess she's just hard to get acquainted with, I mean, at first, but when you do know her she's very frank and sweet and a lot of fun."

"How old is she?" Patrick asked.

Scott grinned at me. "Well, that's no state secret, is it, Jean? She's eighteen years older than Edwina, and Edwina is twenty-four."

"Ten to your one she's not that old, Scott," Patrick offered.

Scott laughed. "Take you up on that, Pat. Though I must say I don't know exactly how we'll prove it."

"There ought to be a way," Patrick said.

I said, "Well, I don't see why she couldn't be forty-two. She's the type that doesn't show her age, she and Karen."

When Edwina was Bee's age, I refrained from saying, she'd be sagging all over the place. Karen and Bee had breasts and thighs, too, but they stayed where they belonged, but of course I didn't say so to Scott and Patrick. I'm the lean kind myself and probably Scott would think I was merely admiring myself and being jealous of Edwina's curves. I did say, though, "Those gaunt women have all the luck after thirty. Karen will be as stunning as her mother, maybe more so, when she's her age."

"I don't see how any woman could be more beautiful than Edwina," Scott said.

"I agree," Patrick said.

Men! I thought. I said, "Well, you guys know what you like, I guess." I was facing a window. I saw one of the nurses coming toward the office. Scott saw her, too.

"We're lucky not to have been interrupted," he said. The lines of his lips tightened. "I feel decidedly that I've been shooting off my trap."

"Me, too," Patrick said. He stood up. So did I. The nurse came in. She was a new one since I had been here and Scott introduced her, and then came to the door with us. "Will you let me know if anything turns up?" he asked. "Anything special, I mean."

"Sure will," Patrick said. "Thanks for everything."

"Sorry it wasn't something definite," Scott said.

"So long," I said.

Scott said, "Listen, I meant to ask you to come to dinner Sunday night. Can you make it?"

Sunday was the day after tomorrow.

"We can try," I said.

"Sure we will," Patrick said.

"Come about half-past six," Scott said. "But I'll be seeing you before then, probably. So long."

"That reminds me," I said, as we walked toward the car, "Hugh Kennicott has asked us up to the ranch for dinner some time next week. I told him I would call him."

"How about tomorrow night?" Patrick asked.

"Too soon. Sky Valley's eight thousand feet, Pat. And the pass on the way is ten thousand."

A Mexican waiting near our car said he was waiting for us.

"My boss, Mr. Ames, he send me to tell you he wants you to call him up on the phone, please," the man said.

Patrick looked at the man for a moment, and then said, "You tell your boss that when he really needs me he knows where to find me."

12

When we got to the plaza a couple of minutes later there was a great crowd around the sheriff's office, and we imagined it had to do with Dorrie Thayer until Patrick left me in the car for a few minutes and came back to report the facts. It was rustlers. The lame and halt and the ill and the aged, which made up a good part of Santa Maria's male population at that time, were clamoring to help catch these criminals and hang them on the handiest limb. Rustling these days is exactly like shooting fish in a barrel. In the great days of the West the rustler at least took a chance. He was a lusty sort of desperado. Nowadays they travel in gangs by truck. When they come on an isolated herd of cattle they pull up along the side of the road. The driver remains in the truck while the others round up the cattle. They carry their cow ponies in the trailer and the idotic cows are circled in the usual fashion and lassoed and roped and tied and unroped after being loaded in. The horses go back in the trailer with the cows and off rolls the truck to the handiest receiver for the black market.

We hadn't had much of that sort of thing in Santa Maria County, in spite of its great size and small population, because most of our green valleys are uplands with what roads as there are filtering off through tight valleys from the one north-and-south highway, and that makes it hard for the thieves to get away if the theft is discovered soon enough. But when a ranch sprawls over an area thirty miles long, like the Kennicott ranch for example, quite a lot can happen that goes unnoticed for weeks, no matter how vigilant the cowboys are. I'm saying all this because rustlers get a community into a high pitch which makes it forget entirely an incident like Dorrie Thayer's plunging her car into the canyon. Santa Maria wouldn't start thinking about Dorrie Thayer again till the rustlers were taken care of.

Well, in a way it was a relief, I thought, because Patrick wouldn't join the mob hunting the rustlers, and if the Thayer case was shelved a few days, swell, considering his health. He was holding up fine, but maybe that wouldn't last.

When we got home Pancho rollicked all over the place, and Toby showed his shy exquisite pleasure in a cat's fashion. We hadn't been away from home so much on any one day since we had been back.

Ten minutes later the sheriff came zooming up the hill. He swung his big muscular body out of the car and came striding through the gate. He looked ten years younger, from sheer purposefulness. He wouldn't sit down. He leaned against the tree. His left hand automatically brought out his cigarette makings.

"I'll have to take every able-bodied man I can get hold of after them polecats," he said. "Well, the widda was under the car all right. She'd been shot."

"Shot?" I cried.

The sheriff ignored me. I knew I had wasted time.

"The bullet went in at the top of her spine and came out smack between her eyes. It got stopped by something in the front of the car and kicked back into some fur she had on. I got the bullet. It fell down when we lifted the body.

"Also got the gun. Cain't say if the gun fired the bullet, but it's the right size. Luckily nobody saw me pick up the gun. Pete Martinez was working around the corpse and I picked up a door which had busted loose from the car and under it laid the gun. I didn't say anything because Pete's kind of a gossip. The rest of the men were fetching up the basket and hadn't got there yet. I reckon I know that gun. It belonged to Mrs. Bee Chandler."

Bee? I thought, agonized, and Patrick said, quietly, "How did you recognize it?"

Trask said, "Seen it often, Pat. It's a Colt .45 her husband used in the last war. His name is etched on the barrel. There's at least one clear print on the gun, Pat. I reckon I misjudged that little widda, maybe because I kind of like Mrs. Chandler and Karen. I resented the way Max Ottoway jumped onto Karen. They don't put on highfalutin' airs like a lot of Eastern folks that have moved out to Santa Maria, like the so-called artists and such." The sheriff lit his cigarette. "It was Karen that usually packed the Colt revolver, Pat."

There was one of their deadly silences.

Trask said, "When Ottoway gets back here tonight he'll start hollering rustlers like hell because they're a lot more interesting to the voters than the late
Widda Thayer." He looked at his big silver watch. "It'll be three or four hours
before Pete Martinez and his helpers get back here with the body." The sheriff
exhaled smoke. "I know a feller in Santa Fe that runs a private laboratory. He's
also a fingerprint expert. He used to work at police headquarters in Chicago, but
he got lung trouble, so he came out here and set up for himself, does work for
the ranchers and prospectors and even for the police when they're in a rush."
The sheriff paused. "It's a little irregular, I reckon, but Ottoway is so set against
Karen Chandler in his mind that it might give her a breathing spell, in case she
didn't kill the woman, Pat, if we could check that fingerprint on the gun. I could
ring up that feller in Santa Fe and tell him I'm sending a deputy on a confidential
matter. I needn't say what for."

Patrick said, in the same tone the sheriff had used, "One of your stars would
look mighty nice on my shirt pocket, Jim."

Their eyes met. They didn't smile. The sun and weather lines on both faces
looked uncommonly resolute.

"Thank you kindly, Pat. I'll fix you up for gasoline and all. I've got the evidence in the car."

They walked toward the gate. I followed.

"See anything of a brown manila envelope in Thayer's car, Jim?"

"Nope."

"Would have been in the glove compartment, maybe."

"Wasn't there. I went over the wreck thoroughly, Pat."

"Determine what time it may have happened?"

"The clock on the dashboard had stopped at five minutes past ten o'clock.
Reckon that may have been about right, considering the stage of *rigor mortis*.
The Indian came along and heard the radio about one o'clock."

"Know the time by the stars?"

Trask chuckled. "Not exactly. He recognized the radio program, one broad-
cast from Los Angeles at that hour. Then he made himself comfortable and waited
for daylight to take a good look."

Their eyes met and crinkled.

"You saw the oil spots, Jim? On the top of The Rock?"

"Yep. I figure she was shot in the back of the head while sitting listening to
the radio. The car was then put in low gear and sent over the rim. The top was
up, and it lit on the top, when it hit the bottom. The canvas top on a good convertible is tougher than it looks, I reckon. She wasn't as mangled as you might
expect."

"Why would the gun go over with the car, Jim?"

"Yeah, why?" There was a pause. "Well, it could have happened by mistake.
It may have been pretty risky making the car go where the killer wanted. Maybe

he had to ride in it a piece, or anyways guide it while walking beside it. Maybe in the excitement he forgot the gun. One thing sure, the widda didn't shoot herself square in the middle of the back of her head and then drive the car over herself."

The sheriff handed Patrick something wrapped in his blue cotton bandanna, gave him the address of the private lab, and told him which gasoline station to use, since we ourselves were rationed.

I was ready to go as I was, needing only a topcoat to have for the trip back at night, and a handkerchief to tie up my hair.

Patrick decided to get into uniform. He kept his clothes in the guest bedroom and used it as a dressing room. This room was separated from ours by the bath.

I sat down at the dressing table and fixed my face, last brushing my eyebrows and doing my mouth. Pancho hung around looking wistful.

"Mind if we take the hound?" I called through to Patrick.

"Not if he stays in the car."

"It's a deal, darling."

Pancho, understanding every word as usual, began to frisk, running big circles, and leaping like a dervish.

"It takes so little to please the critter, darling."

"Good old Pancho!" Patrick said.

Pancho dashed into the other room and whisked and yipped with delight. Patrick played with him, making a gay racket. I raised my voice, unnecessarily loud at that, and said, "Where did you go when you left me in Julia's shop this morning, Pat?"

"To the county clerk's office," Patrick said.

"Whatever for?"

"I was looking for a record of a marriage license. Just between you and me."

"A marriage license?" I shouted. "Dorrie and Ray Thayer didn't get married here, darling. If that's what you were looking for. They got married in Las Vegas, Nevada. Mr. Trask told you that. What has that got to do with Dorrie's getting murdered? I mean, whatever put it into your head that Ray Thayer would ever have got married here?"

The window was open on the lane. I had been shouting.

"Jeanie?" Bee Chandler called, then.

Under his breath in the next room I heard Patrick cussing a streak as I hurried to the window and put my head out.

Bee sat on her horse, near the gate, not twenty feet from the lane window and even closer to another open on the garden.

She was lighting a cigarette, and her face was mysterious as the sphinx. Seeing me she flapped a hand and said, "Hello, Jeanie. Excuse me for not coming to the door. I could hear your voice. Are you and Pat busy? This minute?"

"Oh, Bee," I said. "We are. Pat has to do an errand for the sheriff."

"Shush!" Patrick breathed, from the bathroom door.

Pancho had come over to the window. He stood beside me, with his ears up and his head cocked.

"It's about those rustlers," I lied to Bee. "It's a secret, for God's sake!"

Bee laid a solemn hand on her breast. "When can I see Pat, Jeanie? It's sort of urgent."

I looked at Patrick. He shook his head.

"I don't know, Bee. He's taking a bath right this minute. If . . ."

"I'll tell you what I want to tell him, Jean," Bee said, and her tone was matter-of-fact. "It's about those specs. Before Pat does anything drastic about them, I mean, gives them to the police or anybody, I wonder if he would talk with me? It will be better if I come here, however, if it won't put you out too much." That was so Karen wouldn't know, I thought. "How about tonight, Jeanie?"

I looked at Patrick, and his lips shaped, "Tomorrow. Lunch."

"I doubt if we'll get back tonight, Bee. How's tomorrow lunch?"

"Lunch? Why, that would be lovely, if you're sure it's no trouble?"

She nodded and thanked me again and wheeled her horse to start down the hill, and then pulled it up suddenly, and called back, "By the way, Maurice wants to see Pat. He says it's urgent. I ran onto Julia on the plaza. She was on her way here to tell you, and she relayed it by me."

"Do you think it's anything urgent, Bee?" I asked.

Bee moved her shoulders. "You never can tell, with Maurice. Anyhow, I delivered his message."

She waved again and rode down the hill, sitting very straight, her black hair shining, her tweed jacket trim.

"God damn it to hell!" Patrick said. He walked over and slammed the window shut, and fastened it. "Nothing like telling the world what you don't want it to know. Of all the people I would rather not know about my poking round in Ray Thayer's marriage—oh, hell!" He glared at the dog. "And where were you?" he demanded.

Pancho squirmed. I said, "He was in your room. He was happy. He didn't hear her coming because he was being so happy. Oh, dear."

We filled the gas tank at the station near the plaza and drove south at the hour when the desert begins to take on its evening charm. I watched the Ames house for a long way, wondering what it was Maurice had wanted of Patrick. I thought, he probably wants to apologize about the other night. Explain it away. He is worrying about that money, I guess. He is lying in his bed—or is he?—thinking that Trask and Dr. Johnson and Patrick and whoever else was listening in on the party line that night might get together and hold him to his bargain. Blind? My eye!

Then I thought of Edwina, showing off that concha belt. Why did Karen show her hatred like that? Had she known about it before Edwina came out there?

Maybe she had heard about it in the village, maybe she had gone in the shop when she was on the plaza, at the time when she had heard about Dorrie's accident, and maybe Julia, good old Julia, let the cat out of the bag. Anyhow, it was a pity. Edwina had piled it on so. She had looked so triumphant. She must be very sure of her man, to wear an expression so smugly female as that.

We rode on, covering the long swells of the road as it took the low hills in advance of the saddle which marked the southern boundary of the Santa Maria valley. In a few minutes we began to descend by the hairpin curves to the level of the Rio Grande.

All at once I thought of something. The sheriff and probably everybody else who wasn't too old or too young or too crippled or something would be away after those rustlers. The prosecutor was still out of town. It would be a fine night for another murder.

13

On the banks of the Rio Grande, Pancho had an adventure. While Patrick walked to the river's edge and peered up the boxlike canyon which began, or ended, a short distance north of the point where the road descended to the level of the river, Pancho jumped out and sashayed around. He always hates to miss anything and, right away, as usual, he made a discovery. He was standing with his eyes glued on whatever it was and his body stiff and his tail quivering when Patrick turned back toward the car.

Patrick dived into the jump seat for his rope, and a moment later Pancho, roped and wriggling and furious, was dragged away from his find.

I felt that horror.

"Was it a rattlesnake, Pat?"

"Porcupine," Patrick said. Pancho had been lucky. He had only collected about a dozen white quills. Patrick pulled them out with the pliers and dabbed the wounds with iodine from the car's First-Aid kit and we drove on. For some time Pancho was very quiet and dignified.

"A lariat is quite useful," I conceded, then.

Patrick slanted me a look. "Thanks."

"Darling," I said, a little later, "I like to wait for you to tell me things, but when you don't . . ."

"Shoot," Patrick said.

"Well, what did you think of the way Bee grabbed everything Karen touched this afternoon? I mean the compact and those spectacles." Patrick said nothing. "You did notice it?"

"Right." His eyes remained on the road.

"Is Bee frightened for Karen, do you think?"

"It looked that way. Yet—maybe you noticed—Karen snatched the rifle after Bee had used it, too."

"Did you leave your keys on their terrace on purpose, so you would have to go back?"

Patrick said, "I went back for Karen's riding crop and Bee's teaspoon."

"Oh. Bee missed them, Pat. That's why she rode over to the house, then. She's worried." Patrick didn't say anything. "But, darling, why? You didn't know at that time that Mr. Trask would find the gun with finger-prints on it?"

"There's a good print on the right inside lens of those glasses. They handled the specs, but luckily they didn't touch the lenses."

"Oh. You think it's Karen's, Pat?"

"The expert can tell us, I hope. Everything's in my case—specs, crop, spoon, gun, bullet—in my brief case."

A little while passed. We were out of the narrow valley and in a wide fertile one.

"This Thayer affair is like a Dali painting, Pat. I mean, everything's probably present, but—you know—scrambled all over the place. Two corpses. A blind man looking through a telescope. A gun. Two guns, if we count the one that banged away at you through the window. A concha belt. Faces. Edwina's classic oval face. Bee's and Karen's sphinx-faces. Maurice's strange coffee-colored face. Dorrie's persimmon face . . ."

"Wait a minute. That belongs on one of the bodies."

"I said a *Dali* painting. Who knows where the face might pop up? And, finally, then, the purple-blue specs. The specs ought to repeat all over the picture. Specs, specs, specs, lots of purple-blue spectacles. Do you think they're the real clue?"

"Jeanie, *I don't know.*"

"Did you bring along that little bottle you found in Dorrie's medicine cabinet?"

Patrick laughed. "You don't miss a trick, do you, chum? I told you I've brought everything. Except, of course, the sausage. . . ."

"Don't make jokes, please, darling."

"Okay. Let's skip it. Shall we? When we get to Santa Fe I'll drop my stuff with the expert, and we'll dash over to La Fonda and have a drink and a nice lazy dinner. Like to?"

"I'd love it. You mean you won't have to stay with the expert?"

"Not all the time, I hope. But keep your fingers crossed. And pray that we won't have to go on to Albuquerque."

"We couldn't anyway," I said. "It's too long and too hard a drive for you, darling . . ."

"Tut, tut! Remember your promise not to mention my condition!" He paused. "If we have to go on, for any reason, we might pick up a private plane."

Santa Fe isn't very big but it looks like a metropolis compared to Santa Maria. I felt very happy and light-hearted after we left the stuff at the lab and drove to the plaza.

It was a sweet evening. The air was warmer than we had had it in the mountains, and the wind was blowing just a little, and the town looked gay because many of the shops were open, and people were strolling about the streets and on the plaza itself. The wind ruffled and swished the bright clothes so many people wear in Santa Fe. Some were tourists. You could tell the tourists because their jeans and calicos are stiff and bright with newness. Their jewelry was too shiny, and their Western hats too clean. On the corner near the hotel a Santo Domingo Indian who used to sell me things for my shop was skinning the shirts off a couple from New York. He was a graduate of Carlisle but they thought he couldn't speak English. I smiled at him passing by and his slit eyes gave back a gleam of acknowledgment, but no more.

We entered the hotel by the San Francisco door and Patrick left me in the lounge while he made some telephone calls. From then on for almost two hours everything was wonderful. We relaxed on a leather lounge in La Cantina and had a couple of cocktails. We had dinner in the New Mexican Room. There was candlelight and music. We sat at a slim table, on a *banco*, and I had a special New Mexican chicken dish called *Gallina Lucrecio*, which was every bit as good as any of Maurice Ames' prize recipes. Patrick had a steak.

Always Patrick lives in the moment, when we're celebrating, enjoying things as they come. It was wonderful.

I was spooning up a strawberry parfait and hoping we could stay for the dancing when a bellboy called Patrick to the phone. A few minutes later the boy brought a note. "Have to go along and see about you know what," it said. "Am taking car and Pancho. Have a drink and another cup of coffee and keep the table. Love, Pat. P.S. Will buy the hound a hamburger. Love and Kisses, Pat."

Twenty minutes passed. I had the coffee.

The orchestra moved in from the patio and took their place in the center of the room. Many new people arrived. The tables filled up. There was dancing.

Forty minutes had gone. Fifty. I ordered a cognac. The floor show started.

I kept watching the entrance. Nothing happened.

Now it was an hour. The bellboy came back.

"Sorry," the telephone message said. "Be there as soon as I can. Keep the table and have one for me, too. All my love, Pat."

I tipped the boy, and glancing after him as he left the room, I saw Edwina Ames and Hugh Kennicott. They were standing just outside, under the portals which enclosed the patio. Edwina was looking up at Hugh with a little-woman-in-awful-trouble look on her face. Her lips were parted. Her eyes were wide.

She wore the same blue dress and had a mink coat over her shoulders.

Hugh was talking. He looked as if he were laying down the law. His sudden smile didn't once enliven his somber dark face.

All at once Edwina's gaze shifted. She saw me. She said something to Hugh. They moved away. In a few minutes Edwina came into the restaurant by herself. She came to my table.

"What luck!" she said, in her velvety voice. "Are you alone, Jeanie?"

"For the moment." My eyes, drifting to her waistline, lingered on the silver belt.

"Would you mind if I sit with you a minute?" The waitress had already come up, was pulling out the table. Edwina slid into the *banco* and dropped off her coat. I smelled her musky perfume. "Hugh had to come to see a man, so I came along," she said. "I'm starved, too. Bring me a chicken sandwich, coffee and a chocolate sundae," she said to the girl, who went off with the order, and then Edwina said, "What luck I don't have to kill the time alone, Jeanie. Where's Pat? You did come with Pat?"

I nodded. "He had to see a man, too."

"Don't they always," said Edwina. "Well, I'm glad it's you I ran into, instead of one of the local cats. My Lord, what people can make out of nothing!" She pursed her garnet lips, considered, and then said, "But, as Hugh himself said, it isn't exactly nothing, and it's got to come out sometime, so why beat around the bush. We're here to see a lawyer about a divorce." I felt that sickening feeling you get when something is evil and you know you are powerless to do anything. "Hugh has gone to see the man first, to ask if he will handle the case. He usually doesn't take divorce cases, but he's the Kennicotts' lawyer and we think for that reason he will."

"Does Maurice know, Edwina?"

"Heaven forbid!" Edwina cried. "He would kill me!"

"But I thought he was bedridden?"

"Oh, darling, you don't half know!"

I didn't know what to think. I said, "I had the idea that Maurice was pretty nice to you, Edwina?"

"Oh, my dear! But of course that is what he pretends. He's even got Bee sold on him, and Scott even, and you know how devoted Scott is to me, too." Edwina looked like a trampled flower. "Naturally, they don't know the real truth, how sadistic he is, how brutal! I hope it need never come out. I don't think it will. Maurice is vain, you know. He likes people to think he's a gentleman. Hugh says to use cruelty as grounds, if I must, but we think that Maurice will settle for incompatibility. He doesn't want everybody to know the truth."

"But, while he's ill . . ."

"Ill!" Edwina's drowsy smile was full of mockery. "I wonder if he's ill. He hasn't any temperature. I think he's got Dr. Johnson guessing, too. I think he is deliberately making himself sick in some tricky fashion, just to work on my feelings. I know he gets out of bed and walks around sometimes. Maybe it's all just a trick."

I could see him, as she spoke, a man with too wide shoulders and too short legs, a coffee-colored face, opaque brownish eyes, stiff gray hair, and a smile that made a tight V.

"I'm so afraid of him," Edwina breathed, and her mouth sagged, but she went ahead and cut into her chicken sandwich. "He's awful, Jeanie! You've no idea! You must never tell anyone why I'm here until everything's all set. Or, could we say I came with you, in case anybody else sees me? I'm so terrified, darling!"

I said, "How did you get away tonight?"

"He thinks I'm at Bee's. Bee is sitting up with Maurice—we could get only one trained nurse, you know—and I said I would go and stay with Karen."

"Does Karen know where you are?"

"Oh, my dear, of course not. Nobody knows the real truth, yet. Oh, I shouldn't have told you. I'm so upset."

"Edwina," I said. "I'm going to tell you something. Julia was saving that concha belt for Karen. Did you know that? When Hugh bought it she thought he was giving it to Karen."

Edwina looked devastated. "Oh, darling. Oh, how awful. I didn't realize . . . Oh, and I went over there, and showed it off!"

"But how come Hugh knew exactly what he wanted? I was in the shop when he bought it, Edwina."

"Why, I don't know. He has pretty good taste in Indian things. He's bought a lot for his sister in New York. Maybe he had seen it before Karen reserved it. It's just an accident that he chose it for me, really it is, Jeanie."

"Well, it's none of my business, anyway," I said.

"That's all right," Edwina said. "Listen, don't tell Bee about this divorce business, will you not? I shall, in due time. Bee is kind of strait-laced."

"You mean, she wouldn't want you to divorce Maurice? Not even if he's cruel to you, and all?"

"That's not it. She would think he should be warned first. She simply doesn't realize that he's a—he's a beast, and has to be handled like one. Bee's hard in some ways. Karen is, too. They're both wonderful and I adore them both, but I'm different. I am soft, I know I am, I have to have someone to lean on, to look after me." Edwina sighed. "When Maurice proposed I was dazzled. I mean, I was so young. You see, I was never happy, really, after my father died. He was so wonderful. We had had such a lovely life, there in Paris, always the best of everything, and then he died, and there was a depression in America, and Bee decided it was best to live in Europe because we had so little, but it was enough to give us, over there, what she called advantages. Travel and languages and schools in Switzerland and all. My dear! I loathed every minute of it. Karen was too young to mind, but I was older." Edwina shuddered, and her full breasts seemed to sag a little. "You should rejoice that you never were one of those wretched European little girls in black cotton stockings and a scratchy mohair uniform." Her back eyes filled with tears. "You can't wonder that I took the first man who wanted me, even if I thought him repulsive." One of her plump, exquisitely-cared-for hands caressed her expensive sleeve. "I could think of nothing but his beautiful house, and pretty clothes and—enough to eat!"

She might just as well be really a European woman, I thought. Patrick had told me about the European women he had known in the years he spent abroad before the war. Not even the beautiful grew up with any idea of marrying for love. All they dared hope for was a roof and enough to eat and relative kindness from the man who chose them. It was luck even to be chosen, indeed.

Edwina was American, but she had been reared in such an atmosphere, and, all at once, I could see that perhaps Bee had done her a great injustice. Unknowingly, maybe.

I looked at my watch. Patrick had been gone an hour and twenty-five minutes!

Edwina finished her ice cream. I watched the floor show. A Spanish couple was doing one of those part-song and part-dance things which seem to be characteristically Hispanic.

"Of course," Edwina said, "Hugh simply insists." She smiled. "He's very determined," she said.

"Are you going to marry Hugh, Edwina?"

"Darling! But of course." Her eyes opened wide. "Oh, you mustn't tell that, Jeanie. Hugh wanted to go to Maurice and have it out, but I won't have it. He doesn't know Maurice. Believe me, it is better to see the lawyer first, and tell him what Maurice is like, and take his advice. Oh, I love Hugh so. You've no idea!" Her eyes shone. She said gently, "Hugh is only one reason for my divorcing Maurice, Jeanie. I would do it anyhow, even though I had to support myself with my own two hands."

I looked at those pampered hands. They made me angry.

Why couldn't she be honest? Why didn't she say outright that she was unloading Maurice because the Kennicotts had more money and because Hugh was young and handsome and appetizing? Maybe I could like her, then.

No, I couldn't. I could never like her. If I were her mother, I thought, I would detest her. How did Bee feel about Edwina, really? How did Bee really feel about anything? Bee was a mystery, a walking puzzle.

The room had taken on a dreamlike character. The atmosphere held a kind of exaltation, compounded of smoke, candlelight, the music of guitars and mandolins, the voices of people lifted out of the hardness of daily reality by good food and drinks and congenial companions. This room with its charming decor was a delight to start with. It captivated the senses. I wished Patrick would come back.

Yet I did not want to leave this room to go and find him. I ordered another cognac, more coffee.

"I could have asked Scott to bring me here," Edwina said. "I intended to, to keep from involving poor Hugh. But Scott hasn't any prestige. The best lawyer in New Mexico wouldn't've given one moment to Scott Davies." She laid her hand on mine. It was satiny, spotless, a little cold. "Jeanie, you are so sweet! I know I have bored you utterly." Her eyes expressed her hope that she had not. "Will you excuse me for a moment? I've got to go to the desk and see if Hugh has come back. I asked him not to come to this room till I had a look to see if anyone we knew was here. It doesn't matter your seeing us of course—what luck!"

The waitress moved out the table. Edwina flashed me another smile, and walked toward the door, her figure swaying gracefully, the silver belt catching and giving back the candlelight. She returned in about five minutes and laid five dollars on the table and took her coat. "He's waiting. I can't stay to pay the bill," she said, "but that will take care of it." The waitress had started toward our table when Edwina returned. She now addressed her in the superior way she took with servants. "You can keep the change but be sure you give the wine-boy his share," she said. She went out, giving me a last smile, and the waitress added up her bill and took away the money and the dishes. The waitresses at La Fonda are all educated girls, many of them college graduates learning the hotel business by actually working in all its departments. It wasn't the first time this one had been treated like a menial, I thought, because she didn't betray it by so much as an eyebrow-wiggle.

I looked at the time. Patrick had been gone two hours and five minutes.

Two seconds later he came in. "I'm starved," he said. "How about something to eat and drink?"

"You look triumphant," I said, as he settled into the *banco*.

"I should hope so," he said.

"Did you get all the dope?"

"Everything I hoped for—and more."

"What's the extra item, darling?"

Patrick bent close to my ear. He kissed it. "Dorrie wasn't legally married to Ray Thayer," he said.

"Oh, my goodness!" I said. "How come?"

"Because he was already married," Patrick said.

14

I fell asleep on Patrick's shoulder soon after leaving Santa Fe. I had told him what Edwina had said as soon as we were on our way. He wouldn't listen in the restaurant, because we had only a little time to dance and have fun.

When I woke, the car was making a hollow noise as it rolled across the bridge over the Silver River three miles or so south of the place where the road past the Ames place branched off.

The moonlight shone through a thin skim of gloomy-looking clouds. Its light lay pallid on the earth. The mountains looked gray and dreamlike. The canyon in this pallor did not exist. Desert plants near the highway had a ghostly character, their shadows darker ghosts.

I shivered and moved closer to Patrick, and Pancho, who was curled under my coat on my lap, squirmed and grunted, hating to be disturbed. For some reason a motor-car ride always exhausted the dog.

Patrick asked, "Have a good nap?"

"I guess so," I said. The headlights caught a glint of eyes. "See that cat, darling?"

"Too wide apart for a housecat."

I sat stiff.

"Do you think it's a wildcat?" There were supposed to be wildcats in our valley but I had never seen one. I had never seen one anywhere outside of a zoo. I hadn't even heard one. Once in Yellowstone at night I had heard something screaming horridly like a woman being murdered but they told me next morning that it had been a moose. I never had quite believed that a melancholy, stupid-looking moose could emit such a neurotic scream. All of which is irrelevant except that later we learned that Bee Chandler had taken her gun along that night, when she drove out to sit up with Maurice while the nurse slept, because a wildcat had been seen hanging around the Ames ranch. It was the calving season, and Bee thought—or said she thought—that she had hoped to get the cat before it killed and devoured another calf.

Anyway, riding along, I looked up and felt a little excited as I noted how extra determined was Patrick's profile.

I kissed his sleeve. "What's the matter, darling?"

"Lots of things. I didn't tell you, but that was Karen's thumbprint on the lens of those spectacles."

I felt a sinking. "Then she did leave them in Ray's study? So she did go there? She must have forgotten them. . . . I expect they dropped behind the files and she forgot them, or had to run away in a hurry without picking them up. She must have come back for them and was lurking in the garage while we were there. Then it was *Karen* that choked me!"

Patrick said, "Her fingerprints were also on the revolver. I also didn't tell you, Jeanie, but I found that bullet which was fired through the window at me the other night after we were out and prowled about The Rock. It's the type used in Bee Chandler's rifle."

"Oh, darling!" I said. It was so horrible. "But why on earth? What is it all about? And you said that Ray was already married?"

"That's what's interesting," Patrick said. "Ray Thayer was married to Karen Chandler. Or her mother, if Bee's initials are K.E."

"What?"

Patrick nodded. "I suppose it was Karen. They were married in Bernalillo last September 5th. That was the day Ray left Santa Maria and took Karen as far as Albuquerque on his way to Hollywood."

"How on earth did you learn that?"

Patrick laughed. "Elementary, Baby. I had a look at the county records. Matter of routine. Like to find out what I can about my clients. Dorrie wasn't presumed to be dead when I left you with Julia in her shop and went to do some sleuthing in the county clerk's files. I was curious to know more about Ray's will. It was very simple, left his entire estate to his fiancée, Karen Chandler. It was dated August 10th. I checked on the marriage licenses for the past two years as a matter of routine, too. Maybe it was mostly curiosity. It wasn't likely that Karen and Ray would have taken out a license in Santa Maria, because it would not have remained a secret, but I looked just the same. No dice. My curiosity has been much aroused by Bee and Karen Chandler."

"Darling—they're all right. I'm sure."

Patrick continued as though I hadn't spoken. " 'Suppose one of them did it?' I kept asking myself. 'Why? There has to be a motive. Maybe Karen *was* in love with Ray Thayer? Why not? He seems to have been a right sort of guy.' "

"Also a Marine," I said.

Patrick let it pass. " 'What do we know about it anyway? How can we tell?' I kept wondering. So I checked the records for anything I could find in Santa Maria and in Santa Fe and Bernalillo—and there I found that a Thayer and a Chandler had got married last September 5th."

"But how?"

"Telephoned the county clerks in both places. Told them I was the police. The information from Bernalillo was kind of vague, so I popped down and had a look myself."

"Did you fly?"

"It's only thirty-five miles from Santa Fe. Quicker to drive."

"You should have taken me!"

"If I had, you would have missed Edwina, and we wouldn't know that she was planning to get a divorce, which may turn out to be useful information in this tangled business."

"You win," I said. He always did. "Oh, look at Scott's window, Pat! That's the one his bed is built in. It's fixed so that if ever he has to stay in bed any length of time he will have the sunshine and the view. Let's stop and talk with Scott, Pat. I'm sure he knows more than he lets on. He's been pals with Bee and Karen and

Ray Thayer, all of them, for so long. If he knows you've got the goods on Karen—
I mean, there might be what they call extenuating circumstances—so that—I
mean, if they were justified . . ."

"It's too late, Jeanie."

"It's only a little past midnight, and he's up. Please do stop, Pat!"

Patrick said, grimly, "It's Ames I'd like to surprise with a midnight visit!"

But he turned off on the Silver River road and a little way along we ran into
the short drive in front of Scott's neat white house.

We parked, and, after we knocked, the light in the iron lantern above the blue
door was snapped on, and Scott opened the door wearing a navy bathrobe, and
on his feet felt slippers. He was reading *War and Peace*, and held his place with
one finger. His blond hair was mussed and he looked a little shy at being caught
déshabillé.

"Why, hello," he said.

"Hello," Patrick said. "Kind of late to drop in on you, Scott."

"It was my idea, Scott," I said. "We saw your light, and . . ."

"But come in," Scott said, stepping back and opening the door wide.

"For only half a minute," I said. There was a night chill in the air. I had left
Pancho in the warm heated car, wrapped in a rug.

We stepped into the little hall, and Scott closed the door. The living room
beyond was warm with lamplight. It was a large beautiful room, wood-paneled,
with books and pictures and warmly colored old Indian rugs which gave it much
life. With one bedroom, a bath, an ultra-modern kitchen, and the terrace, it com-
prised Scott's house. The Venetian blinds in this room were closed.

"Sit down," Scott said. "I'll get you a drink."

Patrick said, "Thanks, Scott, but we haven't time to sit down, and . . ."

"And we've had too many drinks already," I said. "We've been on a bender in
Santa Fe."

Scott laid the book on the hall table and stood with his hands in the pockets of
his bathrobe and his feet a little apart.

"Tell him, Pat," I said. "We must sound crazy."

Patrick nodded. "I might as well," he said. "It won't be much of a secret by
tomorrow. Well, apparently Karen Chandler killed both Ray and Dorrie Thayer,
Scott."

Scott's mouth opened, and he swayed a little, and put a hand on the wall to
steady himself.

I looked at Patrick, for I had expected him to start off by asking Scott if he
knew that Karen and Ray had got married. It was part of his technique to ask
abrupt questions. These more or less unhinged his victims, I suppose, so that
they told more than they expected to before they got themselves in hand. But I
could never get used to it.

Scott said, "If this is a joke, kids, I don't seem to get it."

"Sorry," Patrick said gently. "I did it that way on purpose, Scott. I wanted to shock you, to make you realize straight off that things are ganging up against Karen. If she's really guilty, the quicker we know it the better. If she isn't . . ."

"She couldn't be," Scott said. He moved a step to the left and sat down on a chair, his eyes fastened on Patrick's, appealing, incredulous, a little opaque, the way everybody's get from shock. What was it you did in a shock case? Something warm on the stomach, or in it, maybe, or both?

"In that case, if you know anything that will help Karen, the sooner we know it the better," Patrick said again.

"I don't believe it," Scott said, in a toneless voice.

"I'm sorry. The evidence is against her, Scott."

Scott leaned forward. "But why?" A little life came into his eyes. Good. He was beginning to fight. "Why?"

"You knew, didn't you, that Ray Thayer and Karen were married?"

Scott gaped, his mouth twitched, but he said nothing.

"In Bernalillo. Last September 5th," Patrick said.

"I don't believe it!" Scott snapped out.

"Ray didn't tell you?"

"Certainly not!"

"It's in the records. I saw their signatures myself," Patrick said. "I don't know Karen's writing, but I took a sample of Thayer's, and his signature, from his study when I went through it this morning. Yesterday morning, I mean." I glanced at my watch. It was twenty-five minutes past midnight. "She signed herself K. E. Chandler. He signed himself William Thayer. They gave Hollywood as their address, which would be somewhat irregular, for Karen, I believe. I suppose they didn't want any publicity."

Scott said, "Karen was still in school. I suppose she would want to keep it secret, for the time."

"Then you agree it was they?"

Scott said, and now his words came more naturally, "Ray's real name was William. He never had the Ray legalized, but he used it at his bank, everywhere. That William makes me think you might be right, but the whole business knocks me for a loop. It doesn't make sense. Suppose they did get married? Even so, why would Karen want to kill him when he came back here with Dorrie? She was already in love with Hugh Kennicott. She never cared for Ray the way she does for Hugh. She ought to have been relieved, rather than outraged. She could easily have had the marriage annulled, couldn't she, if they hadn't lived together, and if Ray came back here with another woman? Which is another incredible thing! He was my best friend, yet he did these things, married Karen secretly and committed bigamy, and he didn't tell me . . ."

"Did he have a chance?"

Scott said, "Well, maybe not. He never wrote letters. I only saw him once, alone, after he got back. He came here, he was terribly upset, but before he could get himself in hand and say anything much, Dorrie showed up, and he went away with her, back to his place. I didn't see him again. They found him next morning in the canyon. If only he had talked to me—if I had insisted—if I had chucked her out when she barged in . . .''

"Well, these things happen," Patrick said gently.

I sat down on an old carved chest which stood in the hall opposite the entrance, and Patrick, taking out his cigarettes, offered them, was refused because Scott didn't smoke and I didn't want one, lit his own, and sat down beside me and listened as Scott said, "But so much of it doesn't make sense. Why did Karen waive her rights to his property, if they were married?"

"Kennicott has plenty, hasn't he?" Patrick asked.

"That's not it," Scott said. "Karen wouldn't want the property for herself, but why would she let Dorrie get away with it? Karen would give it to the Red Cross or somebody, rather than let a—a creature like Dorrie wolf what Ray had worked for and saved."

Obviously, that was something only Karen could answer. Or Bee.

"What about Mrs. Chandler?" Patrick asked, as if he had had the same idea I had.

"Bee? What do you mean, what about her?"

"Did she want the marriage between Karen and Ray?"

Scott said, "Bee would leave that to them. Bee wouldn't force her ideas in that regard on anybody. Bee is a little hard to understand, I think, but I believe I understand her, and she's the salt of the earth. Ethical as they come."

"Do you think she would know that Karen had married Ray?"

Scott said slowly, "Yes, I think she would. I don't think Karen keeps anything from Bee. I don't know, of course, but they seem such pals, always. Bee liked Ray. There would be no reason for Karen keeping their marriage a secret from her mother."

Patrick said, "Very ethical people are always going off the deep end, Scott. It probably gave Bee Chandler a big jolt when Ray Thayer came back with Dorrie, if she knew that he and Karen had got married."

Scott said obstinately, "Well, you've got to show me. You say that apparently Karen killed them. What about the evidence? Murder has to be proved, doesn't it?"

"Right. I'm afraid I can't discuss the evidence till after I've talked with the sheriff. Were you familiar with Thayer's files?"

"With the outside of them, of course."

"I told you about their being upset?" Scott inclined his head, and Patrick said, "I'd like your opinion of Maurice Ames, Scott?"

Scott Davies looked very stubborn, and Patrick, ignoring it, said, "He's a strange guy, isn't he, Scott?" Scott did not answer and Patrick said, "Maybe Dorrie was right about his stealing something from the files? But what?" Scott shook his head. "And is he really sick, or is he putting it on?"

"I stopped in there this evening," Scott said. "He looks sick to me."

"Was the nurse on duty?"

"Yes. Maurice's eyes were bandaged. He didn't seem to know me. The nurse said he had listless periods that worried the doctor a lot."

"You don't think he's pretending?"

"For God's sake, why?"

Patrick grinned. "I'm asking you. He's supposed to have sent for me today, twice, maybe oftener, as we've been away since shortly after four o'clock. I suppose I should have gone, but this other thing that took us to Santa Fe seemed more urgent. Ames doesn't like Bee Chandler, does he, Scott?"

Scott squirmed, and said, "Well, maybe not. She isn't his type of woman. Too brainy, for one thing."

"She doesn't know something about him he'd rather she didn't know?"

"Not that I know of. Why?"

"I was wondering if he might frame her," Patrick said.

"What for?"

"It's just an idea," Patrick said. "Maybe Dorrie was right. Maybe Maurice did hire somebody to steal something or other from her house. Maybe Ray had something he wanted."

"Good Lord, Maurice has everything!" Scott exclaimed.

Patrick said, "Ames is the kind that always wants something else. That's how he gets his fun. He acquires a thing, and that's wonderful, but the excitement passes and he wants and goes after something else. Suppose Thayer had something Ames wanted. It would be easy for him to plant clues which would pin the blame on Bee. Or on Karen. It's hard to think of a man his age trying to frame a young girl like Karen. He wouldn't be so soft, though, about Bee, and, besides, he doesn't like her."

"He doesn't like Karen much, either," I said. "Remember how he picked on her at that party, Scott?"

"That's superficial," Scott said. "But he really dislikes Bee."

Patrick said, "That's a deep antipathy, I think, which may spring from nothing but that they are extremely antagonistic types." The question was experimental. It got nowhere.

Scott said, "Look here, Pat. If anyone on earth should hate Maurice Ames, it should be me. He married the only girl I ever wanted and he never fails to remind me of it, and he takes a special malice in doing it, but, all the same, I like him, I respect him, and I can't think he would be such a fool as to do murder. He snubbed Dorrie. So did Karen and Bee. So she griped against them. She's like that. It doesn't mean anything. She was a born troublemaker. Maybe she upset the files herself."

"Didn't she confide in you anything about her marriage with Thayer?" Scott looked blank. "Did she suspect him of the previous marriage?"

"If she did," Scott said, "why didn't she take the money when she got it and skip? That was what she wanted, or so I think."

"Right."

"I never could dope it out," Scott said. "But I wouldn't let her talk to me. I thought maybe Ray married her when he was drunk. Two or three times I've seen Ray drunk to the point of not knowing what he was doing. This is between ourselves, see? It happened when he was terribly tired. He drove himself terrifically sometimes. Then he would drink to relax. Maybe that's what happened. Maybe he didn't know what he was doing when he married Dorrie—then he came to his senses, and realized what he had done, and thought he could never make Karen understand—well, you figure it out, Pat. You're the detective."

"We must go, darling," I said. "Scott doesn't belong to the leisure class, like we do."

"Don't worry about that," Scott said.

"I've got to stop and see Trask, too—if he's back in Santa Maria," Patrick said.

We had all risen. "He is back," Scott said. "The rustlers got away, across the state line. Max Ottoway got back in town about five o'clock and when Trask rolled in an hour or so later Ottoway hollered to high heaven because the gang had got away. Wasn't Trask's fault. He wasn't notified in time, but Ottoway means to pin the blame on him if he can. Jim's too much of a local hero for Max Ottoway to shine the way he'd like."

"My money's on the sheriff," I said.

"I hope you're right, Jeanie. The Wild West ain't what she used to be, though. Could you stop in the office in the morning, Pat?"

Patrick said, "Couldn't you say it—now?"

Scott frowned, hesitated, and then he said, "I've got no right to tell you this, Pat, but maybe it will help Karen. Ray Thayer did talk with Bee Chandler. I think he may have told her what you need to know about his marrying Dorrie."

"Thanks," Patrick said.

Scott said, "Don't tell her I told you. I want to tell her that myself when I see her. I don't want her to think me a heel."

"I won't. Thanks a lot."

Scott turned on the light over the door and stood under its glow till we got in the car. Then he turned off the light.

At the road Patrick turned to the right.

"Darling?" I demanded.

"Ames sent for me twice, Jeanie," Patrick said. "Maybe I ought to drop around."

"Is it Maurice you want to see?" I asked. "Or Bee Chandler?"

15

We drove slowly, using the dimmers, following the white line of road past the Thayer place, so dingy from neglect, so shadowed with death.

We drove on, veering away from the river as the road swept left and curved up through the grassy juniper-dotted range country, where the strange night was stranger, the earth gray, the scattered pot-bellied evergreens black as ink.

Cattleguards rumbled as we crossed them. We drove on. Before crossing the last, at the entrance of the lane, Patrick turned off the lights and we crawled over the guard into the slim white perfect drive to the house.

"Why so mysterious?" I asked.

"Might be an advantage to surprise him."

"And it might not!" I said, thinking it dangerous.

"Nothing to worry about," Patrick said. "Only, you do as I say—remember!"

The house sprawled, pale and immense, without illumination, without life, under the clouded moon. It grew larger and taller with nearness. The slim poplars adorning the grounds looked fragile, the shrubbery calculated and dense.

We crept. Patrick cursed the essential rustle of the slowed-down motor. We arrived at the place where the road divided. One branch curved to the parking space at the front of the house. The other led to the back, and further along to the garages, the cowhands' bunkhouse and the stables. We turned to the right, and when the double verandas came in full view, we saw the night lamp in the open doors of Maurice's room, very dim, hardly distinguishable from the moonlight.

The French doors of his room stood open in the upper veranda. At the other end of the veranda Edwina's bedroom doors were closed.

Patrick stopped the car near the verandas, at a point where the planting concealed it from the house.

"What are you going to do?" I asked. I felt a little tingle of fear, yet for no good reason. This was a civilized house. A visit at the wrong time of day might win a rebuke, but what else? Maurice might play tricks, he might hire someone to do murder, even, but surely you would be safe on his premises.

Patrick said, speaking very low, "I am going to ring the doorbell and ask to see Ames."

I laughed. "Well, good luck. I'll wait in the nice warm car, if you don't mind."

"See that you do!"

"Hey?" I said. "Anyway, be careful."

Patrick reached over, gripped my leg affectionately, got out and closed the door softly.

In the jump seat, snug in his blanket, Pancho curled himself into a tighter ball, and griped audibly because another delay was keeping him from his cozy basket. He certainly was a spoiled dog.

Patrick's long-walking shape vanished beyond the shrubbery.

Nothing happened. I waited. I could hear nothing.

I rolled down a window. The night air blew in, sweet-smelling and damp, and Pancho groaned. Then far away, like an echo, I could hear a silvery bell, ringing and ringing.

It was the front doorbell. Patrick had certainly made up his mind to get in.

Oh, he ought not to keep at it like that!

My sense of propriety felt outraged. Sometimes he really hadn't any manners, I thought.

I slipped out of the car to go to Patrick and urge him to come away now and come back tomorrow.

As I got to the edge of the planting which sheltered the car and was less than thirty feet from the double verandas at the front of the house the lamp, which flanked the blue door, swam out. Patrick stood there, brightly illumined in his forest-green uniform.

It made me uneasy. The whole business was fishy. He ought to be careful about making himself—a target.

The door opened slowly—part way. Bee Chandler, in a rose-red flannel robe, slipped out. Even from this distance her annoyance showed.

She turned her head up sideways and put a finger on her lips and looked at Patrick coldly.

"Good evening, Mrs. Chandler," Patrick said, in a clear, cheerful voice, "I'm getting here a little late, I'm afraid."

"Well, rather," Bee Chandler said. She tapped her lips, for quiet.

Patrick said, just as cheerily, "Ames sent for me twice. I think I should see him."

"He's asleep," Bee said, in a very low tone, and she opened the door a little, ready to slip back in. "It would be better to come back in the morning."

"Thank you," Patrick said. His voice was now apologetic, but not quiet. "I'm sorry to have troubled you, Mrs. Chandler."

"Shush!"

"Sorry," Patrick purred.

"It's quite all right," Bee said, civilly. "Good night."

"Good night," Patrick said.

The door closed. The lights went out. Patrick came walking lightly across the flagstones to the drive. He saw me.

"I thought you were staying in the car?" he said. He linked an arm in mine and hustled me back to the vehicle.

"I got out to prevent your having that brush-off," I said. "Unfortunately, Bee got to you first."

"Thanks, anyway," he said. His eyes were gleaming. He elbowed me into my seat and went around to get in at the wheel. Instead he folded the driver's seat down and dived into the jump seat and got his rope. He took off his cap and laid it on the seat. "You'll be safe out here with Pancho."

"What are you going to do?"

"I came here to see Ames," he said, "and, by God, I intend to see him. Now, you stay here. You'll only mess things up, Jeanie."

He shut the car door and headed back toward the veranda.

I waited for about one minute, then I got out and went after him. The hell with him, I was thinking all the time, and still I was worrying about him. Here he was, in the night air, behaving like a commando, when he really belonged in bed.

I was too late. As I arrived at the edge of the shrubbery Patrick's dark lean figure was swarming up one of the white pillars, with the aid of the rope.

He had reconnoitered in advance. An iron table on the upper veranda just outside Maurice's dimly lit room made an anchorage for the rope.

He swung himself over the balustrade and unfastened the rope. It dropped beside me, with a sibilant little splash. I saw him outlined dimly in the French doors of Maurice's room. I waited.

Nothing seemed to happen.

I began to get frantic. I stood there, shivering, waiting, hearing nothing, terrified by the silence, by the night itself. I felt chilled. There was that dankness in the air. That wasn't all. I felt *vulnerable*.

I didn't know what to do. I kept standing there. I could not move.

Suddenly, the way you do, I knew that somebody was watching me.

It was nothing. A sensation. An awareness. A stillness that was not normal. A watching.

I moved closer to the pillar, into its shadow. I listened. I listened for whatever it was, and I listened for Patrick. When he came out again I would call a warning, I decided.

No, I reasoned, I must not make any noise. I must caution him in silence. How?

The rope lay near my feet, a loose reptilian-like coil on the flags, and useless because I had no skill to employ it.

I kept listening. My ears strained upward, outward. Then suddenly there was a light springy footfall on the veranda over my head. Then silence again.

Then I heard a voice. Bee was speaking, from the doors of Edwina's room, at the other side of the upstairs veranda.

"So you came in anyway?" she said, and her voice was dry and ominous, but a little admiring, too.

Patrick said, crossing to her lightly, "I'm afraid I did."

"You seem very determined, Lieutenant Abbott."

"If I have to be," he said. "Will you have a cigarette, Mrs. Chandler?"

"Thank you."

There was a tiny interval. I imagined Bee taking a cigarette, and Patrick putting another between his lips. I heard the quick flick of his lighter.

"Why did you come here?" Bee asked.

"I wanted to see Ames. He sent for me, as you know."

Bee's laugh was deep in her throat.

"Well, you saw him. I watched you, by the way. I was standing outside the hall door."

"Yes, I saw you, too," Patrick said.

Bee laughed again. "Why didn't you wake him?" she asked.

Patrick said, "How could I? He is sleeping under the influence of barbiturates, you know."

Bee said, "Doctor's orders. They won't hurt him and they give his mind a rest. He is so frightened because of the blindness."

"Has the doctor sent for a specialist?"

"He says it is not necessary."

"No," Patrick said. "He's right. Johnson is a good diagnostician. All that ails Johnson is that he hasn't any nerve."

Bee said, "You Marines are extraordinary, really. How does it happen you know so much about medicine?"

"I studied certain kinds of medicine, Mrs. Chandler."

"Oh. To be a Marine?"

"I beg your pardon. To be a detective."

"How amazing," Bee said. "I had no idea."

"Most people haven't," Patrick said. "They read too many murder mysteries, with old maids and such pulling rabbits out of the hat. I'm glad I ran into you here, Mrs. Chandler. I've been wanting to ask you, privately, why you pretend to be five years older than you really are?"

Bee's laugh was a dry flutter. "Why, thank you," she said. "You have a great imagination, Lieutenant Abbott. Or you're only flattering me, perhaps?"

Patrick said, with that deadly nonchalance, "I'm not flattering you. And it's not good enough just to imagine about you, Mrs. Chandler. I should like to know about you—where you came from, where you went to school, things like that."

"I can tell you," Bee said, "in a very few words. My life has been lived in many places, but it has been otherwise uneventful. I grew up in Hartford, Connecticut. I was an only child. My parents died when I was sixteen, both of them within a few weeks of each other. I was scheduled to go to Vassar, I went, then went abroad on a tour the summer after my freshman year, met Edwin Chandler in Paris, and married him after ten days' acquaintance. I never regretted it. We lived in Paris continuously, except for holidays in the Tyrol or in Spain until his death eight years after our marriage, and after that the girls and I lived here or there, mostly in Europe because you got more for not much money over there. That's the story. We were in this country when the war started, and I bought the little rancho, and I expect to make this my home most of the time for the rest of my life."

"The rest of your life," Patrick said, casually, and Bee said, and there was a suggestion of oddness in her voice, "What makes you say it like that?"

Patrick said, "There may not be much left of your life, Mrs. Chandler, if you don't stop poking into things which are decidedly very dangerous. Why did you go to Thayer's study?"

Bee was silent.

"Did you think you would find your daughter's marriage license there?" Patrick asked.

Bee's voice was like a drawn-out gasp. "Why—why—oh, what an idea!"

"You might as well be frank," Patrick said. "And brief, too. I saw the records in Bernalillo, a few hours ago. Jean knows I saw them, and Scott Davies knows it, too, and in a little while I shall report it to the sheriff. It will be his duty to give the information to State's Attorney Ottoway, who was rather unpleasant to your daughter when Thayer was murdered, I believe. They say that Ottoway likes to create sensations, Mrs. Chandler."

Bee was silent.

"One thing bothers me," Patrick went on calmly. "Why did you upset the files? I don't know you very well, Mrs. Chandler, but I've seen your ranch and your house. You seem an extremely orderly person. I can't understand your producing such a deliberate mess—unless it was to mislead people like me, who would think you didn't do it because you are essentially so tidy."

Bee said, "The files were in that condition when I went there."

"Then you did go there."

"Yes, I did. I didn't want Karen to go. I was so afraid for her. I went myself."

"You got the license."

"I got it. It has been destroyed. But I shall never testify to that, never. You can line me up and shoot me," Bee said, "and I will deny having done it. I am merely telling you now so that you won't heckle Karen. I know that if I deny having gone there, you will go to her and accuse her. You found the spectacles; you will use them like a whip."

"On the contrary," Patrick said. "I am sure you didn't leave the specs there, Mrs. Chandler. I think they may have been left deliberately by the person who tore up the files."

"But Dorrie Thayer must have disturbed the files?" Bee said. "I am sure she did. She did it to make trouble, to start a stink."

"Where did you last have the spectacles, Mrs. Chandler?"

Bee hesitated, then said. "Here. And everybody has been here, in and out of this house since I left them here, so their being in Ray's study means nothing, except that someone had it in for Karen. Well, Dorrie did."

"Did Dorrie come to this house?"

"No, she didn't, but she could easily bribe one of the maids to get the spectacles for her. I don't think she would require the specs. Anything that belonged to Karen would do."

"I'm glad you mentioned Ray Thayer," Patrick said. "I believe him to have been murdered. Don't you?"

Bee said, spacing her words slowly, "I don't know."

Fear ran through my heart; her tone was bitter, tense, heavy with meaning. She was a strange woman. She was an enigma. Patrick was deliberately putting himself in danger. Suppose Bee did it? Suppose Karen did it, and Bee knew? Would she hesitate to kill Patrick?

Not for one minute, I thought.

And Maurice Ames! There he lay, within earshot of their talk, perhaps asleep and perhaps only feigning it, as he may have feigned blindness. Lying there! Listening! Given half a chance Patrick could swing himself over the balustrade and drop to the earth lightly as a cat, but he had to have the chance. I must make a little noise, warn him.

"Thayer had something somebody wanted, didn't he, Mrs. Chandler?"

Well, I wanted to know about that, too. I put off making the noise.

"I really don't know," Bee said airily. "Must we discuss this here?"

"Why not?"

Bee's answer sounded hard and artificial.

"The hour is a little unconventional."

"True. But there is also no time like the present. I have in my possession a good deal of evidence which will, I'm afraid, incriminate your daughter for the murder of Dorrie Thayer. . . ."

Bee was natural again, and very worried.

"Karen had nothing to do with that. She was at home all last night."

There was a little note of triumph in Patrick's reply.

"How do you know, Mrs. Chandler? You were out here, weren't you? Dorrie was murdered last night a little after ten o'clock. Night before last to be exact, since it is now after midnight of this night. On your way here you stopped at Thayer's house and finding no one at home you went in and looked at the files and took the license. You must have had it in mind well in advance. When Dorrie started a rumpus about something being stolen from her house you decided to act. It is my opinion that you destroyed it there, flushed its pieces through the toilet." Bee was silent. "I guessed right, didn't I, Mrs. Chandler?" Bee made no reply. "Of course, Thayer probably had a cesspool. It would be a nasty job, but the pieces might be recovered. . . ."

"My God," Bee said hoarsely. *"How do you do it?"*

"Then I'm right about that?"

"I appeal to you," Bee said, and she sounded broken, "for Karen's sake. Karen didn't do it. She didn't kill Ray Thayer and she didn't kill Dorrie. Karen couldn't do that. She's impulsive, she sometimes does foolish things, and she's so sort of—well, wholehearted. Whatever she does she does with all her heart, like being in love—she is so young. Even if she is only accused her whole life will be clouded by suspicion, because people are so anxious to believe the worst."

Patrick said gently, "If I thought Karen had done it, Mrs. Chandler, I wouldn't be questioning you now, but Karen. I think you ought to be entirely frank with me. Tell me, did Ray Thayer talk with you? Did he tell you how he came to marry Dorrie?" Bee didn't answer. "If he did, you'd better tell me," Patrick said, and he sounded very, very determined.

"Not here," Bee said finally, in a very low voice. "Come inside. No, not through Maurice's room. This way. He has a way of waking suddenly. He's taken so many of those tablets that they don't keep him under long now."

I don't know why I didn't call out, prevent it. I didn't. I just stood there, congealed in indecision.

I didn't understand Bee. I didn't understand Maurice. I couldn't make two and two make four.

I could, however, scream. But why? They had sounded so normal, so matter-of-fact.

A twig broke near the house, as though a foot had crushed it, and back came that feeling of being watched.

I heard another queer thing, a motor creeping along the lane. It was a fine engine. It ran smooth as silk and with a minimum of sound. It was a car traveling along the white driver as we had done, slipping in without headlights. The verandas caught the sound and gave back a louder echo.

The fear returned. I stepped out of the shadow and craned at Maurice's window.

I heard another car. This one came fast, up the ascent past the Thayer place, making the wide left curve and taking the first cattleguard with a snappy zoom.

I could not locate the first car when I tried to again. It had taken the left fork of the drive, I decided. It had gone to the back of the house. The motor had probably been turned off. There was something comforting in this. Perhaps it had been some of the cowhands, returning home. Perhaps they had used Maurice's expensive station wagon.

Was I still being watched? I could not feel it now. And there was so much else, so much to hear and speculate on, because the second hurrying car had turned its headlights off at the end of the lane, too, and was coming in, driving secretly like the other, but not silently. The motor was not costly or even new, it stuttered, it had one of those odd little tappets. Now, where had I heard that car before?

Then I heard footsteps on the flagged path which circled the house, and I got a whiff of Edwina's perfume.

Edwina Ames and Hugh Kennicott appeared in the queer moonlight at the farther end of the veranda from where I hovered in the shadow of the pillar. They stopped at the door. Keys jingled. A flat key engaged the shackle of a lock.

"Take it easy," Hugh murmured.

"I'll be all right, darling," Edwina said, and her voice was a caress.

"You said you wouldn't go near him, remember."

"I won't, darling. I'll use the bedroom on this floor tonight. Bee has mine, anyway, you know."

"I wouldn't've consented to your coming back if Bee weren't here," Hugh said. "There is something tough about Bee. In the right kind of way, Edwina."

Edwina laughed softly and said, "Yes, I know, she's very wonderful, she'll look after me, sweet."

"Be careful, remember."

"Darling, I shall!"

"Good night, Edwina."

"Good night, my dear."

Edwina opened the door with a feline softness, and slipped into the dark hall. I held my breath and stuck close to my pillar's shadow. Hugh lit a cigarette. I saw his somber face in the swift flicker of the flame. He waited, standing very still, his head drooped forward a little, listening, waiting to be sure she was safe. Their parting had been without passion, I thought. But Edwina was sly. She wouldn't risk kisses and endearments at the door, with the incalculable Maurice overhead and the double doors of his room wide open to the verandas.

Hugh moved, all at once, and walked back the way they had come. He took long steps, and swiftly disappeared around the house.

I took a deep breath.

Now, there was a deep silence. The stuttering car had stopped, somewhere. If anybody was lurking near the veranda now, no twig cracked, no leftover autumn leaf rustled.

The ground mist was rising and thickening. It caught and held the strange illumination of the clouded moon. The little fat junipers stood around in it blackly.

I stepped away from the pillar and had a look at the upper veranda.

Maurice's night light was the same, dim to the very edge of darkness. His doors stood open. In Edwina's room a lamp almost as dim had been turned on. The doors were closed. I could hear nothing. What had happened? Why was everything so still? My alarm for Patrick came back. I would throw a rock, I decided—no, it would be more natural to go back to the car, and toot the horn, impatiently, like a wife wearied of waiting.

I started toward the car.

A gunshot sounded deep inside the house.

16

I didn't stop and think. I obeyed my impulse and slid for the front door, knowing beforehand that it would be closed and locked. I was panicked to a frenzy, but I would ring the bell without stopping and beat on the door with my other fist, and, if I could, scream.

Screaming is an art, an accomplishment to some denied. I've never been able to count on doing it because I freeze up when I'm scared. I suppose it's the Scot deep within, generations of inhibitions, no doubt.

Someone would hear me ringing the bell. Not Patrick, because, somewhere in that house, he was lying wounded, dead.

I might as well face it. Bee or Maurice had done it, one or the other of those two inscrutable people, or maybe they worked together, and I must find them, get witnesses. Edwina was in there now, and some of the servants. Edwina wouldn't mind being a witness against Maurice, I though, ironically, as I reached the closed door.

First, and automatically I tried the knob.

The door opened! Inward.

I was too astounded to question this, then.

I slipped inside. I shut it. I had escaped from whatever it was outside, anyhow.

I smelled the smells of a beautifully run house, the spice of wax and furniture polish, the dry smell of old, valuable things, the fragrance of the pinon which hangs about any New Mexican house where open fires are indulged in. My footsteps fell soundlessly on the deep-piled, garnet-red carpet.

Now the carpet was black like everything else. I could see nothing.

I took a few steps and then panic stopped me cold again. Why wasn't there some commotion? Why was no one moving about? A gunshot ought to start hectic movement in a house. No one was stirring anywhere. There wasn't a sound, nothing. Why?

And how come I had got into this house? Why was the door unlocked? Did somebody open it purposely to admit me, and close it again behind me?

Was I trapped?

Patrick would be upstairs, I decided.

I hurried in the direction of the staircase—the El Greco staircase. "I seem to have seen this before some place," Patrick had said. Maurice had been so amazed! "I've got it—in El Greco's house, in Toledo," Patrick said. Maurice had been hushed. "I say, old boy! That's amazing!" How his coffee-colored eyes had gleamed, and his thick lips had shaped the tight V smile!

Amazing? Tragic was more like it! If I hadn't told Patrick about the fool staircase and he hadn't pretended to remember it, Maurice wouldn't've thought him a genius and started yelling for him when he thought he was being murdered and so maybe we wouldn't be in the spot we were in now.

Only, where was he? Where was everybody? The house seemed infected with this horrid silence.

The stairs were seven or eight feet broad. I found them and started climbing, avoiding the railing where it is easy to be pushed over, keeping to the wall. The wall felt rough and dry to the touch, reminding me far-fetchedly of Maurice's dry grasp on my bare arm the night we came here to dinner. I hurried. I caught my heel on the edge of a step and stumbled.

My hand touched something icy cold, and my heart almost leaped out my throat, and then I laughed secretly at myself and felt rueful because the cold thing was only one of the tiles in the risers between the steps. Precise copies of those in El Greco's house, brought all the way from Spain.

I moved on, a little calmer and more realistic after that, and on the broad landing I cut straight across toward the upper flight. My shoe kicked something which lay loose on the carpet. I stooped and picked it up. It was the belt of a terry-cloth bathrobe. I tucked it in the pocket not holding the notebook, started on, and then stopped and thought.

The belt must belong to Maurice Ames' robe. That didn't mean that he had passed this way recently, but it would seem possible, if he did get up and wander around—and he did, of course. Was he upstairs, or down? Whichever, I decided to turn and go back down. It was easier to get out, if I must. I could take our car and go to Scott Davies for help—oh, I could fetch Pancho, he would find Patrick in no time and make plenty of fuss—and there were cowboys in the bunkhouse a quarter mile or so back of the house—and there was Edwina . . .

I felt my way back downstairs, moving resolutely now, and guiding myself firmly by the railing. It was pitch-dark. My eyes had accustomed themselves to the darkness, but I could see nothing at all. The curtains were drawn and the blinds closed. No moonlight, even such as it was tonight, entered here.

I got to the bottom of the steps. I laid my hand on the newel post.

I went stiff with terror!

My hand fell upon another hand which, like a waiting, crouching thing, writhed and twisted and clutched mine, and a second hand covered my mouth.

And then I felt deliriously relieved. I knew the owner of these hands by their particular and attractive smell. I laid my head against a row of service ribbons and sighed thankfully.

"Quiet," Patrick said, in my ear.

The hand slowly removed from my mouth. I said, "Let's get out of here, darling."

"Huh-uh." His voice was barely audible. "How did you get in?"

"Door."

"How come?"

"I don't know. Unless Edwina left it a tiny bit open."

Patrick stiffened.

"Edwina?"

"She just came home, Pat. Hugh brought her to the door. She came inside, then I heard what sounded like a shot. . . ."

"Yeah?" Patrick said, bitterly. "I told you I was slipping. Come along. Stay close to me, remember."

He guided me along the hall, away from the stairs, beyond the hearing of anybody on the stairs who might be listening. We spoke in low whispers.

"Where did you think the shot was fired, Jean?"

"I don't know. I couldn't tell, from out there."

"Bee left me in the study," Patrick said. "Upstairs. The windows were closed and she shut the door after her. She was about to tell me something and suddenly she said she would look in at Maurice and come right back, and I'm such a dumb bunny I believed her."

I remembered, and gave him the belt of the bathrobe. He took it without comment. "Come along. No more talk now," he whispered.

"Where?"

"To the kitchen first. I think that's where it happened, from what I remember about this house."

I didn't ask why. We went by way of the dining room, pitch-dark too, and in my mind I saw it as that last time, the table gay with flowers and candles and attractive people, and from the wall Edwina's portrait, in white lace, with rubies, looked down.

Patrick would not risk a light. He felt his way toward the swinging door into the pantry, holding my hand, and moving carefully, to avoid any possibility of noise.

We got to the door. He laid his hand on it and pushed.

It got part way, and stopped.

Patrick pushed harder. The object gave slightly, silently.

I got a whiff of Edwina's perfume.

"Darling!" I said.

"Shush!" He pushed me behind him, stooped, felt around the door.

Then the lights in the kitchen were snapped on and a faint glow lit the pantry and Patrick peeped around at what was blocking the door from the dining room, cursed under his breath, and pushed me back. He gripped my arm and dragged me back across the dining room to the hall and along to the kitchen entrance from the main hall. He knew the way. Maurice had showed him most of the house.

He cautiously opened the kitchen door and then stepped inside and spoke in an authoritative voice.

"Don't touch that!"

The Indian cook was bending down to pick up a rifle which lay on the floor near the icebox.

She straightened up, gave us a dark wordless glance, and stepped a few steps away from the gun. She folded her hands on her ample stomach and stood still. She had her back to the sink and its attendant row of cupboards below the row of small windows.

The swinging door from the kitchen into the pantry was open a little. I saw a mink sleeve and a plump wax-like hand with long garnet-red nails.

"Edwina!" I cried.

Patrick walked over, stooped down, picked up the hand, tried for the pulse, found none, and then examined the body quickly. Edwina had been shot through the heart. He turned to the cook. "Who did this?" he asked.

She shook her head, and stood silent.

"Did you hear the shot?" Patrick demanded.

She nodded, one dark grim nod.

Patrick tried the outside kitchen door. It was unlocked.

"Did you leave this unlocked?" he asked the cook.

"Me go bed, no lock doors," she said. She sounded surly.

"I'm afraid I'm to blame for that," Bee said, from the door we had used from the hall. She was standing there, slim and straight. She wore the rose-red flannel robe. "What's happened?" she asked Patrick.

"You'd better put on your glasses," Patrick said, coldly.

I was frightened then. He thinks she did it, I thought.

Bee walked into the kitchen. At a point near enough that she didn't need her spectacles she saw Edwina's hand.

"What's wrong?" she cried out. "Oh, do something!"

"There is nothing to do," Patrick said. "Except call the police. She's dead."

"Dead?" Bee said. She did not sway or falter. She looked rather indignant. "I don't believe you!" she snapped.

She walked over to the partly open door and bent calmly down and picked up Edwina's wrist. She looked at the face, ugly now with its grotesque surprise, and with the velvety black eyes rolled up and only the whites showing. The mink coat fell away from the blue jersey dress and the silver and turquoise belt shone softly between her curvaceous bosom and thighs.

"If she were your own daughter," Patrick said, "you might not take it so calmly, Mrs. Chandler."

Bee stood away from the body and paled under her tan, and her voice was razor-edged as she said, "You're being melodramatic, aren't you, Lieutenant? Do you want me to call the sheriff?"

"You will stay right in this room," Patrick said mercilessly. "Jean will phone Jim Trask."

"Just as you like," Bee said. She moved her shoulders flippantly. "There's an extension just outside in the hall, Jean."

Patrick stooped and closed Edwina's eyelids and then covered her face with one of his clean linen handkerchiefs.

"Is that your rifle?" he asked Bee, as I started toward the phone.

"Yes, it is," Bee said.

"Did you shoot Edwina Ames, Mrs. Chandler?"

Bee said, "I believe I am entitled to the advice of an attorney before answering such questions?"

"Yes, you are," Patrick said. His voice was a knife.

The door into the hall stood partly open. While I tried to get the operator I could see Patrick, through the crack, motioning for Bee to stand beside the Indian cook. Bee went where he said and at once took her cigarettes from the pocket of her robe and took out a match book. It was a big room. The place where she stood was a good distance from Edwina. Patrick called, "Ask Trask to pick up Karen Chandler and bring her along here, Jean."

Bee's eyelids went down, her hand lighting the cigarette trembled, and for a moment she showed fear, but when she spoke up her voice was matter-of-fact.

"You needn't trouble," she said. "Karen *is* here."

"That's too bad," Patrick said. "When did she come?"

"She just arrived," Bee said. "I heard our car drive up and came down and let her in. That's why I didn't come back to the study."

"You know the car?"

"Why, of course."

"Where is Karen now?"

"In the guest bedroom on this floor. I took her there after admitting her to the house from the back veranda."

"She didn't come through the kitchen, by any chance?"

"No, she did not. She doesn't know anything about what's happened."

"She didn't hear the gunshot?"

Bee said, wearily, "Of course she heard it. I told her to wait. I'll go now. . . ."

"You stay here."

Patrick opened the icebox door and took out something which he dropped into his pocket. He closed the door.

At the telephone I jiggled the hook, trying to rouse the operator.

"She's got nothing to do with this!" Bee rasped at Patrick. "She's been with me ever since I left you—except for the minute or two I took coming downstairs."

Patrick looked at his wrist. "It's just six minutes since you left me upstairs in Ames' study, Mrs. Chandler."

"I'm going to Karen!" Bee said then. "I've got to."

"You'll stay here," Patrick snapped.

Bee moved her shoulders, and stayed where she was.

"If you're such a good detective," she said acidly, "how does it happen you didn't know I was with my daughter?"

Patrick said, "You left me to have a look at the patient. Remember? It was one o'clock. You looked in on him promptly on the hour, you said. You said you'd be right back. Remember that?" Bee said nothing, and Patrick said, "You shut me in the study, closed the door. I took you at your word. Did you really know that Karen was here? Or did you come downstairs because Ames wasn't in his bed when you looked in his room?"

"Number?" the operator yawned in my ear.

"Get me the sheriff," I said.

"Why, what's happened?" the operator asked.

"Please!" I said. "Get Mr. Trask."

"Hello," Mr. Trask said, almost at once.

"This is Jean Abbott," I said. "Will you come out to the Ames ranch at once? Mrs. Ames has been shot. . . ."

"Tell him she's dead!" Patrick called.

"Dead," I said.

"God Almighty!" the sheriff said. "All right, ma'am. I'll notify the doctor and the undertaker." He paused. "And the prosecutor," he said. He hung up.

"Say, how did it happen?" the operator asked.

I hung up.

I wheeled around as a door opened.

Hugh Kennicott was entering the hall from the back door. Nothing surprised me any longer.

All the lights were blazing now. Hugh nodded at me and followed me into the kitchen. Patrick looked up from where he had just covered the rifle with a kitchen towel to protect it from handling.

"Well, where did you come from, Kennicott?" he said.

"I brought Edwina home," Hugh said.

"But why?" Bee asked him.

Hugh didn't answer. He had walked, as Patrick beckoned, into the middle of the kitchen, and there he could see the white waxlike hand, the mink coat, the blue dress, the silver belt with its winking turquoises.

"Oh, my God!" he gasped. "Is she dead?" Patrick nodded and asked Hugh if he hadn't heard the shot. He shook his head. *"So it happened!* I waited outside in my car. I was about to drive away. I started the motor and turned around and then I felt uneasy for her, and waited. It's my fault. I shouldn't have let her come here—back to that beast . . ."

"Oh, fiddlesticks!" Bee Chandler said.

Hugh gave her a look full of horror.

The Indian cook's face did not change.

Patrick watched them from beside the pantry door. His eyes were green and narrow.

"How could you say such a thing?" Hugh demanded of Bee. "Edwina told me how you made her marry him for his money—your own daughter—and now—look—look—look what you have done!"

Bee did not reply.

Patrick said, "I'm glad you're here, Hugh. I wish you would go through the house and bring anybody you find, except Ames, of course, down to the kitchen. Turn on all lights as you enter rooms and leave them on. Be careful. Don't try to do any extra special searching. Trask will be here soon to handle that."

"Want me to go with Hugh?" I asked Patrick.

"You stay here!" Patrick said.

Bee Chandler said, "By what authority can you take charge here and order everybody around, Lieutenant Abbott?"

"It's all right for him to order me, Bee," I said, quickly being a dutiful wife.

Patrick looked at Bee and unfastened one button of his forest-green blouse and showed her the deputy sheriff badge pinned underneath. Bee moved her shoulders and said nothing.

Hugh brought Karen in first. He looked bewildered now. He had found her waiting in the guest bedroom on this floor, he said. That bedroom was in the middle of the house, across the hall from the dining room.

"I was with Karen," Bee Chandler quickly reiterated. "We were together when the shot was fired."

Karen, in the jeans and jacket she had arrived here in, went over and stood beside her mother and the silent cook.

She avoided looking at Edwina.

Hugh next brought down the trained nurse. She was a stocky, swarthy, middle-aged woman. She wore a striped bathrobe and had her tightly permed hair under an ugly brown net.

She declared that she had heard nothing whatever, having been fast asleep.

"I looked in on the patient after this young man waked me," the nurse said. "He's asleep." She turned to Bee Chandler. "What happened to his chart?"

"It was there the last time I saw him," Bee said.

"When was that?"

Bee said, "Exactly at midnight. I didn't go in the room again after that, but I looked in at one o'clock, and . . ."

She broke off, leaving the sentence hanging.

"Never mind about the chart," Patrick said to the nurse. "Suppose you go back and stay with the patient. We'll call you if we want you."

"Yes, sir," the nurse said.

Hugh could find no one else in the house. The cook said that the two regular maids were out for the night. Bee Chandler corroborated this. "Did you know they would be out, Mrs. Chandler?" Patrick asked.

"Everybody who knows this house knows that the girls are out tonight," Bee said. "They're sisters. They go home Friday nights, because Maurice liked to have friends in Saturdays and Sundays."

The cook stood there, and said nothing.

The sheriff arrived twenty-five minutes after I phoned. Dr. Johnson was next, and Max Ottoway next. The state's attorney was a smooth pigeon-shaped pigeon-eyed man in a smooth double-breasted greenish-striped suit.

Close behind him Julia Price and Scott Davies drove up in Julia's car.

"The operator called me up and told me the news," Julia explained. She came into the kitchen by way of the hall, with her arm linked firmly with Scott's. The doctor was washing his hands in the bathroom across the hall. The rest of us waited in the kitchen. Julia wore a checked shirt and flannel pants and a topcoat. Her embroidered Mexican hat was on the back of her auburn head. She hadn't taken time to put on her bracelets. "I got dressed and drove out to tell Scott."

Julia wept when she looked at Edwina, and so did Scott.

It was kind of Julia to think of Scott. I felt guilty that I hadn't done it. I watched him as he stood over Edwina's body, his face twisted with grief. He would always think now she was an angel, no matter what.

"My goodness," Julia exclaimed, then. "That's the belt Hugh bought in my shop, for Karen."

"For Karen?" Hugh said, and he took a step forward from the place where he was standing, near the kitchen door. He glanced at Karen. She was watching Julia. "I bought the belt for Edwina. She gave me the money and told me which one," Hugh said.

Bee Chandler said, "Edwina was with Karen when—oh, never mind," she said, as she realized she was only involving Karen, but Julia piped in, with,

"Yes, she was. Edwina was along when Karen asked me to put the belt aside. I thought when Hugh asked for it . . ."

"It makes no difference now," Karen said, gently.

I looked at Hugh, who was still looking at Karen, with something new and deep and wondering in his dark eyes.

Everything seemed fine—for about a minute.

Then Max Ottoway said, "The Chandler girl's a homicidal maniac. She had good cause to murder Thayer, maybe, or even his wife. A jury might understand that. But to kill her sister, over a piece of Indian junk . . ."

"Junk!" Julia snapped. "See here, Max Ottoway . . ."

"Shut up!" Ottoway said. His eyes hopped around the room, resting on us, one at a time, coldly. "I'm in charge here," he said. "Make yourselves as comfortable as you can. You're all going to have to answer a lot of questions."

17

We found places to sit or to lean and Max Ottoway placed a kitchen chair so that he could straddle it and fold his arms on its back and face all the rest of us across the open middle of the kitchen.

Karen stood next to her mother and the cook. Hugh was near the outside door, beyond the enormous icebox, and I leaned against a table near the hall door.

Nobody at this point seemed very much upset. That was shock, of course. The reaction would set in later on.

In his fidgety fashion Dr. Johnson examined Edwina's body and declared her dead from a bullet which had pierced her heart. He would probe for the bullet when the body had been removed to Pete Martinez's undertaking establishment.

Patrick and the sheriff presumed that the bullet had been fired from the rifle now lying on the floor in front of the icebox, and took various measurements and such to speculate on exactly where, and in what position, it had been fired. They marked the floor to indicate where the body and the rifle lay after these had been removed.

Ottoway sat watching them over his folded arms and chewed a toothpick. "Take away the toothpick and what have you got?" Julia Price had once said about Max Ottoway. Maybe there was something in it. He sat looking smug, all-knowing, smooth. He was one of those hairless-looking men. He looked as if he had to shave only at Christmas or Easter, maybe, and then only for show. His eyebrows were pale like his skin. His lashes were hardly noticeable around his almond-shaped china-blue eyes, and you noticed the pink insides of the lids. He didn't blink his lids as often as most people, and his eyes moved smoothly, as though on pivots.

His smooth wise-seeming glance kept singling out Karen Chandler.

This was his show. Pretty soon he said so, again.

"Leave all that go," he ordered the sheriff, presently. "Waste of time, Jim. Pete, take away the body. Isn't there some place more comfortable than the kitchen? Where's the living room of this house?"

Patrick said, "Why not go up to Ames' bedroom?"

"Now, really!" Dr. Johnson objected. And he looked upset.

"Why not?" Patrick asked. "He can't be dangerously ill. He got out of bed and wandered around the house. It was about the time his wife was shot."

The doctor glanced at Bee Chandler. "Is that true?"

"Not that I know of," she said. She lit another cigarette.

"You gave him the barbiturates?"

"On the dot," Bee said.

The doctor frowned, and waving his hands vaguely he said, "Well, he's had so many lately that they may not have the expected effect but—see here, did you really see him wandering around?" he asked of Patrick. "Or are you making it up?"

Max Ottoway cut in, "Got a fire in his bedroom?"

"No," Bee said.

"Let's sit where there's a fire," Ottoway said. He stood up. "You lead the way, Mrs. Chandler."

"The fire is laid in the drawing room," Bee said. "All that's needed is a match."

Ottoway said, with open admiration, "You're the calmest one here, Mrs. Chandler. I wish I had your nerve."

She led the way. The others straggled along, Karen and Hugh drifting together, catching hands. Patrick, I took notice, lagged behind, and I lagged, too, and when we were near the staircase the others had already vanished into the drawing room. Patrick headed swiftly up the stairs, and I followed.

"Look, what did you take from the icebox?" I asked Patrick.

"Shush!" he admonished me.

In Maurice's bedroom Patrick sent the nurse to her room to get dressed.

Maurice lay in apparent deep sleep in the middle of his vast antique bed.

Patrick walked around turning on all the lights. A terry-cloth robe lay across the foot of the bed. Patrick examined it. The belt was missing. The material of the belt I had found on the stairs matched the robe.

Patrick stood at the foot of the bed, and he ran the belt through his fingers.

"I suppose you know that your wife is dead, Mr. Ames," he said, then, and Maurice's eyes opened quickly and he stirred a little. Patrick said, "Now, we've had enough of your tricks, Mr. Ames. You sent for me today, and I'm here, and first, I want you to answer a question. Did you shoot Edwina Ames?"

"I didn't," Ames said, and the V of his mouth was upside down for a change.

"You know she's dead?" Maurice nodded. "You found her when you ran downstairs after hearing the gunshot, didn't you, Mr. Ames?"

Ames said sullenly, "Yes. I saw her."

Patrick said, very quietly, "The refrigerator door was open and you saw her by the light from the lamp inside the icebox, didn't you?" Ames nodded. "You shut the door of the icebox and you hurried right back upstairs because you thought you would be missed from your bed and be accused of shooting her. Isn't that right, Mr. Ames?"

Ames nodded. "Approximately. You're a clever fellow, Abbott. But I didn't kill her," he said.

"Do you think other people will believe you? You were out of your bed, you know. You dropped this belt on the staircase."

"Good God!" Maurice said. He sat up in the bed. He bristled with his special vitality. "Why should I kill her? I knew she played around, and I didn't give a damn, either. But I suppose people will suspect me. Tell you what, I'll give you a thousand dollars, Abbott, if you'll track down her murderer."

Patrick said wryly, "It was a hundred thousand when you thought you yourself might die, Ames. You seem to put a greater value on your own life than on your wife's."

"Naturally," Ames said. "I make the money, don't I? Okay, ten thousand. I don't want to be a suspect all the rest of my life. I didn't kill her."

"You'll pay it, even though I can prove that you yourself did it?" Patrick asked.

"I didn't do it!" Maurice snapped. And all at once he sounded worried. "My God, would I be hiring you if I did? I've got a pretty good idea of your ability, Abbott. I'm not a fool."

"Can you see me?" Patrick asked.

"Of course I can see you!" Ames yapped.

"It's hard to know what to believe about you," Patrick said. "Reports conflict. Some say you are blind and some suspect you're playing a peculiar kind of game."

Maurice squirmed.

"It comes in spots," he said. "I'm not blind now. I haven't been all today. But that fussy doctor makes me keep my eyes bandaged. I sent for you today, by the way, because I wanted to talk to you about something—something else. . . ."

"About my going through Ray Thayer's files?" Patrick asked, and Ames cried, "My God, Abbott, how do you do it? Are you a mind reader?"

"Not at all. I saw you on your veranda, watching that house through your telescope." Maurice's eyes went opaque as Patrick said, "Who were you looking for, Mr. Ames? Besides us?" Maurice made no answer. "Perhaps I should put it in a different way," Patrick said. "Who did you see, besides us?"

"Tck, tck!" Dr. Johnson hissed, from the door. He trotted over to the bed. "Maurice, you've got no business sitting up! And with all this light on! Tck, tck!" He fussed around, turning off everything till we were again in the sullen gloom brewed by the night lamp. "You're wanted downstairs, Lieutenant. You too, Mrs. Abbott." Maurice lay down again and closed his eyes passively. The doctor took up a stand near the head of the bed. Patrick had not moved. He remained at the foot of the bed, and he rolled up the belt of the terry-cloth robe slowly, with a calculated felinity. "Right away!" Dr. Johnson said. "The state's attorney wants you, both of you, downstairs."

Patrick didn't move.

"Will Ames have to have an operation, Dr. Johnson?" he asked, cheerily.

The doctor shivered and shook. "What a question!" he spat out. "And in the hearing of a very sick man!"

Maurice opened his eyes and looked from one to the other.

"It couldn't be encephalitis, as you diagnosed it at first," Patrick said. "I've seen the chart. No fever has been recorded, at any time."

Maurice's face held a queer glint, like humor, as he watched the doctor twitch.

"Hey, you up there!" Max Ottoway yelled, from the downstairs hall.

"Coming!" Patrick said. He put the belt back in his pocket. Maurice watched him. Patrick gave the pocket containing the belt a little pat. The bright look on Maurice's face changed to sardonic alarm, yet he cast that off deliberately and assumed again that passivity. "Ames is in a way my patient too, Dr. Johnson," Patrick said. "Be seeing you both, after a while."

"He ought not to be bothered like this," the doctor fluttered, as we were leaving the room. "It's enough to bring on a relapse. He's a very sick man. And now, with what's happened . . ."

The doctor rubbed his hands together, as though that would help him get up the courage to tell Maurice Ames that his wife had been shot dead. I wished I could wait and see how the patient would take the news this time, but I ran after Patrick, who was dashing down the steps three at a time. I didn't want to miss anything downstairs either.

Ottoway and Jim Trask were waiting outside the drawing-room door. On seeing Patrick, Ottoway said, "You stay here and keep an eye on those folks, Jim. I want to talk to Abbott." He beckoned Patrick to the relative privacy of a place near the front door. "Jim says you took a revolver to Santa Fe for a check-up on some fingerprints?"

"Right," Patrick said.

"What did you find out?"

Patrick said, reluctantly, "The only entirely clean prints on the gun were identified as Karen Chandler's."

"You're sure?"

"I've got the report here in my pocket."

Patrick took out an envelope and handed it to the prosecutor. He put it in his own pocket without looking at it.

"Well, that does it," Ottoway said triumphantly. "That fixes her. I've had my eye on that gal for a good while. She's a funny one, that Karen. Natural-born criminal, that's what. Last fall she killed a fellow named Ray Thayer that she was engaged to because he showed up here from a trip to Hollywood married to another woman. I knew all the time that that was murder. It was made to look like an accident or suicide by his falling or jumping into the Rio Grande Canyon, but there wasn't enough blood, so I figured he was dead when he went over the rim. But I let it go. I had to. There wasn't enough real evidence to get a conviction. Besides, there was Maurice Ames. He was her brother-in-law, see, and I figured he would hire psychoanalysts and Gods-knows-what-all to prove this or that. And what chance have I got against experts? This county's poor. You got to have money to fight money. So I waited, but all the time I kept my eyes open. I cautioned that widow to be careful. I didn't tell her why exactly, because she couldn't keep her mouth shut about anything, but I warned her not to trust just anybody and everybody. The fact is, I warned her to get out of here, to leave, but she kept staying on. I think she thought maybe Thayer had more property than she'd found out, and she kept waiting to make sure. And now she's dead. The killer picked a time when I was out of town, knowing how the law is administered around here when I'm not on hand and keeping my eye on things."

I stole a peek at Mr. Trask. He stood in the drawing-room door, rolling a cigarette, and giving it apparently his entire attention.

"But they never know when to stop," Ottoway said. "Now it's her sister. This time the motive is just as plain as it was the other two times. Sister is playing around with the new boy friend. Julia Price accidentally supplied me with an immediate and concrete motive. That piece of Indian trash, that silver belt. Boy friend buys belt Karen wanted and gives it to her sister. That's all it took."

Patrick said, "Are you going to accuse Karen? Directly?"

Ottoway shifted the toothpick and grinned smugly and he said, "In due time. I won't rush it. Don't worry, I know how to handle this, Lieutenant."

Patrick said, "There's the rifle, you know. The fingerprints ought to be checked, and we ought to make sure how the rifle came to be in this house . . ."

"I know, I know," Ottoway said.

Patrick said, "There may even have been a witness of the murder, Mr. Ottoway."

"You mean, her mother?"

"No," Patrick said. He appeared to waver. Then he took out the terry-cloth belt. "This was found on the stairs. Ames left his bed about the time his wife was shot. He'll have to be handled with care. He's an odd sort of guy. Doesn't tell all he knows straight off."

"I'll grant you that," Ottoway said. He seemed a little deflated. He wouldn't want an eye-witness to turn up just yet, I thought. It would spoil his showing off what a splendid deduction he can make. "I'll go easy," he said. "Look here, Abbott, I don't make any mistakes. What did you do with the stuff you took to Santa Fe?"

"It's in my car. In my brief case," Patrick said.

"In your car? Good God, man . . ."

"There's a dog in the car," Patrick said. "A good dog," he added, and I was sorry that Pancho couldn't hear it because I was sure that Pancho felt that Patrick rather looked down on his canine ability. "Nobody could take anything away from the car without showing Pancho's teeth marks in some way or other, Mr. Ottoway. But I'll get the things now, if you wish."

"Please," Max Ottoway said. "And hurry, if you don't mind. I want to get this thing over with, and get home to bed."

18

Patrick went out the front door and I left the spot where I had huddled beside the newel post and moved toward the drawing-room door. Mr. Trask stepped unsmilingly aside to allow me to enter. In the room the fire was blazing and the lights were mellow and becoming. All these people around the fire, I thought, as my steps fell soundlessly on the thick garnet-red carpet, were in this room around another fire like this only a few nights ago. That is, all except Julia and the Indian cook, and the sheriff and Max Ottoway. Maurice was here, too. Maurice wore the formal attire of a Spanish grandee and buzzed around serving his special Scorpion cocktails and talking about this New Mexican food. Edwina had sat in the chair where Julia Price was sitting now. She had worn a red dress which harmonized with the red in the carpet and the draperies, and her lip rouge and fingernail enamel matched her dress. She had languished her drowsy velvety glances on Patrick and it had made me uneasy deep inside, but all the time it had been Hugh Kennicott she'd wanted. Tonight Scott sat nearest Julia, on a sofa, and Bee sat beside him, and facing them from the other sofa were Hugh Kennicott and Karen Chandler. You would think of the two that it was Hugh who was craziest in love, though of course with him it had only just happened, while Karen had been carrying her tragic torch for Hugh such a long while. The cook occupied a chair at the end away from the fire and the sofa where Hugh sat with Karen. She did not look uncomfortable sitting among us, as a white cook might have done. She simply looked like an Indian, sitting down instead of standing. Taking things as they come. I sat down beside Bee. She at once offered me a cigarette, which I accepted and was lighting as Ottoway sidled into the room and took charge.

He pulled up another straight chair, turned it backward at the apex of the semi-circle, straddled it and folded his arms across the back and then slowly let his gaze rove over us, one after another, until he apparently felt that we were all sufficiently cowed. He even made me feel that he suspected me of a part in this crime.

Mr. Trask remained near the door. Patrick had not yet come in.

Ottoway said, "First, you're going to tell me, all of you, how you happen to be out here at this hour of the night. We don't have to ask you," he said to the cook. "Or you, I suppose," he said to Bee Chandler, glancing at her dressing gown, and having heard, I imagined, that she was spelling the nurse by staying with Ames. "You," he said to Karen, "can talk later. We know why Miss Price and Scott Davies are here. What about you and that husband of yours?" he said to me.

I hesitated, and Bee Chandler said, "Maurice has been asking for Lieutenant Abbott all afternoon, Mr. Ottoway. He got here as soon as he could, even though it was rather late."

Ottoway shifted the toothpick, looked at her, looked at me, looked doubtful in general, and then said, "All right. Next, Hugh Kennicott—how come you're here?"

"I brought Mrs. Ames home," Hugh said.

"How long ago?"

"Not very long. I must have just started up my car when she was shot. I didn't hear it, by the way. I may have been turning around just then. Another car had come in behind us. I couldn't see where it went and on second thought I waited— to make sure Edwina was all right."

That would have been Karen. Ottoway let it pass.

"How does it happen you were out with Mrs. Ames at this time of night? A married woman, too!"

"There wasn't anything funny about it," Hugh said.

"Maybe not," Ottoway said, "If you can explain it to my satisfaction."

Hugh said, "I took Mrs. Ames, at her request, to Santa Fe. We didn't leave Santa Maria till quite late, and when we got back I—I brought her here."

"Why did you go to Santa Fe?"

"I went to see a lawyer—our lawyer, to be exact."

"And you took Mrs. Ames along?"

"She waited at La Fonda while I talked with the lawyer. Perhaps Mrs. Abbott will verify that."

I nodded. "Edwina sat with me a long while," I said to Ottoway. "It was while Pat was taking care of—of the business you know about, Mr. Ottoway. We sat in the New Mexican Room and listened to the music and all."

Ottoway asked, "Did Mrs. Ames tell you that Hugh Kennicott was down there to see a lawyer?"

"Yes," I said. "She did."

"Did she say what for?"

I wriggled, and glanced over one shoulder at the door, wishing Patrick would show up. I said, "I don't see any use in repeating what Edwina said to me. She's dead now. It can mean nothing."

"I'm the judge of that," Ottoway said.

"I don't want to tell you what she said," I said. "I don't have to, you know."

Ottoway moved his plump shoulders. "Not here," he conceded. "Maybe it isn't important. We'll get back to you in your turn, Mrs. Abbott. Did you come straight back here from Santa Fe, Hugh?"

"No, we didn't. Mrs. Ames had left her car on the plaza."

Ottoway grinned around the toothpick. "I wondered if you would remember that. It isn't every evening a Lincoln Zephyr spends a whole evening parked on our modest little plaza, you know. But how come the car isn't here? I had a look for it when we drove in, Hugh."

Hugh flushed. "Mrs. Ames planned to pick the car up tomorrow. I assure you it's all right."

"It's at our house," Karen said.

Ottoway glanced at her, and his unctuous voice went spiteful, "Speak when you're spoken to, Miss Chandler!" he snapped.

"Oh, sorry," Karen said. She sounded flippant, and I quaked inside, knowing she should not antagonize this man.

"But what's the idea?" Ottoway asked Hugh then. "Gasoline and rubber are scarce as hen's teeth around here, yet you put an extra twenty miles on your car and your tires going out of your way to bring her home when she might as well have driven herself out here? How come?"

"She had a good reason not to come home alone," Hugh said. He looked stubborn. He looked as if it would take dynamite and then some to get anything more out of him. But you were aware of his fire and innate toughness. I thought he was nuts, but I liked him very much.

"Why did she take the car to her mother's?" Ottoway asked.

Bee's breathing quickened, and she did the answering.

"She intended to spend the night at our house," she said. "She—changed her mind after she got out to our house and Hugh drove her out here in his car."

"You followed her out to Mrs. Chandler's *from the plaza?*" Ottoway asked Hugh Kennicott. "Why?"

"She was afraid at night," Hugh said. "It's only a little way out to the Chandlers', you know, in fact it's only a mile or so out of my way home." The Sky Valley road forked off the main Colorado highway between the plaza and Bee's rancho. "But—when she decided to come on home she left her car there and drove out here with me. She said her mother had their car out here and she would go back with her in the morning and pick up hers."

Karen and Bee's eyes met, flicked apart.

Patrick came in, crossed to the center of the room and handed his brief case to Ottoway, who nodded, and then patted the case with satisfaction and set it on the low table at the end of the sofa where I sat. Patrick pulled up an ottoman behind the sofa where Karen and Hugh were sitting. I watched him for signs of fatigue. I saw none. It must have turned a little foggy, I thought. His hair was shining from dampness, and his tanned skin had a slightly moist look, very becoming, too.

"Did you go to Santa Fe to see a lawyer about a divorce for Mrs. Ames?" Max Ottoway asked.

Hugh said nothing.

"You might as well come clean," Ottoway said. "You're wasting time if you think you can keep anything like that quiet, Hugh. What about it? Why did you go?"

"I'll give you the name and address of my lawyer," Hugh said. He mentioned the man's name. Max Ottoway at once looked a little less sure of himself. His smooth face for a moment was a trifle awed. "If he wants to disclose why I came to see him, he probably will," Hugh said.

"He'll have to," Ottoway said. But he sounded less sure of himself.

Julia Price leaned over and spoke to Scott Davies. His furrowed brow twisted with renewed anxiety, and Julia laid a consoling hand on his arm.

Ottoway said, "Mrs. Ames expect to marry you after she divorced Ames, Hugh?"

"Certainly not!" Hugh said, and he looked shocked.

"You were pretty thick, weren't you?"

"We were good friends," Hugh said. His voice was deep and sincere. "She was very kind to me when I came out here. I was pretty much bushed, thought my life was ruined because I'd been disqualified for the air force. Edwina and Maurice were very swell to me."

"Therefore you were willing to help her get a divorce?"

"I was not!" Hugh shouted, in a mounting rage. "That was her own business, not mine, but I could hardly refuse to take her to see our lawyer, could I? She had her reasons—which it isn't my right to reveal here."

Oh, dear, I thought, he's getting in deep now.

"So you did take her to see your lawyer, Hugh?" Ottoway was fairly purring over his folded arms. His eyes were set neatly in their pink-lined lids, as neatly as if by a stonesetter, and they were changeless as stones, and hard and cocksure. "Well, you took her to a good one, all right. Even if she had no grounds . . ."

"She had grounds!" Hugh cried. "Why should we try to hide the truth? Ames is a sadist. He abused her until—well, she only needs incompatibility in this state to get a divorce, so why talk about anything else? I'm sorry. Please do her memory the kindness of not repeating what I have just said."

Bee listened with a peculiar expression on her face, startled and then a little sullen, and again her glance met Karen's, and flicked away.

Julia Price said, "Maybe Maurice killed her himself?"

"No, he didn't," Max Ottoway said, and, glancing swiftly his way, I saw Patrick's eyes narrow and go green for a second the way they did when he had to hang on to himself to keep minding his own business, and then assume once more their lazy blue-green norm. "Ames had good reason, maybe, and he may even have had the opportunity, but he didn't shoot his wife. Now, there's a little matter about a belt. Mrs. Ames was wearing a silver belt which needs looking into. I think. What about that belt, Hugh?"

Hugh said, "I bought the belt in Miss Price's shop, and you yourself heard her say so, Mr. Ottoway."

Ottoway lolled the toothpick around.

"And Karen Chandler wanted that belt, didn't she? She had asked Miss Julia Price to save it for her, hadn't she?"

"You heard me say so," Julia said, her big eyes very wide and round with her anxiety. "That didn't mean anything, except that I don't like people thinking I would sell something to somebody else if I had promised to hold it for them."

"When Karen Chandler wants something she wants it bad," Ottoway said. "Even when it is only a piece of Indian trash . . ."

"Trash?" Julia cried. "Well, I like that!"

I glanced at the Indian cook, and her expression had not altered a whit, not even when the prosecutor had called the lovely silver and turquoise belt a piece of Indian trash. You would never get a word of any kind out of her, I thought.

She must know plenty more than she talked about. Too bad the Mexican maids weren't here, though. They would be more talkative. They probably knew plenty, too.

"Well, how come *you* bought the belt? Why didn't she buy it herself, if she wanted it so much, Hugh?"

Hugh said, "Well, she told me that her husband disliked Indian jewelry intensely, and . . ."

"That's true," Julia Price said.

Hugh continued. "She said she loved it and would like the belt to wear while Maurice was ill and would not be annoyed with it. She said she wanted it specially for a dress she had, a blue dress—the one she was wearing tonight. She said that the belt was exactly the right touch."

"It was, too," Julia Price said.

Her remark made Ottoway wince. This was *his* show.

He said acridly, "Of course, I wasn't intimately acquainted with Edwina Ames, but she looked to me healthy enough to walk into a shop and buy a belt for herself."

Hugh moistened his lips. "She was afraid someone would see her buying the belt and talk about it and Maurice would hear it and be angry. She said if he saw it by accident and asked her about it she would say it belonged to Bee."

Bee's long lashes rested on her triangular brown cheeks. She blew out cigarette smoke.

"You seem to have been kind of a sucker, Hugh, from your story," Ottoway said, and you thought that he didn't believe a word that Hugh had said. "You seem to have been left holding the bag, Hugh."

Hugh said, "Edwina paid for the belt. I couldn't foresee, could I, that my buying the thing would look queer? I'm sorry. But, believing what I did about Maurice Ames, I would buy the belt again, only I would tell a few people— Karen and Bee Chandler, for instance—why I bought the belt. The rest of you could go to hell."

Ottoway's grin slid around his face and he looked his wise look and said nothing, but he picked up the brief case then and fiddled with the zipper, opening it, peeking in, pulling it closed again, tapping the case with smooth well-padded hairless fingers. The fire clicked, and his fingers made stealthy noises on the leather of the case.

Julia Price spoke up.

"See here, Max," she informed the prosecutor, "if you are going to play cat and mouse much longer, I'm going home. And I'll take Scott with me. We belong to the working class, in case you don't know, and since we probably can't answer any questions anyway."

Ottoway cut in. "Maybe you can!" he said.

"Well, fire away then," Julia said. "If I'm any judge, so far you've got nowhere fast."

Ottoway's expressionless eyes gleamed as he drew the lids tighter and the light on them was reflected differently.

"If you weren't a good friend, Julia, I might need to remind you that I am the state's attorney," he said.

"That oughtn't to keep you from being human," Julia said. "Listen here, Max! This is a big shock to all of us. I feel funny. There in the kitchen when I saw Edwina dead I didn't feel so funny as I do now. It sort of creeps up on you slowly. I feel awful, and so does Scott, I can tell by the look on his face. Maybe we'll get sick." Her brown eyes traveled around the room. "Everybody looks awful, except you, Max. Pat Abbott, for another, has no business staying up like this. Come on, ask Scott and me what you need to, so we can beat it."

"I'll be all right, Julia," Scott said, but his lips were pale.

I said, recalling my First-Aid course, "People who've been shocked need something hot on their stomachs."

Patrick unfolded himself. "Maybe *in* them would do," he said. He stood up. "I've got some whisky in the car."

Bee came to life. "There's plenty right in this room," she said. She stood up, straight and very elegant in her old rose-red flannel robe. The men rose, automatically. Even Max Ottoway unstraddled himself from the chair, in due time. It's funny the way just anybody can sense the lady in a woman. Bee crossed to a portable bar which stood like a side table in one corner. Patrick went with her and wheeled the bar back to her sofa and stood by until he had handed all the drinks.

Ottoway had shifted his chair to allow the gadget to pass, then settled back in the same position, but he spoke more politely now.

"I'll let you and Scott go as soon as I can, Julia," he said. "But you're here. You came here, no doubt, to sympathize with the family, but you are, nevertheless, material witnesses in the murder of Edwina Ames. There will be an inquest, of course, and you can tell all you know then, but while you're here there are a few questions that you can answer for me. In a few minutes," he said then.

Bee was still asking what people wanted. Everybody who wanted anything at all asked for whisky, except Julia, who stuck incredibly to her favorite gin, and Scott, who said what he needed was hot milk, but the prosecutor wouldn't let the cook go out to fix it for him so Scott compromised with a very small whisky and soda.

"I would just as soon stay, Julia," he said, as Patrick handed him his glass, and the firelight caught it like liquid amber. "I—well, I've decided to tell something that—well, that was told me. I hate betraying a confidence, but I think I must."

"You can tell it at the proper time," Ottoway said. "I've always had a hunch that the whole kit and boodle of you people knew a lot more about that Thayer business than you let on. I wish I had camped on you closer. How could I? This is a big county. It's dead broke. And a man never has a minute of his own." He dwelt on this for a few minutes and more time passed. "That was your rifle in the kitchen, wasn't it, Mrs. Chandler?" he said finally.

"Yes," Bee said.

"How come you had it out here?"

"I brought it with me. I thought I might get a shot at a wildcat."

Ottoway snorted. "You came out here to nurse Ames through the night, didn't you, Mrs. Chandler?"

"Yes."

Ottoway said, "The Southwest is a remarkable place. People out here do remarkable things. But I never heard of anybody yet who combined nursing a sick man with shooting wildcats."

"I don't see why not," Bee said. "All I had to do was give Maurice his medicine on schedule and look in once each hour to see if he was in bed and properly covered. The house was dark, save for his very dim night light. The cattle have a way of coming as close to the house as the fences permit at night, and a wildcat has sneaked in and torn to bits and eaten two of Maurice's young calves, almost under their noses here, and besides, I'm crazy to shoot a wildcat."

Everybody felt a little stirred by her definiteness. She rang true. And she made shooting a wildcat something even I thought I would like to do, and me terrified of guns, too.

But it didn't make sense to Max Ottoway.

He said, superiorly, "And where did you keep the rifle? While you nursed the patient?"

"I left it in the kitchen."

"Why?"

"Well, there was no light on that side of the house. It was the logical way to slip out, if I heard the cat, and I kept the back doors unlocked so that as little noise as possible would be made when I left the house, in case I heard the cat."

"I see," Ottoway said. I *don't* see, he meant.

He reached for the brief case.

"You like guns, don't you, Mrs. Chandler?" He made a little bow at Karen. "And Miss Chandler?"

"I like to shoot," Karen said.

"I don't think I like to shoot," Bee Chandler said. "But I am trying to learn how."

Learn? I thought. In my mind I saw her, popping on the amethyst specs, taking instantaneous aim. I saw the hawk, falling.

Ottoway unzipped the brief case.

"You own a revolver, don't you, Mrs. Chandler?" She inclined her head. "What kind, by the way?"

"It's a Colt," Mrs. Chandler said. "A .45 which my husband used in the last war."

"I see. When did you have it last, Mrs. Chandler?"

Bee's glance avoided Karen's deliberately, and Karen spoke up. "I was the one who had it last," she said. "It was in my car, on the plaza. Somebody snitched it, Mr. Ottoway."

"When?"

"Four days ago," Karen said.

"You don't say so?" Ottoway said. His eyes rested on her, cold as a snake's. "Well, well. I wonder what we have in this satchel? Let's have a look, what say?"

He reached into the brief case and took out the revolver.

I felt like ice. My heart simply stopped beating. Of course, I knew about the gun, and had known this would happen all along, but I didn't think I would feel like this. How did the others feel, the ones who didn't know what was in the case?

I glanced around the circle.

Hugh Kennicott was frowning. His hands were doubled in fists, hard-gripped. He recognized the gun, I could see that, and his expression asked what Ottoway was doing with it. Why the revolver? Hugh's dark, solemn face was questioning as his eyes moved from the revolver and fastened on the prosecutor.

Bee and Karen stared at the gun, looked at each other, looked away.

Scott Davies looked puzzled and worried. He opened his mouth as though to ask a question, then he consulted Karen with his eyes, and apparently decided to wait. I felt a little tinge of hope. Scott knows something, I thought. Maybe he knows the real truth about this Thayer business. Maybe he will tell us, now that Karen is going to be arrested.

Julia's funny face was a wide-eyed circle of astonishment. Her red hair circled the face. Her black Mexican hat circled the hair.

Patrick looked so diffident I would have pinched him, had I been close enough, and the Indian woman's slant-eyed countenance was just the same, and the sheriff, leaning against the doorjamb now, was rolling another cigarette.

"I'm going to be kind and hurry things up," Ottoway said. "I'm not going to beat around the bush any longer. This is the gun which killed Mrs. Thayer. Sheriff Trask found it in the wreck. He also found the bullet. He deputized Lieutenant Abbott to take the gun and the bullet to a man in Santa Fe, who identified fingerprints on the gun as Karen Chandler's."

There was a hush, and Bee's voice came first, and low and rapid, "That's ridiculous."

"You can't fake a fingerprint," Max Ottoway said.

"You said *in the wreck*," Hugh Kennicott said. "You mean, the revolver was down in the canyon?"

"It was," Ottoway said, and he handled the gun, running his hand along its dark gleaming barrel, and patting it. "I guess the murderer didn't mean for the gun to go over the rim along with the car. These things happen, don't they, Miss Chandler? You always leave something behind, don't you, Miss Chandler? The first time—remember?—it was your glasses."

"I left those glasses in Ray Thayer's car!" Bee Chandler said. It didn't go over at all. It was an over-obvious gesture, a futile attempt to avert disaster from Karen.

Hugh's hand reached for Karen's, to comfort her.

Scott Davies spoke up, anxiously. "Don't say anything, Karen," he said. "You have the right to have a lawyer. I don't think you killed Ray, or Dorrie, either. You wouldn't. I know a few things, myself, too. Dorrie Thayer talked to me. I won't tell what I know here, though," he said, and his face was full of his clean-eyed angry indignation over Ottoway's cruelty. "You're a damned heel, Ottoway. You don't play fair. She needs counsel before she does any talking. You let her alone, see?"

"She'll have the best lawyer in the Southwest," Hugh Kennicott said.

Ottoway squirmed.

"Oh, heck," he said. He avoided Hugh's eyes. "Don't be so god-damned noble, Scott!" he said, then, but the bravado had gone out of him apparently.

Patrick's voice eased in, as he stood up from the ottoman and gazed down at the prosecutor.

"Who first found Mrs. Ames' body tonight?" he asked Ottoway. "Sorry to bother you with the question, but I got back to this room after you had started, Mr. Ottoway."

"Well, who did find it?" Ottoway asked. He stared around. "Speak up!"

"Me," the Indian woman said. Her voice was surprisingly musical. "I find it," she said.

Ottoway eyed her.

"You? Did you hear the shot?"

She nodded darkly. "My room over kitchen. I hear shot and get up and put clothes on. Take some time, though, but think maybe all the time it was Mrs. Chandler shooting the lion maybe. I come down, turn on light, and see gun, then the lady, everything."

Patrick said, "Was the icebox door open when you came into the kitchen, Geronima?"

She shook her head. "No open. Shut."

Ottoway gave Patrick a searing look. What time-wasting was this then?

Patrick, ignoring his impatience, said, "There is more than one belt in this tangle, Mr. Ottoway." He took out the one dropped from Maurice's toweling bathrobe. "Have a look at this. Ames is supposed to be confined to his bed, but he got up when he heard the gunshot and came downstairs in the dark. He dropped this on his way down. Indeed, he admitted to me a few minutes ago that he saw his wife's dead body lying near the half-open pantry door. He saw it by the light from the icebox. He ran across the kitchen and shut the icebox door and then beat it back to bed."

"Hooey!" Ottoway said. "Boloney!"

"Why?"

"Would he run back to bed and leave his own wife lying there dead?"

"Maybe. There were several people about, you know. They might ask embarrassing questions, considering that Edwina was trying to divorce him, and that he was supposed to be confined to bed. And blind, too. Don't forget that!"

"Are you crazy?" Ottoway asked Patrick.

"Maybe, a little," Patrick said. "Why don't you talk with Ames?"

The faces in the circle had pinkened, the pinched look had gone from them all, and there was hope in some of the eyes, at least.

The sheriff beside the door was watching Ottoway with a quickened look on his weather-worn honest face.

Patrick stood lean and casual and—determined.

"I'll run up and talk to him," Ottoway said. "He is upstairs, isn't he?" Bee inclined her head. The prosecutor got to his feet. He handed the brief case to the sheriff. "Don't let this get out of your hands while I'm away, Trask. And watch them, mind. You help him, Lieutenant. I won't be long. Just a matter of routine, you understand."

19

When the prosecutor was gone everybody perked up. Quick smiles and hopeful glances flitted among us. The sheriff came away from the door and sat down nearer us. Patrick turned Ottoway's chair about and seated himself upon it, with his long legs crossed. He offered his cigarettes and lit one for himself and Julia.

Karen said, with a childlike simplicity, "From the way Mr. Ottoway treats me I really do think he thinks I'm guilty. I don't understand it."

"He has to pick on somebody," Hugh said. "But, by God, if he doesn't lay off you when he comes back I'm going to sock him one if it's the last thing I ever do."

Trask drawled, from the little distance, "I wouldn't try that, son. Just make you worser trouble."

Patrick said, "Well, somebody killed them." Bee's eyes assumed too quickly a harassed look. Patrick went on, "Mrs. Chandler, I asked you a short time ago, while we were in Ames' study, if you talked with Ray Thayer after he came back here with Dorrie."

"And I said I did not," Bee answered.

"You lied."

"Yes," Bee said, after a moment. "I lied."

"It's all right to lie if you have a good reason, Pat," Julia said.

Patrick said, "Why did you leave me in the study, Mrs. Chandler? Did you anticipate that your daughter—Mrs. Ames—was to be shot?"

Bee sat up straight.

"How can you even think such a thing?" she asked, angrily.

"You deliberately left me in the study," Patrick accused her. "You deliberately closed the door."

Bee gave herself a moment, and then said, calmly, "I had you come into the study because I had something to say, and—well, I'm never quite sure about Maurice. Several times tonight I thought he was only feigning sleep."

"And you didn't want him to hear what you *thought* you might say?" Patrick asked, slyly.

I glanced at Karen. Her mouth was unsteady.

"You don't like Maurice Ames very much, do you, Mrs. Chandler?"

Bee said, "I admire Maurice very much."

Her statement was trite and flat, as though she had made it too often.

"I said *like*," Patrick said. "That is so obvious, however, that we needn't discuss it. But you don't dislike him enough to poison him, do you? Edwina isn't your favorite *daughter*, after all."

"Why, what horrible things you say!" Karen burst out.

"What," Bee asked, shaking her head at her favorite daughter, "would be my motive for poisoning Maurice Ames?"

"It was only a routine question," Patrick said. "Maybe Ames knew something that you—or your daughter—was afraid he might tell. Maybe he knew about—Bernalillo?"

My heart was pounding now, and I felt a little sick, I hated Patrick's forcing them to disclose that secret. And I knew I couldn't stop him, if he had determined to do it.

"You've got no right to do and say what you do," Bee said bitterly.

"But I have," Patrick said. "I've got all kinds of rights. I am at present a deputy sheriff. Your sheriff here will confirm that, so I am acting on the side of the law. Also, Maurice Ames is once again my client. And as you know, Mrs. Dorrie Thayer asked me to find out who had stolen something from her house. Who has better right to question you than I? Excepting, of course, Mr. Ottoway."

Karen looked at her mother and said resignedly, "We might as well tell it, Bee. The problem is to make people understand it." She turned and said to Hugh Kennicott, "Ray Thayer and I were married, last September 5th. I would have told you, of course."

Hugh stiffened, then his hand closed over Karen's.

"I didn't see any point forcing that," he said to Patrick. "It's Karen's business, not yours."

Patrick said, "How long do you thing it will be a secret after Ottoway starts screaming murderess at Karen, Hugh? A marriage license has to be bought and signed for, and there have to be witnesses. The secret has been kept until now, but how long will the witnesses be silent after the newspapers start yelling murder?"

"For heaven's sake!" said Julia Price. "My goodness!"

Bee snapped out of a momentary paralysis. She began an appeal to Patrick.

"It wasn't a real marriage," she said earnestly. "And, besides, it was my fault. I adored Ray Thayer. I'm afraid Karen married him mostly to please me. She was rather impulsive, and there were so many sudden war marriages and all— and I am afraid I influenced her . . ."

"No, you didn't," Karen said. "I adored him, too. I hadn't been in love then, I didn't know the difference. Honestly, we never planned it. Ray took me back to school on his way to California. Bernalillo is a place where you can get married in a hurry and he said jokingly as we drove into the town that we could get married and I could still make my ten o'clock class. Well, I said, why not? Ray said, no fooling? And I said of course not, but when it was over I felt badly because it seemed a dirty trick to pull on Bee, so I said I wasn't going to tell her, or anything, and we would have a proper wedding when I was finished with school. Ray agreed. I did tell Bee about it right away, in a letter, and she said it would be better to keep it a secret at least until Ray got back."

"You rather make your daughters' decisions for them, don't you, Mrs. Chandler?" Patrick asked.

"She does not!" Karen said.

Patrick said, to Karen, "I was speaking to your mother."

"I heard you," Bee said. She weighed her words. "I tried not to influence Karen, I did, really. I couldn't Edwina. She always did what she pleased, regardless."

Scott Davies said, in an agonized voice, "I don't get it. I don't get it at all. I thought Ray was a swine when he came back here with that Dorrie, simply because I knew he was engaged to Karen—it was such a dirty deal—but if he was married to Karen, why on earth . . .?"

Julia piped in, "That's what I say! Why on earth did you let her get away with it, Karen?"

"But—don't you see? By that time, I really didn't care," Karen said. "I mean, I was sorry Ray had got mixed up with a person like Dorrie, but I—I was in love by then with somebody else. With Hugh." She turned her glowing eyes to him. "He couldn't even see me then, but there just wasn't anybody in the world for me after I saw him and honestly I didn't care much then what anybody thought or did. I felt kind of stunned about Ray, but only because I couldn't understand why he had shown such bad taste."

Scott said quietly, "So Dorrie lied to me then! She told me she and Ray were married in Las Vegas, Nevada."

"They were, Scott," the sheriff spoke up.

"But it couldn't have been legal, Jim?" Scott said.

"It would seem not," the sheriff said.

Scott said, "She admitted that Ray was drunk when he married her, but she didn't care, she said. She had had a hard kind of life. Her father deserted her mother before she was born and her mother deserted her later on and she grew up just any old way, and she was hard as nails about men. I think Ray looked like something that had dropped in her lap. She didn't expect him to live with her. She thought he had picked her up for the usual reason and she turned the tables by getting him drunk and driving them to Las Vegas and getting them married. It was across a state line, of course, and Dorrie thought he would have to buy her off. She kept him drunk till she got him here."

"I suppose the more state lines she crossed the more money she thought Ray would have to give her!" Julia said furiously.

"Dorrie never knew he was married, did she?" Patrick asked Scott.

"I don't really know. She examined his papers in Los Angeles, right after she had—shall we say—kidnapped him—and—well, I'm sure she had no idea there was any woman in his life, in any way. She looked at his driving license and his draft exemption papers. I don't suppose he had anything on him to show he was married."

"If she hadn't been so—stand-offish—about his files, she might have found out the truth," Patrick said.

Bee said, "Now don't put that on Karen, please."

"What?" Karen asked Bee.

Bee rested her eyes on her daughter.

"I went to the Thayer house, Karen. At night, when Dorrie was out. A window was unlocked on the porch. I pushed it open and went in and looked in the files and found your marriage license. I tore it up."

"And then I went there, and found your purple-blue specs," Patrick said.

Bee said, "I didn't leave the glasses in Ray's study. The last time I had them was in this house, the night we were all here to dinner." There was an appeal for understanding in her voice as she asked, "Hugh, my dear—what you must be thinking!"

Hugh glared at Patrick and said, "What I'm thinking is that I don't see why you and Karen have to endure this third-degree . . ."

"Oh, let's out with it, all of it," Karen broke in. "Anything is better than all the uncertainty. Who left the specs in the study, then? The same person, I suppose, as the one who left them in Ray's car? To throw suspicion on *us*. Well!"

She sat stiff and violent, and she looked first at one, then another, of us.

Julia said, "But, see here, Karen, if you were married to Ray, why did you waive your property rights to that little bitch? You didn't have to, you know."

"Why should I want his things, Julia?"

"That's not it," Julia said. "Why should she have had them? Even if you didn't want Ray's money, Karen, it was your duty to see that something useful and good was done with it."

"Julia is right," Scott said gently. "But also, Julia, you weren't emotionally involved in the mess. That makes some difference in your point of view."

"I suppose it does," Julia agreed. "Still, it was too bad. She was such a dirty little thing."

Patrick was again looking at Bee Chandler. "So you never saw Ray Thayer after he came back married?" he said. She lowered her eyelids. "So it wasn't you who left the spectacles in his car there at The Rock that night?"

Bee said, "You heard me say that I did."

There was another dramatic pause, and then Bee said, and now she sounded simple and sincere, "Yes, I saw him. I lied to you all. I talked to him. And I left the amethyst spectacles in his car that night at The Rock. I suppose Maurice told you, didn't he, Pat?"

Patrick did not say yes or no, and Bee said, "When Ray came back here with Dorrie, Karen happened to be at home again for the weekend. I heard about Dorrie from Edwina. It was in Julia's shop—perhaps you remember it, Julia, because it upset me terribly. For a moment I couldn't think. I was terrible to Edwina, and it was because, for a little while, I could only think that Ray and Karen were married, and that this would be a terrible thing for her, start a lot of talk, ruin her life, perhaps, because, always, wherever she went, people would always remember the scandal. I went home and told Karen and I asked her to keep silent. That wasn't easy, for her. Then Ray sent me a note, by post. He said he could explain what had happened, but he must see me alone, and that it would be better if no one knew, as yet, that we had met. I ignored the note. Then he sent Maurice to me."

"Maurice?" Scott Davies asked.

"Maurice went to see Ray about some work Ray was supposed to have done for him while in Hollywood. I didn't know anything about that, but Ray told Maurice at that time that he had to see me, and I think he may have even told him why, because Maurice would not have disclosed anything that would hurt a young girl. I am sure he would not. He annoys and irritates one, and all that, but deep inside himself Maurice is true. Ray told Maurice that he would go to The Rock that night at ten o'clock. If there was no one around, he said, he would park so that his headlights shone up the road. If there was anyone else around, he said, the parking lights only would be on, and I was to turn and go back. It was urgent, he said, for Karen's sake, that our interview be kept secret. That was because he was terrified of Dorrie.

"I drove out there. The headlights were gleaming up the road so I joined Ray and we sat in his car and talked. Ray had the glasses. Karen had left them in the car the morning Ray drove to Hollywood—the day they got married. He gave them to me—but I left them in the seat. Next morning he was dead and the spectacles were there and the state's attorney jumped on Karen. She had no alibi. I had left her at home alone. While I was away she took her horse and rode over a trail in the desert. She didn't come back for a couple of hours after I myself returned. She had not seen a soul. We had no phone. There was no way to prove that she had not met Ray Thayer except for me to explain the presence of the glasses, and that would let the cat out of the bag. Then Dorrie began to scream because of the will, which Ray had made when he and Karen became engaged, and it seemed best to keep quiet. For Ray's sake, too."

"Ray's?" Scott asked, and his brow was a tangle of questioning.

Bee said, "Ray didn't tell me how he happened to marry Dorrie. He said the truth was he didn't know how it happened. He said he remembered nothing clearly from the time he stopped at a drive-in and ordered her something to eat and himself a bourbon and soda. He said theirs wasn't a bona-fide marriage and he asked me what he should do. I knew that Karen didn't really love Ray and I advised him to get rid of Dorrie any way he could and, as quietly as possible, to arrange to have his marriage with Karen annulled. He was heartbroken." Bee said then, "I thought he killed himself, and that it was so needless, such waste."

Scott said, "I am sure he got mixed up with Dorrie quite innocently. Ray liked to pick up strangers and talk with them. They would reveal themselves, he always said, the way people you knew well wouldn't. He had a good ear, too. He liked the dialogue of certain lower-class types, and he could remember it. I wish he had talked with me, Bee. I'm afraid I've been pretty unkind in my mind about Ray."

"Well, why wouldn't you be?" Hugh Kennicott said. "It would be pretty hard to explain a thing like that."

"Not too hard," Bee Chandler said. "Of course, as I agreed with Ray when we talked, ridicule might be pretty hard, on himself as well as Karen. Ray had a 'reputation.' "

"Ridicule is tough for anybody," I said, and my mind flew to our Pancho, and the way he moped when people laughed at his utilitarian silhouette.

Patrick was again looking at Bee.

"Did Ray Thayer mention knockout drops?" he asked her.

Bee tilted up her head. "What?"

Patrick said, "Usually it's the other way round. The innocent girl is snatched and betrayed with knockout drops in her drink. In Dorrie's sphere perhaps no nice girl feels safe without her own little bottle of knockout drops. I suspect Thayer was drugged, not drunk, when he mumbled the formula—if he was able to mumble it—which passed for Dorrie as a legal ceremony."

"What put that in your head?" Scott asked Patrick.

"A little bottle," Patrick said. "I found it in Dorrie's medicine cabinet. I had it checked in Santa Fe, and found that it contained chloral hydrate, as I thought."

"Funny," Bee said, "but maybe you're right. Ray said he had only one drink that he remembered, there at the drive-in, and he supposed he had got some horrible wartime bootleg stuff. As you know, he always left Los Angeles at night, to drive across the desert when it was coolest. How awful! He took time out when he was starting home just to feed Dorrie, because she looked half starved. And he didn't blame her for what happened at all. He blamed himself. If you're right—well . . . Ray didn't deserve to be the victim of such a horrible trick."

"Makes you sort of fatalistic," Scott said, and his voice sounded husky, as if from unshed tears.

Patrick said, "Are we to believe, then, that Ray committed suicide by jumping off The Rock? Then who killed Dorrie? And why? You weren't as detached in your feeling toward Dorrie as Ray Thayer was, were you, Mrs. Chandler?"

"I had nothing whatever to do with her," Bee said stiffly.

"Naturally," Patrick said. "When she was such a menace to your daughter," Patrick said wryly. "Did anyone except Maurice Ames know of your meeting with Thayer at The Rock, Mrs. Chandler?"

"No one that I know of," Bee said.

"Why didn't you tell Ottoway that you left the glasses in the car?"

"Because it would mean explaining why I went there."

"But when Karen was accused?"

"Nothing could be proved against Karen. And, as I told you, she had no alibi. It was better, I assure you, to be silent."

"And you trusted Ames' silence?"

So it *was* Maurice, I thought? So that is why Patrick asked him if he would pay the ten thousand even though he himself was proved the murderer? Maurice must feel pretty sure of himself. Had Maurice then also killed Edwina?

Of course, with Edwina, the motive would be obvious. Maurice was a vain fellow. He might not care a hoot for Edwina, really, but he would hate having her leave him in the lurch and sneak in a divorce, for instance.

Bee said slowly, "I have never been certain that I understood Maurice Ames entirely, but I do sincerely think he is fine, inside."

Hugh opened his mouth and closed it, not saying a word.

There was another tiny silence.

Then Patrick took something from his pocket. I recognized it as the thing he had removed from the icebox. It was a small cream-colored jar, something like those in which we used to buy *pâté de foie gras.*

Patrick held this in the palm of one hand.

"You are a bacteriologist, aren't you, Karen?" he asked.

"Yes," she said. Then she grinned. "You'd better not play any tricks with Maurice's *pâté,*" she said. "He's only got two jars. They're the pride of his life."

"I suspect he has only one now, hasn't he?" Patrick asked the cook.

The Indian nodded slowly. "Not my fault the other was broken and the *pâté* burned up. Mrs. Ames, she make me."

"That's all right, Geronima," Patrick said. He again addressed Karen. "You are familiar with the bacillus *clostridium botulinum*, I suppose?"

Karen nodded, and Julia Price said, "The *what?*"

"An extremely toxic bacillus," Patrick said to Julia, and his eyes were getting narrow. "Was anyone in this house likely to eat any of this *pâté*, except Mr. Ames?" Patrick asked the cook.

She shook her head. "Nobody," she said, emphatically.

"He was experimenting with it," Bee said. "There was only a little. Edwina didn't like it, anyway."

"And nobody else want it, 'cept Mr. Ames," said Geronima.

Patrick almost jumped on Bee.

"You knew that?"

"Everybody knew it," Karen said. "Maurice talks about his hobbies every living minute. Doesn't he, Julia?"

"My Lord, yes," Julia said.

Patrick turned back to Karen. "I suppose you learned about sausage-poisoning in Europe?"

Karen laughed. "I didn't know a bacteria from a horse when we lived abroad, Pat. I was only a kid."

Patrick was at Bee again. "Well, you weren't a kid," he said. "You know what I'm talking about, don't you, Mrs. Chandler? You know what's wrong with Maurice Ames, don't you?" Patrick reached inside his tunic and brought out a kind of notebook. "Here is his chart. Ames never ran any temperature at any time. He suffered the blindness which is characteristic of this type of poisoning. He . . ."

Patrick stopped speaking as Dr. Johnson appeared in the door from the hall.

He looked positively jittery from irritation and anxiety.

"What's the use in being a doctor when people won't take your advice?" he complained, as he nervously crossed the room and thrust himself briefly into our circle. "You," he said to Patrick, "ought to be home in your bed. I can't promise what will happen to you if you continue disregarding my orders. You," he said to Scott Davies, "know what I have told you repeatedly. Only by the strictest care of yourself during your leisure hours can you go on holding down that routine job you've got now. Ames wants everybody to come upstairs. *He* won't listen to me, either. He's a sick man, and not out of the woods yet by any means, but he will not heed my advice. Please go up quietly and don't stick around up there any longer than you can help."

20

In Maurice's room the night lamp distilled its eerie gloom. Maurice Ames sat like an oriental fakir in his immense antique bed. He had pillows at his back and he had on the white bathrobe, which made his skin look very dark, and his eyes were bandaged. He was a queer and sinister-looking figure in the peculiar dusk of the bedroom.

The prosecutor prowled with his hands thrust in the pockets of his smooth trousers. He chewed his toothpick with less cocksureness than downstairs.

The light, or rather the entire scene, was unreal, actually theatrical. I moved to a chair with a feeling of watching a play. Involuntarily and without any directions from the state's attorney, or the doctor, or our bedridden host, we drifted in and sat down, making the bed the center of our semi-circle, just as the fire had been before. But what a difference! That cheery focus had uplifted and stoked the spirit. This depressed.

Maurice, I thought, and it made every nerve tense, knew something pertinent, and probably unpleasant, and he had summoned us here to tell it. He sat with his lips in their V. He looked decidedly like the cat who had swallowed the cream.

Suddenly I remembered something. As I stood below that veranda outside this room tonight two cars had slipped into the lane. After the first had arrived and was silent I heard the second distinctly and I had wondered where I had heard it before. Now I remembered. *It was the car I had heard start up at the foot of the hill the night Patrick was shot through the window.*

I looked at Bee, on my right. I looked at Karen, on the opposite side of the circle, on a divan, next to Hugh Kennicott.

Had one of them been so distracted because Patrick had been summoned by Maurice Ames, when he thought himself dying, that she had sneaked out to our house that same night and tried to kill him?

I glanced at Patrick, on my left. I leaned over and whispered that it was Bee's car I had heard that night he was shot.

Max Ottoway said to us, "Please!"

Then Karen spoke up. "I'd like to explain why I came here to-night, Mr. Ottoway," she said. Her mother shook her head at her, but Karen said, "You see, I followed them out."

Ottoway stopped pacing.

"Followed who out?"

"My sister and Hugh Kennicott."

Ottoway gave her a terrible look. "You mean to say, *you just got here?* You mean to say you followed them here intending to murder . . ."

"Nonsense!" Bee Chandler cut in.

"Speak when you're spoken to!" Ottoway said.

Karen said, "I would have told you downstairs how I happened to be here if you had given me a chance. I came out to apologize."

"Apologize?" Ottoway barked. "For what?"

Karen said, "Because I wouldn't let Edwina come in, when Hugh brought her to our house tonight."

"Jealous, huh?"

"Well, maybe I was," Karen said. "Anyway, I was mad."

"Mad enough to kill," Ottoway stated.

Karen said, "Well—yes, maybe . . ."

Hugh said quietly, "Don't answer him, Karen!"

And Bee said quickly, "Karen wasn't near the kitchen when the shot that killed Edwina was fired."

"How do you know?" Ottoway said.

"Because she was with me. I was standing in the door of this room looking in on the patient when I heard the two cars coming along the lane. The front verandas exaggerate noises from that direction, and the doors were open then, as now. I recognized our car. I went downstairs. I didn't turn on any lights; you see, I was hoping not to frighten away a possible wildcat. I didn't see Hugh and Edwina. I went to the back door leading from the main hall to the back porch. I saw Karen coming across the lawn. I spoke to her and she came into the house and we went into the bedroom on the ground floor, which is across the hall from the dining room and at some distance from the kitchen. We were there when the shot was fired."

"Naturally, you'll lie for her," Ottoway said.

"You've got a filthy sort of mind, Mr. Ottoway," Karen said.

"Don't, Karen!" Bee said.

"That'll do now!" Ottoway said, stiffly.

The doctor and the nurse stood at opposite sides of the head of the bed. There were two matching night stands and the doctor was next to the one which held the lamp. The patient sat looking very alert, in spite of the blindfold, against his pillows.

Now that my eyes had adjusted to the dim light I saw everyone plainly. Eyes glistened. Backgrounds were shadowed. Everyone was tense, still, of course, from shock.

Max Ottoway pulled a straight chair not far from where the doctor was standing, reversed it, straddled it, and spoke across his arms folded on its back.

His voice was lower than in the drawing room, and more respectful. Maurice was not only his senior, and ill, but rich.

"Mr. Ames insisted on having you come up here, but it's against his doctor's orders, so please be brief. I mean, answer your questions, but don't be long about it."

He enlarged on this, taking a good many seconds which he himself might have spared poor Maurice.

The patient bore up well. He sat turning his blind-folded head from side to side, smiling, looking very pleased with himself.

"Mr. Ames has some information which he insists everyone must hear," Ottoway said, finally. You could tell that he did not entirely agree, but was deferring to the whim of a heavy taxpayer. "All right, Mr. Ames."

Maurice made a kind of jerky bow, as if he were giving an after-dinner speech, and began talking in his quick aggressive manner.

"I saw something through my telescope this morning," he said. "Yesterday morning, I should say, and it was very late in the morning—indeed, it was in the early afternoon. I was having one of my good spells. Sometimes I see all right and sometimes I don't, you understand. Anyhow, Edwina had been in to tell me about what had happened to Dorrie Thayer in Ray's Cadillac, and how many people had gone to The Rock to see what they could see, so when I got the chance I slipped out on the veranda and had a look through my glass. I saw something I didn't expect. I saw a Mexican in a black peaked hat steal around the west side of Ray Thayer's house and choke a woman on the terrace and wrap her head in what seemed to be a green jacket."

"Why, that was me!" I cried.

"So they tell me," Maurice said drily, as if that particular item had no importance.

"What became of the—Mexican?" Patrick asked.

"He ran across the lawn to the steps which lead down the cliff, and disappeared."

"Which way did he go?" Patrick asked.

Maurice said impatiently, "I couldn't tell. The cliff hid him from view. And then the nurse came back and made me get into bed." Patrick started to say something, but Maurice said, "In just a few minutes she left the room again and I went back to the veranda. The woman on Ray's terrace was standing up, walking. I recognized you then, Jean. You seemed dazed, but you went into the house under your own power so I assumed you were all right. That's about all. The nurse—you!" he said, turning his face toward the woman, and not then or ever using her name, "you stole my telescope!"

"My orders," Dr. Johnson said, delicately.

"I don't really see what connection this has with the murder of your wife, Mr. Ames," Ottoway said.

"Don't you?" Maurice said. His tone was almost an insult.

Patrick asked, "You're sure it was a man?"

"Well, he wore pants," Maurice said. He laughed his dry shadowy laugh. "Of course, who doesn't, in Santa Maria? He—she—or it—wore jeans and a black peaked Mexican sombrero."

My eyes went to Julia. I couldn't help it. Dear old Julia, sitting there close to Scott Davies, and dressed, as usual, in her slacks and her black peaked Mexican hat.

Such suspiciousness was insane. Julia would have no motive for killing anybody. Certainly she would never choke me.

Lots of people wore jeans. Lots had Mexican hats. There were two, I recalled suddenly, which hung as ornaments on Bee Chandler's terrace. On the walls of her house, near the place where she had hung up her rifle, when she shot at the hawk.

Maurice asked, "What were you and Jean doing at Ray Thayer's, Lieutenant?"

Patrick replied with another question, "Is that why you sent for me? Twice?"

"Well, yes," Maurice said.

"I thought so," Patrick said lazily. "I guess that must have been why I wasn't in any great hurry to get here, too."

Maurice threw back his heavy shoulders.

"I also wanted you to do something for me," he said arrogantly. "After all, I haven't died, Lieutenant, so the other job I gave you can't come off, can it? See here, I want you to find something for me, Abbott. Something which must be in that house."

"What is it?" Patrick asked.

"That's confidential," Maurice said.

Ottoway's fishy eye was on Patrick.

"Now, just what were *you* doing in Thayer's house?" he demanded.

Patrick said, "Mrs. Thayer had asked me to find something she believed stolen from her house."

"She was dead!" Ottoway snapped. "You'd no business being on her premises after she was dead."

"I didn't know for sure that she was dead," Patrick said.

"Everybody else knew it!"

"I beg your pardon?" Patrick said. "Everyone surmised it, because the car was in the canyon and a hat she was known to have worn, and one slipper, could be seen from The Rock. But no one knew then that she was actually under the wreck."

"Well," Ottoway said petulantly, "did you find what you were looking for?"

"Yes and no," Patrick said.

"Really!" Dr. Johnson fluttered. "If this is going on much longer . . ."

"What was the person who strangled Jean doing there?" Maurice cut in.

"He apparently dropped in to pick up a sausage," Patrick said.

It sounded like an uncouth joke. I frowned at my husband.

"A sausage?" Maurice spat out. "Don't be pixieish, Abbott!"

"I had no such intention," Patrick said, and his voice was crisp. "Tell me, Ames, was it you that left things in such a mess in Ray Thayer's study? And was it you that left those amethyst glasses behind the files?"

Maurice shrugged. "I didn't mean to leave them. I can explain that. I had them in my pocket when I went into that house. Bee had left the glasses here the night before, the night of our party. I was taking them to her. I went into the Thayer house on an impulse. I was driving past. The garage doors stood open and the car was gone and I thought, by God, I would do right then what I had been wanting to do ever since Ray died—in short, go in there and help myself to something that in a sense belongs to me. But in the middle of looking through the files I suddenly realized what a spot I would be in if she came back unexpectedly. I bolted, and drove away. I didn't discover that I had lost the spectacles till I got to Santa Maria. I suppose they worked out of my shirt pocket when I was stooping over the files."

"Just what were you looking for, Mr. Ames?" Max Ottoway asked, politely.

"That's none of your business!" Maurice said. "The point is, don't jump on Karen on account of those glasses."

"What makes you so sure you lost them in the study?" Patrick asked.

"It's the only place I could have lost them," Ames said, with some annoyance. "It's the only place where I bent over. They were in my shirt pocket, you understand. Karen's a foolhardy brat, Ottoway. But she is honest, which is more than I can say for my wife." There was a sort of round-robin gasp, and Maurice said, sardonically, "I mean, my late wife."

Oh dear! How could he be like that?

Karen said, "Thank you, Maurice. I suppose they would have jumped on me, too—but for you." She smiled a wan smile. "I wouldn't go into that house for a million. Anybody ought to know that."

"Well, that's all I wanted to say," Maurice said.

Ottoway nodded, then said, "Now, listen, Mr. Ames. He still spoke respectfully. "About tonight. You admit having gone downstairs about the time your wife was shot. . . ."

"I didn't *admit* it. I volunteered it," Maurice drawled.

"Yes, of course. But be sensible, Mr. Ames. You adm—I mean, you said you were going downstairs when you heard the gunshot. You thought at once that it was in the kitchen. You thought that Mrs. Chandler's gun had been shot off, perhaps by mistake—you said you knew it was there, that she had told you about bringing it to shoot at mountain lions." Ottoway's lips curled. "When it went off you hurried on to the kitchen, by way of the main hall. You opened the door, you said, and there was a very dim light in the kitchen, made by the light inside the icebox—the icebox door stood open. You went across to close the door and you saw your wife lying dead—you felt her pulse and found none, you said—and then you shut the icebox door and left the kitchen by the way you had entered, you said."

Hugh Kennicott said, "Do you mean to say you found Edwina dead and—*just walked out?*" His voice was thick with disgust. "Don't you have any feelings at all?"

Not any, I was thinking. Maurice hadn't any feelings, only taste. Everyone here felt the shock of Edwina's death more than he did.

Maurice said, "I hadn't much feeling for Edwina, Hugh. She was so merce-

nary. But she was very decorative. She always looked just right in this house."
He shrugged his big shoulders. "There are thousands like Edwina. Maybe next
time I'll be lucky enough to get one who also has a heart."

How terrible to say such things, when she was only just dead! They were true,
but he horrified me.

Dr. Johnson was fidgeting, rubbing his hands.

The nurse stood rigid, and watched the doctor.

Patrick asked, "But why did you go downstairs?"

Maurice smiled. "I wanted to see if my *pâté de foie gras* was really in the
icebox," he said.

Ottoway cleared his throat. "You ought to have called the police, Mr. Ames. I
know you are telling the truth, but no jury will ever understand your going into
the room and seeing your wife lying dead and then going straight back to your
room without doing anything whatever, Mr. Ames."

Maurice laughed the shadowy laugh.

"You amuse me, Ottoway. What jury in Santa Maria County ever understands
anything? Most of them don't even speak English. I've seen monkeys in the zoo
that looked far more intelligent than one of your local juries." Maurice turned
his head from side to side, as though he could see through the blindfold. He kept
smiling his tight three-cornered smile. Ottoway stared at the doctor. The man is
crazy as a bedbug, the prosecutor's glance was saying. I looked at the sheriff. He
was anchored near the door into the hall. His sunlined face was blank. His eyes
were shining. "Besides, I wasn't the first one, if I must be brutally frank," Maurice said. "I saw a red bathrobe disappearing through the door into the servants'
staircase as I opened the hall door into the kitchen." He lifted up the blindfold
and looked at Bee in her rose-red dressing gown. "How about it, Mother-in-
law?" he asked.

21

My chest felt hollow again. The sickening uneasiness went all through me, and
I felt limp, and all in.

Bee did not answer Maurice.

I said, as the idea abruptly came into my head, "Look, Maurice, how does it
happen that I didn't meet you on the stairs, either coming down or going up? I
ran into the house from the front veranda the minute I heard the shot."

Maurice smiled the V smile.

"I know, darling," he said, in the bantering tone he liked to use with young
women who weren't his immediate family. "As I came back into the hall from

the kitchen I saw you come in the front door. The moonlight, you know. So I came up the back way."

"By the stairs leading out of the kitchen?" Patrick asked.

"Of course not!" Maurice blurted. "Those lead to the servants' rooms. Would I want the servants' wing connecting directly with my own on this floor, Lieutenant? I used our own back staircase. But my mother-in-law left the kitchen by the servants' stairs and then no doubt escaped into the main hall by the short flight from the landing—a convenience planned for the girls to answer the front door or a call from the front of the house when they happened to be in their rooms—not as a corridor for my mother-in-law to bolt through when she had shot and killed her elder daughter."

Bee said, "Maurice, will you kindly refrain from referring to me as your mother-in-law?"

Maurice laughed his peculiar laugh. He said nothing. You could see him gloating because he had got under her skin.

Max Ottoway said, "Didn't you turn on the hall lights, Mrs. Chandler?"

Bee replied, "Maurice's door was open. I was afraid any light, even one downstairs, might disturb him."

Maurice chuckled. "And I didn't turn them on because I was afraid my—I beg your pardon—afraid Mrs. Chandler would catch me gallivanting around."

There was a silence. Bee's defenses were down now. She gave Maurice Ames a look of acrid hatred.

I remembered Patrick's seeing Hugh Kennicott on that little landing, and myself—looking over the balusters of the El Greco staircase—seeing him emerge from the door of that stairway to meet Edwina. The night we came to dinner.

I put that out of mind and said, "Then you dropped your belt *on the way down*, Maurice?"

"Evidently I did, my darling," Maurice purred.

Ottoway said to Bee Chandler, "Is it true that you were in the kitchen when Mr. Ames arrived there, Mrs. Chandler?"

"Yes, I was there," Bee said, and she now spoke calmly. "I heard him—that is, I heard someone coming and I hastily stepped onto those stairs. When I saw it was Maurice I shut the door softly and went back to the hall by way of the servants' stairs. Karen was sitting just where I left her, in the guest room."

"Then you were the one who found Mrs. Ames dead?"

"I didn't find her at all," Bee said. "I saw the gun lying on the floor, I saw the icebox door partly open, but I didn't see Edwina. I'm short-sighted, you know— also I hadn't time. I had just stepped into the kitchen when I heard Maurice coming. I—well, naturally, I ducked out of sight because I thought—I—thought— well, that is, I saw the rifle lying on the floor, and I thought . . ."

"Well?" Ottoway jumped at her. "What did you think?"

"I didn't think," Bee said. "I was just sort of muddled."

"How ridiculous!" Maurice snorted. "How very lame!"

"No more so than your accusing me," said Bee.

"I didn't like Edwina enough to kill her," Maurice said.

Across the room Hugh Kennicott stiffened, darkening like a thundercloud.

"I was not the judge of that," Bee said icily to Maurice.

"You didn't like her yourself," Maurice said. "Don't get snooty with me, Mother-in- . . ."

"If you ever call me that again!" Bee cried, and she looked like a demon, "I'll-I'll . . ."

I saw Patrick looking at her. I wondered what *he* thought of her burst of temper.

"Now, now," Dr. Johnson said. "Are you finished, Max? Can't they go now?"

"Why, we haven't gotten anywhere," Ottoway said.

Patrick leaned forward. "May I ask a question or two, Mr. Ottoway?"

"You heard what the doctor said," Ottoway grumbled.

"Thanks," Patrick said, just as though Ottoway had agreed to his request. He looked at Maurice. "Can you see? Or can't you?" he asked.

"Can I see?" Maurice said. "Sure I can see, except at intervals when this crazy blindness comes on like a fog."

"That's the trouble," Dr. Johnson murmured. "He keeps thinking he's cured. I can't make him understand that this condition may continue indefinitely and that he must do everything possible to avert strain."

"I understand you've ordered a wheel chair?" Patrick said to Maurice.

"That was my idea," Dr. Johnson put in hastily. "I don't think Maurice ought to exert himself. I proposed the wheel chair, since he so dislikes staying in bed."

"And it takes a good while, doesn't it, Dr. Johnson, to get over an attack of botulism?" Patrick asked softly.

Ottoway's eyes bulged and pivoted.

The doctor grunted, "Who said anything about botulism?"

"I did," Patrick said, in the same quiet voice, so quiet that those across the room leaned forward to listen. "I took the liberty of checking up Mr. Ames' symptoms in your medicine books, Dr. Johnson, the morning after he sent for the sheriff and me."

"What is all this?" Ottoway said. "Why didn't anybody tell me?"

"Shush!" Maurice said. He motioned eagerly to Patrick to continue.

The prosecutor subsided. Patrick said, "I dropped in at your office to talk with you about Mr. Ames, Dr. Johnson. You weren't there, so I consulted your books. I know a little about forensic medicine, as it happens . . ."

"How come?" Ottoway asked.

"Stop interrupting!" Maurice snapped.

Patrick said, "Of course I could only guess at what ailed the patient, and I was pretty sure I had guessed right when I heard later that he hadn't any temperature.

According to your books, Doctor, he is very lucky to be alive."

Maurice snatched off his blindfold again, and gaped.

The doctor said, "Well, we needn't go into it before the patient. . . ."

"And why not?" Maurice demanded. "Go on, Abbott!"

"I don't think Ames exposed himself deliberately to the bacillus, do you, Doctor?"

The doctor's hands fanned the air, and Maurice cried out, "What on earth are you talking about?"

"I said I didn't think you made yourself sick intentionally," Patrick said. "The bacillus is too dangerous. Seven or eight out of ten of its victims die, and you don't want to die, do you, Ames?"

"This discussion is superfluous," Dr. Johnson said. "That specific bacillus is endemic here. Anybody might swallow it, any time."

"For that very reason an excellent means of murder," Patrick said. "If Mr. Ames had died, you would certify that he died from natural causes, wouldn't you, Dr. Johnson? You would say that anybody might get the bug, anywhere, at any time. You wouldn't even be able to prove where he got it, would you, even though from contaminated food in his own house—because all the food in the icebox had been destroyed, burned up in an incinerator. A bacillus doesn't show up in any ashes, does it, Doctor?"

The doctor sputtered. "Ames himself ordered the food destroyed!"

Patrick's gaze stabbed the doctor like a knife. "A patient often senses what ails him, even though he can't name the specific disease, or even the exact location—isn't that true, Dr. Johnson?" The doctor nodded, once. "Your patient was suffering very much when the attack began. So much, that he even forgot that one jar of the precious *pâté de foie gras* he was experimenting with was in the icebox, and it would be burned up with the rest." Patrick put a hand in one pocket. "Luckily, there was another," he said.

The hand came out. Cupped in its palm, like some wicked eye-compelling jewel, was the small cream-colored jar Patrick had removed from the icebox.

It caught the dim light. It looked glossy, snug, precious and dangerous in Patrick's brown long-fingered hand.

Maurice Ames sat in his great bed as if frozen, his coffee eyes glued on the jar.

Others merely stared. Max Ottoway asked, "What is that thing?"

"Sausage," Patrick said.

"Sausage? That little thing?"

"Goose-liver sausage, Mr. Ottoway. A perfect medium for our deadly bacillus. Easy to open the jar, which is sealed lightly with paraffin, and then easy to inject the bacillus through the congealed goose-grease coating over the sausage—by means of a hypodermic syringe—and then easy to seal the jar with paraffin again. Our bacillus thrives best without air. There are no doubt enough in this little thing to kill everybody in Santa Maria." There were several gasps, then Patrick said, "Of course, not everyone would think of a bacillus as an instrument for murder. So few of us know anything about bacteria."

"Bacteria?" Ottoway's eyes swung back to Karen. "Isn't that what you majored in, at the university?"

"Why, yes," Karen said.

All at once Maurice lunged forward in his bed and tried to jump out. The nurse seized him and forced him back on his pillows. "For God's sake!" he managed to cry out. "Be careful with that jar, Abbott. It's all that's left to show for a full year's work. There's money in that stuff, when I work out a first-rate formula. . . ."

"There's death in this particular jar," Patrick cut in. "How many people knew about your goose liver *pâté*, by the way?"

"Everybody knew about it," Julia Price said.

"How do you know it's been tampered with?" Ottoway asked, suspicious again.

Patrick said, "When I went to the car to get you my brief case I examined it. I've got a lens in my pocket, and a strong flashlight in the car. The jar had been unsealed and resealed. I located a perforation which could have been made by a hypodermic needle on the solidified grease. It will have to go to a lab, of course, for a report on the bug."

"Any odor?" Dr. Johnson asked.

"Not discernible."

"Then maybe it's all right!" Maurice cried, happily.

"There doesn't have to be an odor," Dr. Johnson said. "Sometimes the most deadly of those bacilli are in food which seems perfect. You can put the same bacilli in another food and it will stink to high heaven."

"Yes," Patrick said. "There was a sausage in Dorrie Thayer's icebox, too—a liver sausage from the grocer's, that smelled very badly indeed."

I glanced at Karen, who was gazing at Patrick with eyes that seemed sunken in her head. Beside me, Bee Chandler was tense.

Dr. Johnson said, "Did you eat any of the stuff in the other jar, Maurice?"

"I ate a lot of it," Maurice said. "It did taste a little funny, too. I blamed it on Mexico."

"Mexico?" I said.

Maurice smiled. "I had to use some tinned truffles to season the stuff. They were sent up from Mexico City. I thought they had gypped me, darling."

Patrick asked, "Did you think your wife was trying to bump you off, Ames?"

"Edwina? Of course not. Why?"

"You asked me to shadow her, remember."

Maurice laughed. "Oh, that. Just an excuse, Abbott. To have you on tap. I wanted you to get something for me, but I wanted to get acquainted with you first, so I thought you could hang around and watch Edwina." There was a sob from Scott Davies, and Maurice gave him a look of mingled irony and compassion. Then he said, "I was scared pink of that little bitch Dorrie. Did she put the bugs in my goose-livers, do you think?"

Patrick said, "The sausage in her own icebox was infected—must have been—or the killer wouldn't have bothered to steal it. When a rotten sausage is pinched, that's news!"

"She was back of it!" Maurice declared. "She's to blame!"

Patrick said, "When that sausage was stolen Dorrie was already dead, lying in the canyon under her wrecked car, shot in the back of the head, with Karen Chandler's pistol."

Bee gasped. Hugh threw Patrick a bitter glance. Karen looked dazed, Scott freshly hurt.

Ottoway unstraddled himself. "Remember me, folks?" he asked, breezily. "Well, it all gets back to the same one every time. Let's break this up. Take her in custody, Trask. Sorry to have bothered you, Mr. Ames."

"See here!" Hugh Kennicott rumbled.

Maurice let out a sudden scream.

"Oh, my eyes!" he shrieked, and he clapped the palms of his dry stubby hands over them. "Do something, Johnson! Get out of here, the rest of you! Get out—get out—get out!"

He threw himself against his pillows.

The doctor motioned us to go. The nurse removed the extra pillows and settled the patient flat on his back.

22

Well, I was thinking, that settles it, Maurice did it all right, yes, he was the one, but the prosecutor has a single-track mind and how on earth is Patrick going to prove it and make Ottoway let Karen go? There was too much against her. Her secret marriage with Ray Thayer, followed by his return with another woman. Her falling in love with Hugh Kennicott before that happened. Her spectacles in Ray's abandoned car, her guns, her dislike of Edwina, her majoring in bacteriology at the university. Maurice was right about the Santa Maria juries. They were made up usually of very simple people. They understood killing for love or hate or greed, and the prosecutor would talk their language. A clever lawyer might get Karen off, but suspicion would linger and ruin her life.

Only, how had Maurice got poisoned? Had he accidentally infected his own goose livers with the bacilli he meant for Dorrie?

Dorrie, however, hadn't got poisoned by her sausage.

Patrick explained this to me later. Many people suffered at some time in their lives attacks of poisoning from this bacillus, he said, and called it ptomaine or acute indigestion, and recovered, and afterward were immunized. Feeding as Dorrie had, she might very likely have been one of those. Or maybe her sausage had smelled too evil even for her taste, but she hadn't got around to throwing it away.

The shooting part was more simple, in my estimation. Maurice could easily lay hands on Bee's guns, and hire somebody to do the dirty work.

We had risen. Some were moving irresolutely toward the hall door, when Patrick said, "It's a pity Mr. Ames isn't able to hear what I'm about to tell you. May we stop in the living room, Mr. Ottoway? I'll need only five minutes at the most."

The bedclothes stiffened as Maurice listened.

He mumbled, "Nothing wrong with my ears."

"I won't have him worried further!" Dr. Johnson said.

Patrick said, "You'll put Miss Chandler in jail, Mr. Ottoway?"

"Don't know where else," Ottoway said gruffly. He was being unpopular, risking future votes, and he didn't like it, but the law is the law.

"I'll stand her bail," Maurice croaked.

"I'm afraid bail is out of the question. It's murder," Ottoway said.

Everybody had halted. We stood, each of us, not far from where we had sat. Julia was crying again, Karen and Bee looked frightened, Scott was white as a sheet, Hugh Kennicott dark and angry. No one, I thought, except Scott, was mourning for Edwina to a point which took him out of the present moment.

"There'll be an inquest," Ottoway said. "She'll get a fair chance, Mr. Ames."

"You all sit down!" Maurice said now in a full-sized voice. "I want to hear what Abbott has to say."

He is worried, I thought. He's scared.

The doctor protested, the nurse hovered, Ottoway screwed up his mouth so that the toothpick assumed a jaunty angle.

We again sat down.

I glanced at my watch. It was a few minutes past three.

I looked at the windows open on the veranda. The ground mist had risen to a level with the roof of the big house. The moonlight laced it strangely.

On my right Bee Chandler fumbled in the pocket of her bathrobe and on my left Patrick reached inside the blouse of his uniform and brought out the amethyst spectacles. He polished them with the handkerchief which had wrapped them and handed them to Bee. She thanked him crisply, put them on, and glared furiously at Maurice Ames and Max Ottoway.

The sheriff remained all the time by the door. He looked tireless and vigilant.

Patrick said, "Karen would have no motive for killing Dorrie Thayer, Mr. Ottoway."

The prosecutor moved his shoulders, an ugly gesture.

Bee sighed, Karen brightened, and so did Hugh, and Scott and Julia cheered up visibly. Maurice Ames lay listening.

"Edwina Ames' death was, in a sense, accidental," Patrick said. "She walked into the kitchen as the killer was about to remove the *pâté de foie gras* from the icebox. She was moving very quietly, because she didn't want her husband to know she had come home. She didn't turn on any lights. Edwina didn't relish what had happened out at her mother's—her quarrel with Karen—even though she—being conceited—thought she could keep Hugh believing her lies. She didn't want an encounter with her mother, either, because Edwina was afraid of Bee."

Bee gave Patrick a questioning glance.

"Bee," Julia spoke up, "I'm sorry, but I told them about your jumping on Edwina in my shop that day. I didn't want Pat to get mixed up with Dorrie, so . . ."

"That's all right, Julia," Bee said.

Max Ottoway said, "Hurry up, Lieutenant. I want to get home and get a little shut-eye before morning, see."

Patrick continued. "So Edwina tiptoed into the kitchen, and got shot. Would either her mother, or her husband, shoot her because she surprised either opening the icebox? Couldn't that be explained easily enough? Bee Chandler was sitting up with the sick man. She would naturally be using things from the icebox. Maurice Ames has explained why he went downstairs. To see if his goose-liver *pâté* was really in the icebox. He is a person who becomes obsessed with an idea—obsessed enough to kill, maybe, but there would be no point to his shooting his wife because she happened to catch him looking into his own icebox." Patrick paused. "Karen Chandler, on the other hand, would have no real excuse for arriving here in the middle of the night and rushing straight into the kitchen to the icebox."

Ottoway gloated. His eyes gleamed.

Maurice groaned. "Well, if you're ganging up on Karen too, Abbott, stop it right now. I want to call the whole thing off."

"This is murder," Patrick said.

"But why?" Maurice wailed, under his covers.

"Just be patient," Patrick said. "My wife was choked at the Thayer house because she happened to be in the way of the murderer when he—or she, Mr. Ottoway—was running away from that house with a sausage. Edwina Ames was killed because she happened to walk into the kitchen while the murderer was about to remove the goose-liver sausage." Ottoway grinned sarcastically, and Patrick said, "Maybe it sounds silly, Mr. Prosecutor, but the murderer stole the sausages to destroy the bacilli he had planted there himself. Or she—if you wish. In other words, he wanted to destroy evidence of intent to murder."

"But, my Lord," Julia Price cried out, "why did he do it all? What was he after?"

"He wasn't after anything," Patrick said. "He already has it in his possession."

"Has what?" Ottoway asked impatiently.

"A manuscript," Patrick said, and Maurice sat right up. He snatched off the blindfold again, too. "Writers may be a dime a dozen, Ames, but not writers like Ray Thayer. He had done the manuscript for your cookbook, hadn't he, Ames? But he was murdered, and it fell into the hands of Dorrie Thayer, and there you were—another of your ideas, which obsess you, had fallen into the hands of a very unfrienly young woman and was unprocurable . . ."

Maurice spoke submissively. He seemed licked.

"I could have got it," he said flatly, "but I wasn't going to let that little drab hold me up, the way she must have done him. He never married her of his own free will, I'd swear to that. The manuscript was mine by rights. We had a verbal royalties agreement, and I didn't want to be held up for that, either, in case it didn't come up to scratch. I never even saw it, you see. He was to do it while he was away."

"Are you talking about that everlasting cookbook?" Bee Chandler asked. She was tense with anger. "Do you mean to say, Maurice Ames, that you have let that—that *thing*—make all this trouble? You ought to be drawn and quartered!" She rose from her chair. "Maurice, did you kill Ray Thayer—for *that?*"

"Oh, don't be so silly!" Maurice said.

"Did you?" Bee was blazing. "Answer me! Did you do a filthy thing like that and let suspicion rest on Karen all this time? Did you?"

She started toward the bed. Everyone looked stiff with fright, including Maurice, who was seeing all right again, for some reason. He looked quite paralyzed with fear.

Patrick said, "Sit down, Mrs. Chandler!"

Bee hesitated, then wheeled on him.

Patrick stood up in one quick movement and grasped her by one shoulder and backed her to her chair and seated her.

He came back and sat down.

"Thayer's death didn't worry Ames half so much as the loss of the manuscript . . ." he began.

"You make me seem inhuman," Maurice wailed.

". . . but he didn't kill Thayer, Mrs. Chandler. I know who killed Ray Thayer and Dorrie Thayer and Edwina Chandler. I know who choked Jean. I know who hung around our house the night after we went out to The Rock, after Sheriff Trask had told me about the death of Ray Thayer. I know who shot at me through the window and gave me a very bad headache the night after Maurice Ames asked the sheriff to bring me here when he thought, correctly, that he had been poisoned. Mrs. Chandler—did you by any chance lend your car that same evening? And were your guns in your car?"

Bee gazed at Patrick. Her tense face went pale. She emitted a tiny sigh. She fainted.

Everybody jumped up. The doctor rushed away from the head of the bed. Scott Davies took two long steps and was where the doctor had stood at the head of Maurice's bed. He opened a drawer in the night stand. He took out an automatic pistol.

"I sat there wondering if this would be where you always kept it, Maurice!" he said. "Stay where you are, everybody. You leave people who faint lying down, Dr. Johnson, so you can face me like everybody else. Sit down where you were, everybody. Doctor, stand beside Bee Chandler, please!"

We all sat down.

Scott stood, his eyes shining strangely, his blue-eyed face looking exalted. The black gun gleamed dully in his white hand. The thing seemed to point straight at me.

"All right," Scott said. "Now, don't move, anybody."

Patrick sat casually. The sheriff, with a big gun on his hip, leaned against the open door and watched Scott, his head lowered, his eyes lifted and steady. He could have acted, I thought, had he wished.

Scott said, "What happens when a man injects eight grains of morphine in his veins, Dr. Johnson?"

"Why," the doctor stammered, "he dies."

"Why don't I die then?"

The doctor made a vague motion to go to him. Scott motioned him with the pistol to stay where he was.

The doctor said, "Well—er—well, morphine is rather unpredictable. If you will let me, I'll get you some strong coffee—You're sure it was morphine?"

Scott's lips twisted.

"I don't know. I got it in Juarez, when I went down to Mexico for some things for my house. I haven't wanted to live since—since I killed Ray Thayer. I got the dope to bump myself off. But, till now, I haven't had the nerve."

Patrick asked, "Scott, why did you kill him?"

"He laughed at me," Scott said. "I thought he was a swine when he came back here with Dorrie. That made me sick—sick in my very soul. I went to The Rock that night. I saw Bee meet Ray. They talked. Then Ray walked over to the canyon and I thought he was going to jump. I got scared. I yelled at him. I begged him not to do it—and he laughed!"

There was intense silence.

Scott tried to take a firmer grip on the gun.

It got away from him. His fingers couldn't hold onto it. It hit the thick carpet with a deathlike thud.

Ottoway jumped up. "Get him, Trask!" he shouted.

"You keep out of this!" Dr. Johnson shouted back. All at once he had plenty of guts. "Come along, Nurse. Julia, you and Jean look after Bee. Karen, get a bed ready. The rest of you, help me with Scott."

"Well, I'll be darned!" Max Ottoway said.

23

It was ten days later, and ten o'clock at night. Bee Chandler, Julia Price, Patrick and I were sitting around a log fire in the fireplace of the big living room in Hugh Kennicott's cow-camp. The cowboys had had dinner with us, had sung for us afterward, and had gone off to bed in the bunkhouse. Hugh and Karen had put on warm jackets and had gone out—they said to look at the stars.

Julia said, "Hugh didn't waste any time when he finally got the idea, Bee. Isn't it funny? I always thought he was in love with Karen, but nothing seemed to happen."

Bee smiled. "Hugh's protective," she said. "And Karen never made him feel she needed him till that night Edwina was killed."

Julia said, "I suppose Edwina simply crawled with needing-protection."

Bee said, "Don't be too hard on her, Julia."

"But I hated so what she did to Hugh! He was a different boy."

"He was worried and upset," Bee said.

I thought of Hugh in the hall that night, opening his arms to Edwina because she was, he thought, distressed and hurt. She had made use of his need to protect. If she could involve him in her divorce, he would have felt he had to marry her, she probably thought.

"Well, Maurice does look like a brute," Julia said.

"He does take a good deal of understanding," Bee said.

Patrick said, "Ames is a good guy, really. He wouldn't have let Karen be arrested, Bee."

"What makes you so sure?" I asked.

Patrick said, "He told me yesterday that he recognized Scott, when he strangled you there on the terrace, Jeanie. The Mexican hat fell off. But he couldn't bring himself to accuse him."

"He was pretty callous about Edwina," Julia said. "She asked for it though, I suppose. I'm glad you told me she wasn't your real daughter, Bee. I mean, I always thought you were partial to Karen, and while I didn't like Edwina, it didn't seem quite fair."

"I tried to feel toward Edwina as my own," Bee said. "She was four years old when Edwin and I were married. Her own mother deserted them. Her father didn't want her ever to know it. I was eighteen when we married, and there I was, with a daughter four years old! Edwina was like her own mother, I'm afraid. How did you guess my age, Pat?"

Patrick smiled. "I didn't *exactly*, Bee. But your amethyst specs gave me ideas. A few years either side of forty can make considerable difference in the vision. It's quite possible that if you were forty-odd instead of thirty-something you and Karen wouldn't be using the same glasses." He moved his shoulders. "It wasn't sure-fire, but it did rouse my curiosity."

The glasses jutted from the pocket of Bee's shirt. She glanced at them and said, with a small shudder, "I'm glad they had no real connection with the murder."

Julia started raving. "You're simply wonderful, Pat. Really, however did you come to suspect Scott?"

"Scott was a logical suspect from the time I knew what ailed Maurice Ames."

"But why?"

"In the Public-Health Office he would probably have a good deal of experience with food poisons. The subject must have been covered in several of the reference books beside his desk."

"How did he get those bugs, Pat?"

"A whole Mexican family in a remote village died from eating home-canned corn. The office sent a sample of the stuff to the state laboratory for analysis. Scott secretly took the rest home, intending to use it to poison Maurice Ames and Dorrie Thayer."

"Then how did you know how Maurice took the stuff?"

"Something you told Jean about his experimenting with goose-liver *pâté* gave me that cue. Botulism is called sausage-poisoning in Europe. *Pâté de foie gras* is a sort of sausage, of course. The other one, stolen from Dorrie's icebox, clicked." Patrick turned to Bee Chandler. "I would have asked you sooner if you had lent your car to Scott that night he banged at me through the window, and whether your guns were in the car, but I was afraid you might talk and word would get to him. I wanted him to confess, if possible, because I couldn't feel certain about his motive for killing Ray Thayer. I was pretty sure all along that the manuscript figured in the attempt on Maurice's life and in Dorrie's death—I was sure of it when I saw Thayer's study—but I wanted him to say why he had killed his friend."

"I suppose it was all in his character," Bee said soberly.

"Right. He idealized Thayer out of all reason. When he imagined him a heel he went temporarily out of his head."

Julia said, "He shouldn't have left Karen's fingerprints on that gun, Pat."

"He didn't think of that. He wore gloves himself and it never occurred to him that earlier prints would remain on the gun. Besides, he didn't mean that the gun should go into the canyon with the car. He meant to bury it in the desert. Dorrie stopped at his house that evening on her way back from Santa Fe. The poisoned sausage—if she ate any—hadn't affected Dorrie. And Maurice hadn't died. Their feud would soon flare up again. So Scott decided to kill her quickly and get it over with. He suggested her driving him out to The Rock. They arrived and turned off the lights and sat listening to the radio. He made some excuse, got out, shot her in the back of the head, got in, started the car toward the rim, and jumped out. When he jumped, the big revolver jumped from his pocket into the car. He fortunately had a lucid interval and told us everything before the morphine finally got him, as you know."

They had carried him into Edwina's bedroom. He died in her bed.

Julia sighed. "Anyhow, Dr. Johnson had told him some time ago that he hadn't long to live."

Patrick said, "Yet, before that, he had wanted to die—ever since he'd killed Thayer. Curiously enough, when he was told that t.b. threatened his life again, it made him right-about-face and fight to live. Remorse and its consequences were what brought on a recurrence of his disease. Yet, paradoxically, when he knew he again faced death from tuberculosis, his instinct was to fight it."

"And he had no money to live on till he would be well again," I said.

Patrick said, "So he decided to steal the manuscript. If that seems odd to you, remember that he thought that manuscript was a gold mine. Hadn't Ames said so—and wasn't Ames a financial wizard? Anyone who questions his stealing the manuscript must remember that Ames had talked and talked about there being a mint in that cookbook, and also that Thayer didn't write anything there wasn't money in. So Scott decided to steal it to finance himself while he recuperated. Then he attempted to kill Ames and did kill Dorrie because they were making too much noise about *something* having been stolen. Ames never said what he himself was after because he didn't want Dorrie to know. And Dorrie didn't know, but she did know that someone had been in the house, and her natural conclusion was that the motive was theft."

"I blame myself," Bee said. "I shouldn't've carried my guns in my car. . . ."

"Oh, Bee, darling! Stop it!" Julia said. "Pat, dear, do start at the beginning, tell everything."

Patrick passed his cigarettes.

"I have told you everything," he said. "There were little things, of course, hunches and clues, that I may not have mentioned. For instance, a crack I made to Jean about their letting a man with t.b. run the health office made me ashamed of myself, but it also set me thinking about Scott and gave me a slant on his character. He would have made himself pretty tough inside, I thought. He would have to. First he would have had to lick his physical illness. Then, all his life, even though cured, he would have to buck public suspicion that he was still afflicted. Many jobs would always be barred to him. Many homes, perhaps, also.

"Like Dorrie, Scott had got the bad breaks. He had spent his best years in hospitals. He was poor. Work he could do was scarce. He had lost the one girl he loved.

"For a little while, however, he had had a run of luck. He had landed a WPA job he liked. He had got a federal loan and had built himself a house he was crazy about. Yet, ironically, his neighbors and best friends were Maurice Ames, who made money hand over fist, and Ray Thayer, who earned considerable pretty easily.

"Scott didn't care deeply for Ames, but he stimulated him. He idealized Thayer.

"The war came. His job went. He was allowed to manage the health office, temporarily.

"Then Thayer came back here with Dorrie.

"Now, people with tremendous self-discipline, such as Scott Davies had had to develop in himself, are not very kindly as a rule toward weaklings. Scott was terribly upset by the Dorrie business. His great friend had betrayed everyone. Scott adored Karen and you, Bee, and of course he loved Edwina. He was shocked out of his mind. Remember, he never knew the story Ray had told you about how it happened—not until you told us, the other night, at Maurice's. Incidentally, Scott tipped me off that you and Ray had probably had a talk. I wondered how he knew, and that was another clue."

Bee said, "I couldn't have told what Ray told me, after he was dead, Pat."

Patrick asked, "Because you thought it would make him ridiculous, didn't you?"

Bee nodded. "I didn't know about the knockout drops—which would have subjected him to even more ridicule—and neither did Ray. He thought he got some bad liquor. He never blamed Dorrie, in any way. I felt that telling it would hurt his memory and wouldn't help anybody living—or so I thought—so I kept mum."

"Ridicule is a terrible thing," I said.

A somber moment passed, then Julia said, "Pat—please go on."

"There isn't much more. Scott saw Thayer drive to The Rock that night he met you, Bee. It was dark, but he knew the car by its lights. He felt alarmed because Ray was going out there at night. It is faster to walk across the desert to The Rock from Scott's place than to drive. The road is out of the way, as well as slow. Scott walked—ran—across the desert. He got there about the time you did. He hovered in the darkness out of earshot. He never knew what you talked about. You left. Ray looked sunk. He strolled over to the rim. Scott thought he was going to jump. He forgot all his hard feelings in his terror for his best friend. He screamed at him not to jump—and Thayer laughed. That laugh doomed him."

The fire settled. We sat in a little silence.

"That laugh threw Scott—already emotionally overwrought—into a hysterical rage. Thayer never knew it, probably. He returned to the car. He suggested that Scott ride back with him. He bent to put the keys in the switch. Scott, out of his head in his frenzy, picked up a rock and bashed in the back of his head. He then carried Thayer to the rim and threw him into the canyon. He found the lethal rock and left it somewhere in the desert on his way home. Remorse set in hours later, tortured him, weakened him, finally brought on a recurrence of his disease.

"He said the other night that the subsequent conflict inside himself—the longing to die because he had killed Ray Thayer, and the urge to live which is instinctive in us all, turned him into a monster. He felt no remorse for killing Dorrie or poisoning Ames. He considered them both vermin—his word. But to have killed Edwina accidentally was like a punishment visited on him for all his crimes. He was glad to die."

"Just how did that happen?" Julia asked.

"On our way home after doing the errand for the sheriff in Santa Fe the other night, Jean and I stopped at Scott's. He knew then that the jig was up. Yet, he still tried to cover up. He thought that he at least could get and destroy the other jar of poisoned *pâté de foie gras*. He dressed and got into his car and started for Ames'. He didn't know we had gone on there after leaving him. I turned out our lights when we entered the lane—he must have come about that time because neither Jean nor I heard his car. He drove without lights. There was moonlight. He knew every inch of the road. He drove well past the end of the lane and left his car. He walked then to the house. Both Karen and Hugh Kennicott passed along the lane when he was near the house. Scott hid behind the juniper trees. The kitchen door was unlocked. He entered and went to the icebox.

"He thought he was in great luck. The jar was there!

"Then he heard a step. He glanced around. He saw Bee's rifle. He left the icebox and got it.

"The swinging door from the pantry opened. A dark figure appeared. Too late, Scott realized that the light from the open door of the icebox gave him away. He took aim, fired, and Edwina, who was slipping about silently so that her husband and her mother would not hear her, slumped down dead. Scott put down the gun and again in a panic ran out, got his car, went home, and had just arrived there when Julia telephoned him."

Julia said, "When I told him Edwina was dead he told me he didn't believe me."

Patrick said, "He didn't want people to know all that he had done. Had the morphine worked immediately we might never have been sure of all of it."

I said, "He was clever, though. That day he choked me on the terrace of the Thayer house he went home, left his Mexican hat, and was back on the plaza coming from the restaurant as though he had lunched there when we got back to town. All the same, I feel sorry for him."

"Rather," Patrick said.

"What is Karen going to do with Ray's money?" Julia asked Bee.

"Scott left a will," Bee said. "He wants his house to be used for people sick like himself. Ray's money will finance it."

Julia asked, "Are you going to take Maurice's ten grand, Pat?"

"Oh, oh," Patrick said.

I said, "That's a delicate subject, Julia. I want it. Patrick doesn't."

"Maurice could afford ten times that," Bee said.

Patrick said, "It tempts me, in one way. It would help pay for a ranch. I've got to get out of the detective business after the war."

"Oh, why?" Julia asked.

"It's a girl's racket," Patrick said.

I could hardly let that pass!

"Pat's just being mean," I said. "He gets cross when I get in on one of his cases. He has dozens of he-man cases to the one mild number I'm lucky enough to get in on, once in a blue moon."

"Jean won't mind me," Patrick said. "She's always getting into trouble. I've got to turn rancher or something," he said solemnly. "The detective business is much too dangerous—for my wife."

THE END

About the Rue Morgue Press

"Rue Morgue Press is the old-mystery lover's best friend,
reprinting high quality books from the 1930s and '40s."
—Ellery Queen's Mystery Magazine

Since 1997, the Rue Morgue Press has reprinted scores of traditional mysteries, the kind of books that were the hallmark of the Golden Age of detective fiction. Authors reprinted or to be reprinted by the Rue Morgue include Catherine Aird, Delano Ames, H. C. Bailey, Morris Bishop, Nicholas Blake, Dorothy Bowers, Pamela Branch, Joanna Cannan, John Dickson Carr, Glyn Carr, Torrey Chanslor, Clyde B. Clason, Joan Coggin, Manning Coles, Lucy Cores, Frances Crane, Norbert Davis, Elizabeth Dean, Carter Dickson, Eilis Dillon, Michael Gilbert, Constance & Gwenyth Little, Marlys Millhiser, Gladys Mitchell, Patricia Moyes, James Norman, Stuart Palmer, Craig Rice, Kelley Roos, Charlotte Murray Russell, Maureen Sarsfield, Margaret Scherf, Juanita Sheridan and Colin Watson..

To suggest titles or to receive a catalog of Rue Morgue Press books write 87 Lone Tree Lane, Lyons, CO 80540, telephone 800-699-6214, or check out our website, www.ruemorguepress.com, which lists complete descriptions of all of our titles, along with lengthy biographies of our writers.